"You do not reco
do you, Executi

Without warning, the knife in Pham's left hand shot forward in a low arc. As Bolan twisted away, the other knife darted in and slashed his cheek slightly.

Feinting with his hands, the warrior launched a kick that connected with the Vietnamese's lower ribs. The man grunted with the impact, but Bolan knew he'd avoided most of the force of the blow. The knives streaked out in search of his body as Pham was transformed into a whirl of glittering blades.

"You took my eye years ago, Executioner," Pham accused. "Now I will take your life."

Bolan backed away from the sheer ferocity of the attack, waiting for an opening. When his adversary left the ground in a flashing snap kick, Bolan grabbed the striking foot in both hands and yanked. They crashed to the mud, locked tightly in a death embrace.

The warrior landed a solid jab to the man's head, but it didn't seem to have an effect. The mud on Pham's arm caused Bolan to lose his hold, and he watched helplessly as the killer drew back his knife hand for a final blow.

"Now, Executioner," Pham whispered. "Now you die."

MACK BOLAN.

The Executioner

DON PENDLETON's EXECUTIONER
MACK BOLAN.

War
Born

A GOLD EAGLE BOOK FROM
WORLDWIDE.

TORONTO • NEW YORK • LONDON • PARIS
AMSTERDAM • STOCKHOLM • HAMBURG
ATHENS • MILAN • TOKYO • SYDNEY

First edition March 1989

ISBN 0-373-61123-4

Special thanks and acknowledgment to
Mel Odom for his contribution to this work.

Nothing can excuse a general who takes advantage of the knowledge acquired in the service of his country... This is a crime reprobated by every principle of religion, morality, and honor.

—Napoleon I
Maxims of War

There is no excuse for treason, for handing over national secrets to the enemy. If a man sells his country, he has sold his family, his soul . . . his life.

—Mack Bolan

THE
MACK BOLAN®
LEGEND

Nothing less than a war could have fashioned the destiny of the man called Mack Bolan. Bolan earned the Executioner title in the jungle hell of Vietnam.

But this soldier also wore another name—Sergeant Mercy. He was so tagged because of the compassion he showed to wounded comrades-in-arms and Vietnamese civilians.

Mack Bolan's second tour of duty ended prematurely when he was given emergency leave to return home and bury his family, victims of the Mob. Then he declared a one-man war against the Mafia.

He confronted the Families head-on from coast to coast, and soon a hope of victory began to appear. But Bolan had broken society's every rule. That same society started gunning for this elusive warrior—to no avail.

So Bolan was offered amnesty to work within the system against terrorism. This time, as an employee of Uncle Sam, Bolan become Colonel John Phoenix. With a command center at Stony Man Farm in Virginia, he and his new allies—Able Team and Phoenix Force—waged relentless war on a new adversary: the KGB.

But when his one true love, April Rose, died at the hands of the Soviet terror machine, Bolan severed all ties with Establishment authority.

Now, after a lengthy lone-wolf struggle and much soul-searching, the Executioner has agreed to enter an "arm's-length" alliance with his government once more, reserving the right to pursue personal missions in his Everlasting War.

PROLOGUE

Ho Chi Minh City

Solly Taggert swung a big hand at a fly and took another chug of his flat beer. Being at room temperature didn't improve it any.

Pham sat across the table from him, watching with his single eye. In the shadowed corner of the small tavern, his black eye patch seemed to be part of the darkness, a gloomy fragment, in relief, that covered the upper left side of the man's face. The other eye was bloodshot and squinted against the cigarette smoke that curled upward from yellow-stained fingers. Pham gazed intently at the American's face.

Taggert had never liked dealing with the man. As always, an almost physical feeling of dread had settled into the pit of his stomach as soon as the Vietnamese had pushed his chair against the wall, the same chair Taggert had had to vacate to the man because that was the only way Pham would do business—with his back to the wall. Too many people knew of Pham, and most of them wanted him dead. The small man was a ''cowboy'' in the bastardized Vietnamese street language, a man living by his wits.

But Taggert sat there as he had before—feeling threatened by the smaller man and exposed to anyone who might suddenly feel the need to kill an unsuspecting American—because he wanted what Pham had to give. For a moment he regretted arranging to meet with Greenberg later, wishing he'd kept the black man with him to cover his flank. But that would have meant that Greenberg would know everything that Pham revealed. And more than anything else, Solly Taggert tried to be a careful man.

He'd been drafted right out of high school and dumped into the war. There hadn't been much to go home to afterward, and his involvement in an ex-CIA agent's black market pipeline had been too profitable to leave once he found out the guy had been willing to keep operating after Uncle Sam called everyone home. The two men had enjoyed a good relationship for the next few years, until the ex-CIA guy got axed in 1982 by one of his own men when he tried to get too big. Creativity, Taggert had told himself. The guy had had a good thing going and had blown it by trying to get fancy.

From that time on Taggert had lived one day at a time, picking operations that promised the highest yield for the lowest amount of risk. He'd worked at everything, from courier for Vietnamese officials involved in black markets, to field boss for different drug operations, and as a mercenary warrior in various skirmishes in Southeast Asia whenever Vietnam got too hot for him. But he had always returned.

The way he figured it, with every bit of Viet currency he was able to wrest from whatever source he found, he was getting even for every American soldier who died in the jungles. Safe currency, though. No creativity. Just good, solid operations like the one he and Greenberg were on now.

He'd done this routine before. Finding Vietnamese children fathered by American GIs and ransoming them back to the families stateside had proved profitable. Only wealthy families, though, for Taggert charged a lot for his services. He had to. Sometimes the children didn't want to go. And he had to hire men who were as skilled as Greenberg and himself at surviving in this war-torn land. They didn't come cheaply.

And the time involved had to be taken into consideration. It was easy enough to find children who fit the scam, but finding the families, that was sometimes a problem. Most returning vets didn't have the kind of money Taggert demanded for the recovery operation. Some of them didn't believe him. Many of them didn't want their families to know a child had been fathered.

But there were those cases where military men had been forced to leave their Vietnamese wives and girlfriends, as well as children they hadn't seen since infancy. Taggert had to make sure they could pay his bill before taking any steps that might endanger him.

This would be the thirteenth recovery operation since he'd gone into business in 1983. He wasn't superstitious. Not really. But thirteen was pushing the operation to its limits. And the children weren't really kids anymore. Most of them were in their teens, tied tightly to their Vietnamese families.

But Greenberg had assured him this case was well worth the risk. And it wasn't a father this time. No, this time the grandfather would be making the buyback. The son had died in Vietnam, a hotshot pilot who'd been executed in a prison camp.

Taggert took another drink of beer and shook out a cigarette. Pham watched him dispassionately, as if he had all the time in the world. Only the sudden twitching of the Vietnamese's eye when the door opened to admit a new customer betrayed him. Knowing the fear Pham held locked up inside him made Taggert feel a little more at ease.

A humorless smile twisted Pham's thin lips. Taggert had never seen any genuine warmth in the man.

"So, Sergeant Taggert," Pham said, "did you bring the gold with you?"

Taggert reached under his shirt and pulled a leather pouch from behind the belt. He dropped it solidly on the wooden tabletop. The sound of clinking coins barely reached his ears.

Pham picked up the pouch with his left hand, weighing it for a moment before putting it inside his loose clothing. Taggert never even heard a rustle.

He waited for the man to speak, curbing his growing impatience.

"You know, Solly," Pham said in English that held only the trace of an accent, "I think even at this price you're getting a bargain."

Taggert remained silent, wondering if the man was going to try to get more money out of him.

A smile flickered briefly on Pham's face, as if playing hide-and-seek. "How much do you already know about Stuart Wingate?"

"He's got his own business in the States. Munitions." Taggert shrugged and got the nagging feeling he should have pumped Greenberg a little more. He didn't like the interest Pham was showing in the subject. He felt as if he was standing on the edge of a bottomless abyss and the man was an oncoming high wind, blowing in the wrong direction.

Pham nodded. The fingers of his left hand toyed with the beer glass on the table. "To begin with, the man has a lot of money. And he isn't just a bourgeois weapons maker. Wingate handled a lot of government contracts in the war for your Uncle Sam. From there, after the war, Wingate branched off into more sophisticated weaponry."

Irritation made Taggert want to say something sharp, but he kept his voice low, professional. "So far you haven't told me anything I didn't know already."

"Maybe I can't tell you anything new. Maybe all you wanted me to do was confirm what you believed to be true." Pham's gaze was piercing, and Taggert got the feeling the man was really interested in how much he did know. "Did you know Wingate was working on an addition to your President's Strategic Defense program?"

At first Taggert didn't believe him, but when he looked into that depthless eye he knew it was true. How much would Wingate be willing to pay for a grandson he had never seen? *Would* he be willing to pay?

"You know I usually don't ask," Pham continued, breaking into his thoughts, "but this time you've made me curious. What are you working on?"

Taggert remained silent. The Vietnamese already knew too much. Pham would eventually ferret out information from other sources about what Solly planned, but with luck—and timing—the deadly little man wouldn't get involved. The old fear, the one Pham had inspired in him the first time they met, reached fever pitch.

"You can tell me, Solly," Pham prompted, leaning forward conspiratorially. "Who am I going to tell?"

Taggert ignored him, ignored the icy snake coiled in his bowels, caused by the knowledge of what he had to do. For the first time in his life since the war, Solly Taggert was entertaining visions of a small dream. If Wingate really wanted the kid, how much money could he get his hands on?

Or maybe there was something else they could bargain for. If Wingate was working on the Star Wars defense system, he had to be privy to certain national secrets. How much of that might the man be willing to barter away?

He fought to contain the excitement he felt, hoping none of it showed to Pham. Not even Greenberg knew this much. The guy would have mentioned it.

"You're thinking, Solly," Pham drawled mockingly. "It's one of the few times I've seen you sit and digest something. Usually you're a machine, plodding through whatever routes and goals you've set for yourself. Is this thing you've planned perhaps bigger than you had at first thought?"

"Maybe too big."

The Vietnamese laughed. "Afraid you'll be eaten by the big fish you're after, Solly?"

"Let's just say I'm not really sure what I'm going to do with it once I land it." He stood to go, pushing his chair back.

Pham continued to stare at him, as if he could see inside Taggert's mind. "What I'd like to know is what you're planning to use as bait for this fish of yours."

Taggert remained quiet, enjoying the upper hand for the first time in their years-long association. His fear of the man abated. What he had to do was something simple and necessary. Something he had done before. And Pham wouldn't be expecting it.

But Solly Taggert's dream, the first he'd had in more years than he really cared to remember—maybe the first since he'd slipped his hands under Diana Jankco's blouse his senior year and wondered what making love to her would be like—was demanding to be born.

And nothing could make it go wrong.

Except Pham.

"If you don't know," Taggert told him, "then maybe I was overcharged. Maybe I didn't get a bargain at all." He felt satisfied when he saw the mirthless smile on Pham's face freeze so tightly it couldn't fade away. Then he turned and left the bar, feeling the vulnerable itch between his shoulder blades intensify.

"How long we going to wait here, Sarge?" Greenberg asked. They sat in cane chairs in front of a brothel across the street from the bar, where Greenberg had been whiling away the afternoon.

Taggert had thought Pham would leave before he had a chance to rouse Greenberg. Usually the Vietnamese left within a few minutes after his business was concluded. Perhaps Pham was trying to find out what he could from the men in the bar who Taggert sometimes drank with. There had been no mistaking the hunger that had burned in the informant's eye.

"Not long," Taggert heard himself say. He again estimated the distance separating the brothel and the bar. "Just be ready to move when I say to."

How much, he wondered, could you get for the plans to the Star Wars system—provided you could safely contact people who would be interested?

He had already decided he wasn't going to be fancy about it. Find a buyer, dump the goods and split. Kick around for a while before finding another place to hang out.

Taggert got to his feet automatically when Pham started out of the bar. He raised the M-16 from its position at his right side and brought it to a quick halt at his hip so Pham wouldn't have as much time to react. He had complete confidence in his ability to fire a killing shot. The assault rifle was a part of him, and he'd never felt that more than at this precise moment.

Pham was centered in the doorway of the bar when Taggert's finger tightened on the trigger. The first 3-round burst slammed into the man's chest. At least one round of the next burst connected with Pham's head, which jerked back suddenly.

Taggert emptied the rest of the clip across the front of the bar, hosing the area around Pham's body.

"What the hell's going on?" Greenberg yelled from beside Taggert, bringing his own rifle to bear.

Taggert didn't answer, feeding another magazine into the M-16. He gave one last glance to Pham's body and felt an immediate release of tension. Life had just become one hundred percent simpler.

Then he turned to Greenberg and said, "Move out, soldier."

1

Clad in his skintight blacksuit, his face covered with combat cosmetics, Mack Bolan looked as if he'd just stepped inside his own shadow.

Sequestered under the spreading oak trees, thirty yards from the electrified security fence that surrounded the Wingate mansion, Bolan knew he was invisible to the two men in the telephone repair van.

He peeled back a sleeve to reveal the luminous hands of his watch for just an instant. The van had been parked with the engine running for almost fifteen minutes. One man had climbed to the top of a pole earlier, then climbed back down while the other man retreated to the back of the van.

Sensing no immediate danger to the household, Bolan continued to watch. On this one, there were too many representatives from the different ABC groups in the government to go hard yet. Thus far he'd been able to preserve his anonymity, a wild card in the deck for whomever the KGB had managed to plant in Wingate's defenses. If Brognola's intel had been good.

He breathed deep to relax the tension the past two days had generated. Both men were in the rear of the van now, and the warrior decided to give them a few minutes more before he made his move.

The Wingate mansion had never been attacked before, Stuart Wingate had told the Executioner two days earlier, when they'd first met. Bolan had quietly responded that the stakes had never been so high before, either. The munitions man had said nothing as they sat at the big desk in Wingate's den. Between them, lying atop other file folders Wingate had been going over when Bolan arrived, was a letter bearing the presidential seal. The message was brief and to the point, asking Wingate to allow Bolan free access to the mansion and the factory over the next few days. Bolan would be undercover. Wingate hadn't seemed impressed by the Chief Executive's concern for his safety.

Bolan shifted in the darkness, surveying the grounds of the estate. His AutoMag, Big Thunder, was a familiar and comfortable weight on his right hip, and the Beretta 93-R occupied the speed ring under his left arm.

The mansion itself was a fortress—the warrior had seen that firsthand. The walls of the twenty-room house were constructed of heavy rock hewn from granite quarries back East, erected on a flat plain a little southeast of Oklahoma City proper, as were the walls that posed the first line of defense. There was considerable landscaping on the grounds, but nothing grew within the walls that would hide a man. Powerful searchlights had been mounted at frequent intervals, and Bolan knew they could illuminate the entire area in seconds. A rotating security team lived in-house while serving their shifts. Some stayed at the mansion at all times, while others dogged Wingate's every step.

On top of that were the teams the Department of Defense and CIA had arranged for during the time it took Stuart Wingate to finish his work on the Star Wars project.

Yet Hal Brognola had gotten wind of a KGB effort that would be directed against Wingate before the end of the week, when the weapons designer was scheduled to make his presentation to the Department of Defense and the President. An agent had died en route to Wonderland to bring even that much information, which came after months of deep undercover operations.

When Brognola had talked with Bolan at the request of the Man, the big Fed said the feeling was that the enemy had an insider, someone close to Wingate.

Bolan had almost dismissed that notion. Wingate didn't seem to let anyone get close to him, and usually kept to himself even in the company of others. Employees at the factory had revealed that the old man had been more outgoing and more involved with people once upon a time. Things had changed, they said, after Wingate's firstborn son had been shot down in Vietnam. It was as though the man had withered and died inside.

When Stuart Jr. had been killed, one of the secretaries told Bolan, Wingate had turned away from everyone, including his other son, Lee. His wife had been dead several years, and his interest in Lee had been only passing at best. According to the secretary, Wingate had ensured the boy's education and financial freedom, but both of these were later rejected.

Lee Wingate had left home to serve a tour in the Marines during peacetime. No one at the factory seemed to know what he had been involved with during the past few years.

Yet Lee had returned home two days earlier, a man now, with a bearing about him that Bolan recognized as military. The family reunion had been conducted without any real warmth.

Stuart Wingate had greeted his son with the attitude that the arrival had been a normal occurrence. In fact it had been arranged at the elder Wingate's behest.

Since his arrival at the family home Lee had kept to himself, seeing less of his father than Bolan. The behavior had intrigued the warrior enough that he put through a call to Aaron Kurtzman to learn what he could of the man through the Bear's computers.

The report Bolan had gotten back had been surprising. Lee Wingate had been involved in mercenary work since leaving the Marines. A lot of it was unconfirmed, but lately he'd been seen fighting with the Contras. From what Kurtzman had been able to dig up, Lee only worked for anti-Communist factions, sometimes free if he could bankroll his own mission.

All of which left Bolan wondering what the man was doing here now.

This wasn't really Bolan's type of operation. He preferred to gather his own intel, draw his own conclusions about the enemy force and execute his own plans. A "bodyguard" was too deeply seated in a defensive posture, with reaction capability only, and by then it was always too late to keep from losing something.

But Hal Brognola had requested assistance, and he had never let the man down.

And the President was taking a very personal interest in Wingate's work. The Star Wars program had been the Man's pet project from the beginning. Bolan didn't know much about it except that Wingate's addition to the system would increase tracking capabilities.

The past two days had been routine, with Bolan finding no chinks or cracks in the flesh-and-blood security system around the mansion, or in the technical apparatus, which included state-of-the-art equipment, some of it designed by Wingate himself.

If it hadn't been for Brognola's insistence, Bolan would have discarded the inside operation yesterday and opted for something more active. Patience was a useful tool only if you knew for sure something was coming and you couldn't get to it any quicker. But tonight, while making his usual rounds after everyone in the mansion was asleep, Bolan had seen the van parked across the street from the entrance to the estate and decided to investigate.

Wingate would have enough influence to get a phone repairman out at this time of night, but there had been no problems with the phone lines in the mansion.

It was possible that someone else in the area had called in and that the lines happened to connect to the same pole as the ones in the mansion. But assuming was too easy. Too unsure.

Mack Bolan had lived his life on a thin wire of justice—above both law and chaos—for too long to let an assumption go unchallenged. So he'd slipped out the back of the estate without setting off any of the mansion's security defenses.

No one but Stuart Wingate knew his true identity. To the rest of the household and the security staff, he was Mike McKay, a free-lance political reporter assigned by the President to prepare a news brief for the press once the new addition was safely logged with the Department of Defense people in the Pentagon. Brognola had figured it would be safer that way, allowing Bolan to slip through the different security teams without rubbing anybody the wrong way. Or warning the suspect parties that he was operating in their theater. A watchdog to watch the watchdogs.

When the first man left the rear of the van again and started to don his climbing gear, Bolan moved, taking the silenced Beretta from his shoulder leather and fading back into the safe embrace of the night.

Trained by years of using stealth as an ally and shadow as a partner, Bolan catfooted up behind the man just as he reached the pole and was about to hook his safety belt. He let the guy feel the tip of the 9 mm behind his left ear.

Reacting by reflex and instinct, the repairman reached inside his coveralls for a weapon, wheeling to face Bolan.

The Executioner rapped the guy expertly on the temple with the butt of the 93-R and caught the loose folds of the coveralls in his left hand as the man dropped. He reached inside the uniform and tugged a government-issue .45 from a shoulder holster.

Bolan pitched the pistol into the ditch, then crossed soundlessly to the open side panel of the van, holding the

Beretta level to his ear, ready to lock into target acquisition if the need arose.

The other man was absorbed by the bank of machinery covering the opposite side of the van. He wore a set of headphones and sat at a small chair, making notes as he adjusted dials on the communications equipment.

Bolan recognized the equipment immediately—he'd used similar setups before. Somewhere in Stuart Wingate's castle, someone had planted a bug. Or bugs. They were different from the usual type, though. These had recording units attached to them that would store conversation for hours at a time, waiting for a communications vehicle like this one to come by and bleed the memories from time to time. For the most part they were untraceable by conventional means because the bugs transmitted stored information in mere seconds, at a call from a communications operator, instead of broadcasting full-time on a single open frequency.

Very neat and very efficient. Someone had gone to a lot of trouble to set the communications network into operation. The Executioner had little doubt that it had been set up by one of the domestic agencies. But why? Maybe whoever was behind the operation had a definite idea about who was the KGB plant. If so, the agency definitely wasn't sharing its intel with the rest of the defense teams.

Bolan intended to rectify the situation.

The Executioner stepped up into the van, with only the reddish glow from the digital readouts to light his way, and saw the guy take off his headphones and start to turn around. Knowing the darkness inside the van and the combat cosmetics would keep him from being recognized, Bolan let him.

The guy's hand darted for the inside of his coveralls.

"You feel any luckier than your partner?" Bolan asked in a graveyard voice. He made sure the Beretta's silencer was a prominent point of reference in the man's field of vision.

Slowly the hand came away empty.

"Good thinking," Bolan said. He kept the Beretta motionless. "Put your hands up and get on the floor, facedown."

The man did as Bolan commanded, keeping his hands clasped behind his neck.

"Who's setup is this?" the Executioner asked as he surveyed the equipment. The controls were pretty much as he remembered them. A cassette was already loaded into the recorder and he switched it on, holding one side of the headphones to his ear, hearing the unmistakable voice of Stuart Wingate. From the nature of the call, Bolan judged the bug was on the munitions king's personal phone. At least this one was. Later he would have time to figure out where the others were.

"Forget it, asshole," the guy sneered. "I don't have to tell you a goddamned thing. You got a problem with anything, take it up with my superior. You come in here playing hardass and you aren't getting squat."

"That's tough talk from a guy lying on his face."

The man tried to get up, but Bolan pressed his booted foot on the guy's neck.

"The last I heard was that Wingate's on our side. If he found out about this he could slap a court suit on your section chief so fast it would make his head spin. I doubt it would do your career any good, either."

The agent remained silent, and Bolan knew it would take a more physical threat to get him to talk. His involvement in the Wingate matter wasn't really an issue, anyway, but it wouldn't hurt to know his connection. If whoever had set up this operation could penetrate Wingate's defenses, it meant others could. And maybe they already had.

Bolan removed the cassette from the recorder and dropped it into one of the pockets of his blacksuit. He used wire from the communications equipment to tie up the agent, knowing the guy's backup outside would eventually free him. A brief inspection of his prisoner revealed no ID.

Then the warrior was out of the van and moving into the night, once again a part of the shadows.

BOLAN HEARD his bedroom door open and close. He stepped from the shower cubicle and tossed his towel on the sink. Big Thunder filled his hand. He had left the bathroom door open so he could hear sounds coming from the bedroom. It made no noise as he eased it open a little wider and looked out, holding the AutoMag at waist level.

Lee Wingate, dressed in blue Nike warm-ups and unlaced Reeboks still white in their newness, stood in the center of the bedroom, looking at the portable word processor on the small desk. He wore his brown hair short, and it curled tightly against his scalp. His mustache was thick and bushy. Bolan would have been willing to bet the bulge under the man's warm-up jacket was no less than .38 caliber. He looked up at Bolan. "I noticed you were still up so I let myself in. I knocked but nobody answered. Hope you don't mind."

"Have a seat," Bolan said as he wondered what the man wanted. "Let me grab a towel and I'll be right with you."

Shutting the door, Bolan put the AutoMag back in its holster. He finished drying with one towel and wrapped another around his waist. When he'd returned to his room earlier he knew that it had been searched—but there had been nothing for anyone to find. Had Lee Wingate been there earlier?

"Are you really a public relations writer for the government?" Lee asked when Bolan reentered the bedroom. He was sitting at the desk, the bulge of the hidden weapon less obvious now.

"I'm an independent free-lancer," Bolan replied as he took a seat on the bed.

"A free-lancer with government clearance." Lee's tone of voice revealed his disbelief.

"Yeah."

"Dad told me the President asked for you to cover federal involvement with the Strategic Defense program. He said that after the Contra fiasco the President wanted coverage on all arms dealings."

"That's right."

"Mackie McKay. That *is* your name, isn't it?"

"My byline," Bolan corrected him.

"What's your first name?"

Bolan gave him a small grin to let him know he was willing to go along with the question-and-answer game, beginning with who had sent him to do the interview. Because Stuart Wingate hadn't appeared to have a real interest in Bolan's activities since he'd arrived, he couldn't see this being the elder Wingate's doing. Which meant Lee Wingate had taken it upon himself. But why now?

"Mike," Bolan said. "I use Mackie because it looks more commercial on an article."

Lee Wingate stared at Bolan as if trying to fix him into some mental file. "According to the dossier you brought to my father, you got your start doing stories on the Vietnam War."

"Yeah," Bolan said, knowing that didn't explain the collection of scars that crisscrossed his body. He wished he'd had the chance to get dressed before Wingate barged in. At least it would have covered a few of the more recent additions. He added, "I did most of my stuff after I got back."

"You toured in the war?"

"Two successive."

"Regular Army?"

"Special Forces."

"I just missed the war by a few years," Lee said. His voice was flat, but Bolan could detect something in the absence of tone. Resentment? Or something else?

Bolan shrugged.

"From the looks of it, you've been in a few other hot spots since then, McKay," Lee observed.

"A few. You look like you've been in your share of scrapes, too. For a man who hasn't been in a war."

Lee smiled at him good-naturedly. "Don't play naive with me, friend. If the Prez requested that you be here for the unveiling, then you're no happy-go-lucky political reporter. You know something about me."

"I've been told you operate a merc unit."

The smile on the younger man's face remained in place, but Bolan knew it was covered with an inner frost. "Not just a merc force," Lee Wingate told him. "My men and I fight communism wherever we can find a country with people willing to sacrifice themselves to fight for freedom."

The words were spoken with such conviction that Bolan didn't doubt the sincerity of the emotion behind them.

"I hate watching anybody having to knuckle under to Communist forces. I've seen what they can do to a people once they get started."

"What brings you back here?" Bolan asked.

"My father."

"The way I've heard it, you and your father don't have a very close relationship. Is your visiting now just a coincidence?"

"Let's just *say* it's a coincidence. That seems to be the prevalent thing here. It's just a coincidence for the President to send in his own journalist, right? A journalist who spends a lot of time checking out the security, both technical and human, around my father's business. As well as getting the red carpet treatment and being invited to stay at the family house. The same reporter who looks like he's been hit with damn near everything that will fire or cut."

Bolan felt the treacherous footing beneath him, sensed the younger man's aggressive frame of mind. Lee recognized him as a threat. But a threat to what? His father? Surely he realized if Bolan had wanted the elder Wingate dead it would have already happened.

A threat to the project? Maybe, but why? And why had
Stuart Wingate sent for his son? There had to be some motive. Bolan just couldn't put his finger on it yet. Puzzles
within puzzles, he thought as he recalled the tape he'd in-
tercepted a little earlier. It had contained only calls from
Wingate's personal phones in the den and the master bedroom. If nothing new cropped up in the next day or so, he
would give Brognola a call and pull out of the immediate
operation to tackle it from another perspective. It was always easier to look at something from the outside in. Less
confusing without the personal contact.

"You know, McKay, I look at you and I think to myself,
Lee, this guy's CIA. I mean, that accounts for your being
able to check out the hardware and for the way you've been
treating your body. Woodward and Bernstein didn't get shot
up the way you have, and they took on E. Howard Hunt."

Bolan flashed him an easy smile. "Maybe you've been
watching too many spy movies."

"They don't have HBO where I've been, McKay. But they
do have CIA wise guys who like to get involved from time
to time when the politics are right. The problem is they like
to keep playing politics. Ask the Contras. They'll tell you.
Another thing I don't like about CIA guys is they'll get you
dead damn fast if you don't learn to watch your back. I
learned the hard way, but I was lucky. A few of my friends
weren't. You might keep that in mind. Just in case you decide to change careers while I'm still here."

Bolan said nothing. The bitterness in the other man's
voice was an oppressive force daring him to refute what was
said.

"I'm going to be leaving tomorrow," Lee continued,
"and I wanted to talk to you before I left. To give you some
advice." He stood and fixed Bolan with a penetrating stare.
"If anything at all happens to my father while I'm away, I'm
going to hold you personally responsible. Anything at all,
including acts of God."

Bolan watched as the man turned to leave without another word, pulling the door closed behind him.

What made Lee Wingate think his father was in any danger this late in the game? Bolan checked the lock on the bedroom door and tucked the AutoMag under his pillow, within quick reach.

If Bolan hadn't made a move by now, why did Wingate think there would be an attempt in the near future? And what had the merc colonel meant when he said "while I'm away"? From the sound of things he was planning on returning soon. That didn't fit with the impression Bolan had received from the rest of the household. According to the secretary he had talked with, the last time Lee Wingate visited his father was three years ago. And the visit had been cut short by a violent argument. Why had things suddenly changed?

Bolan's thoughts churned and spun inside his head like mounted ducks in a shooting gallery, shifting directions as each new tangent touched them. Why had Stuart Wingate sent for his estranged son? And why was one of the security teams involved with the project listening in on the munitions man's private conversations?

Something was wrong. But what?

If it had been something to do with the addition Wingate was making to the SDI package, the Defense Department supervisors would have known, and the information would have reached Brognola and gradually filtered down to Bolan.

No.

It was something else, Bolan reasoned. Something that hinged on the top-secret project. But what had forced Stuart Wingate to rely on a son he rarely got along with? What was it that prevented him from taking care of the matter himself or calling the State Department?

He tried to match answers to his questions but nothing meshed. Giving up for the night, he set his alarm to coincide with the seven o'clock schedule Wingate Sr. kept, allowing himself several hours of sleep. Tomorrow would provide a fresh start. With Brognola's help he could start working on the bug angle and also learn where Lee Wingate was going.

Closing his eyes, he wished the plush bed was really as worry free as it was designed to be.

2

"What the hell were you trying to do?" Stuart Wingate demanded as he strode into the mansion's private gym, where Lee was working out some of the pent-up frustration that his discussion with Bolan had generated. The elder Wingate glared at his son until Lee dropped his eyes.

Lee was surprised by the depth of his feelings. He hadn't been around his father much for several years, had hardly even talked to him during that time. Yet their roles had slipped back into place, so easily to the time when he was a young man who had feared his father's wrath. He still couldn't bring himself to face his father directly. Not even after all the years, wars and deaths. What didn't surprise him was that his father had been listening in on his conversation. The Wingate home had more bugs than the Watergate.

He picked up the .38 automatic from the bench he'd put it on and slid it inside the waistband of his pants, making sure the drawstring would hold it up. "That guy's no reporter, sir," he said. "I don't know what he is yet, but I know he's no reporter."

Glancing up at his father's stern face, Lee felt the impenetrable wall that had always stood between them. Was it love that had compelled him to respond to his father's summons, or merely duty? It was something he'd been asking himself since he received the telegram, less than a week ago, asking him to come home. He only knew he was on a plane the next day, after turning control of the unit over to Sergeant Phillips, his second-in-command. Thankfully the unit was between campaigns.

"I know that," his father said dismissively. "Nobody who comes from the government as highly touted as our Mr. McKay is exactly what he says he is. But it was a piss-poor move on your part to warn him that we had our suspicions. I've got a large security force here, Lee. They get paid well to make sure I'm protected. It will be harder now to find out what he's doing here."

Lee looked at his father, marveling at how the old man had seemed to diminish over the years, as if he'd used himself up. Age had settled in on Stuart Wingate, kneading the once tight muscularity the man had possessed into a slackness. The gray hair Lee remembered had turned white, and the ruddy complexion was gone, which told Lee that his father didn't get outside as much as he used to.

Recluse, a recent issue of *Time* had labeled him. A genius with the new Star Wars weaponry. Even the years-old file photographs in the magazines hadn't shown the fierceness and hardness Lee remembered most about the man. There had been a gentleness about him, Lee was sure, but it had been something needing to be mined out of barren earth, accessible to only his mother and brother, Stu. Somehow the supply had run out before Stuart Wingate's second-born had gotten his fair share.

For the past few days Lee had been hoping there would be some indication of change in his father, a softening. But there was none. He'd been picked up at the airport by a chauffeur and shown to his rooms, had never seen his father until later that afternoon. The conversations they'd had so far had all been perfunctory, a fencing session on the elder Wingate's part and a hesitant parrying on Lee's.

"Where did you get the gun?" Stuart Wingate asked, putting a stop to Lee's musings.

"At a place not far from the airport," Lee replied. "There's a guy in my unit who knows a guy who knows a guy. He made a phone call before I got to the States and set up a deal for me."

"You're perfectly safe in my home, Lee."

"I know that, sir. It's just that I'm used to carrying a side arm." Lee pulled the warm-up jacket lower to completely cover the pistol. The reference to "my home" stood out, making him even more aware that he was an invited guest.

Stu would have been thirty-five if he had lived, Lee thought. Six years older than he. It had been fourteen years since his brother's death in Vietnam and ten years since he had lived in this house as a family member. By now Stu would have been involved in the administration of Wingate Munitions, perhaps a liaison for the government. He would have had a pretty wife to come home to every day. His father would have made certain of that. And grandchildren. At least one, anyway. A boy. Stuart Wingate would have had it no other way.

Lee had often wondered what kind of life he would have had if he'd stayed, had thought about it many nights when he was on guard duty alone or trying to sleep on muddy ground under a tent that leaked. But there was never a closeness between him and his father. Even a distance between him and Stu had developed as they grew up because their father doted on his firstborn. Stu had been successful in sports, in studies and with women.

Lee had lived a solitary life, having few friends at school and none who were allowed at his home. His mother had been his best friend, but she had died when he was thirteen. By that time Stu was at West Point.

Lee remembered the pride Stuart Wingate had taken in his son's service in the armed forces, the going-away party that had been given in Stu's honor the night before he left for his first tour.

Some of the old hurt washed over him as he looked at his father, but he put it out of his mind. He had learned a long time ago to deal with the here and now and to shelve the personal introspection for later.

Lee watched his father as he sat on one of the weight benches. The older man's shoulders sagged, and he looked exhausted.

"Are you feeling all right, sir?" Lee asked. He wished he could drop the "sir" so they could talk as equals, but it was too much a part of their relationship.

"I'm fine," his father replied, though his voice betrayed him. Lee could hear the strain in it, sense the tiredness.

Stuart Wingate massaged his temples with his thumbs before speaking. "There are a lot of things going on right now that you don't know about, Lee. Just let me handle them. I've been taking care of myself for years."

"Yes, sir," Lee said, just as if he'd been on parade drill back in the Marines.

His father pinned him with a steady gaze. "We've never talked much, have we, son?"

"No, sir."

"I don't even know you now. Except from a distance. I've kept up with your activities, you know. Different people I've employed have mailed me reports on your efforts in all the countries you've been through since you left the military."

Lee restrained the "yes, sir" at the last moment, trying to maintain silence, as if he was a civilian—but he didn't feel like one, and this was his father's camp. He wasn't surprised that his father could keep tabs on him, but he wondered why the man had even gone to the trouble.

"They tell me you've become quite a soldier, Lee. More successful than not, even in those backwater republics you've lived in for the past few years."

"I haven't done all that well, sir. I've had several setbacks, and the effort in South America isn't going very well now."

"Still, you've managed to save several lives at considerable risk to your own. It's something the Wingates would have been proud of." The smile his father gave him was man-to-man, one he had seen him share with Stu often. But never for him. Not once.

"Yes, sir."

"I know I haven't been a very good father, Lee. I see that now. I guess I saw it then, too. Your mother always told me I was too hard on you, demanded too much of you. I accused her of mollycoddling you. She sat by and watched me mold your brother into the image I wanted and drew the line after you were born. I resented her, and you, for that. I had an ideal I wanted my sons to live up to, and Stu was the one I ended up cursing with it. I'm only glad your mother didn't live to see him die in Vietnam."

Lee shifted his weight uneasily from foot to foot, wishing he could leave. That his father would ever open up like this had never crossed his mind.

"I don't know what made you come when I asked you to," Wingate went on, "but I want to thank you for that."

The sincerity in his father's eyes caused Lee to look away. What was going on?

"Something has come up," Wingate said. "Something I had never counted on, never even speculated about." He pushed himself up from the weight bench and turned to face the darkness of the overhead running track.

"You loved your brother, didn't you?"

"Yes, sir."

"I knew you did. Even though you grew apart as you got older. I can't begin to tell you how much I loved him. He was my future, my chance to take myself just one step farther. I worked hard to give him the things I never had. Not financially, no, because there has always been money in the Wingate family. But I tried to help him build a solid foundation, taught him the things I'd found important in *my* life."

Like winning, Lee thought. A cabinet in the den held all the trophies and awards Stu had ever won, from the first trophy he had received for outstanding player in grade-school baseball to the Purple Heart that had been post-humously awarded.

"I wanted him to be the man I had dreamed of him be-coming. I wanted a political future for him, a position where he could influence affairs of state." Wingate turned around and Lee could see the hurt burning in his eyes.

"Part of me died with your brother in Vietnam. But you knew that. Part of you died then, too. I saw it in the way you behaved around this house, in your face when we shared a dinner from time to time. For a long time I was numb in-side. I had my work, and it was easy to expand the routine of my daily life to carry me from morning to midnight. Un-til I could sleep enough to make it through the next day. I shut you out then, Lee, and I knew I did. I just couldn't help myself."

For the first time in many years Lee didn't know what to say or do. When under sniper fire, tending wounded or putting an operation together on the planning board, he never hesitated about which direction to start out in. He had never considered the possibility of this kind of confronta-tion with his father. He was used to the resolute, unforgiv-ing man he thought he'd grown up with. But where was this all heading?

"You've never set a time limit on how long you could stay," Wingate said.

"I'll stay as long as I can, sir, but I do have other press-ing commitments."

Wingate nodded. "I know. I've been informed about the ambush you and your men were subjected to last month. I know it must be a trying time down there right now. Who do you have that you can trust?"

"A few men. But for now we're pulling out to the border and refortifying ourselves. The Sandinistas can't come any farther without sustaining heavy casualties."

"How many men from your unit could you spare for a few days? Certainly no more than a week."

The question caught Lee off guard even though he thought he'd been prepared for anything. "How many were you thinking of?"

"I was told a four-man team. But they'll have to be very good men if you're going to expect to survive."

It all seemed unreal. He hadn't been out of the jungle in a long time, certainly not in surroundings as pleasant as his father's estate. But even standing amid the heavy Nautilus equipment he'd been using only moments ago, remembering the big reporter who held his own secrets, his father seemed to be the most unreal thing of all—asking his estranged son to undertake a mission.

"You never asked me where I wanted you to go when I asked you to make a trip for me tomorrow," Wingate said.

"I knew we would talk about it."

"It's time to talk now."

"Yes, sir."

"Have you got three men you can trust, three men who can take care of themselves in a firefight?"

"I've got a handpicked unit," Lee replied. "They've all been under fire. It's a well-seasoned crew."

"And loyal?"

Lee nodded. "And loyal. You can't be in the business we're in and not have values and ideals. Not if you want to survive, anyway. You have to share convictions and dreams with the men you fight with."

"Are any of them Vietnam veterans?"

"Yes, sir."

"You'll need the best of those men then." Wingate resumed his seat on the weight bench. "How well do you think you knew your brother?"

"Pretty well when we were kids. Afterward, I'm not really sure. We moved in different circles."

"Would it surprise you to know he had taken a mistress in Vietnam?"

Lee remained silent, not sure of what to say.

"When I was told I didn't believe it. Then I used a little political pressure on one of the commanding officers of Stu's base in Saigon and found out it was true. I even got the girl's name, but that's not important." Wingate fell silent and Lee felt the stare probing him, taking his depth and measure. "Last week I got a call from an associate about a man named Solly Taggert. Taggert is an ex-American soldier still living in Vietnam. This associate told me Taggert had located Stu's child by the mistress. My grandson.

"Taggert wants three million dollars for the boy. I agreed to give it to him."

"It could be a trick, sir," Lee heard himself saying.

"I've checked it out. Taggert told his man the boy still wears Stu's dog tags. The commanding officer checked the story with other men on the base, Stu's friends, and found out the girl was pregnant with your brother's child." Wingate was quiet for a moment. "It's true, Lee. I can feel it. I wish I'd known sooner. To think of the hardships that boy has had to endure..."

"Why hasn't the boy's identity come out before? Surely this guy, Taggert, would have pulled in a chit this size earlier. Why now?"

"No one knew."

"What happened to the mother?"

"She's dead. The boy has been living in his grandfather's village."

"And now?"

"And now Taggert will get him. For three million dollars."

"You want me to deliver the money?" Lee asked, then he tried to decide what his feelings should be. But there was too much going on inside him to know at this point.

"Taggert said I should send a four-man team. One small enough to get through the army patrols and big enough to protect itself in case they're discovered. You and your men will have to live off the land with no base support."

"That won't be a problem," Lee said mechanically as his mind analyzed the possibilities. Sergeant Phillips, his second-in-command, had done three tours in Vietnam. Briscoe had been in the SEALs there and, God knew, nobody came tougher. And Kelley. Kelley had been a door gunner on a gunship. "We've lived off the land with no support most everywhere we've fought."

"Will your men accompany you on this? I'll pay them for taking the risk."

"I understand that, sir, but money isn't everything to the men I'll be taking with me. They fight with me because they believe in the things I do."

"And will they be interested in something as personal as this?"

"All of them served in Vietnam, sir."

Wingate nodded. "You understand there can be no official sanction on a mission like this."

"Yes, sir. We haven't had anything like that since we left the regular military forces."

Wingate gave him a wry grin. "No, I suppose you haven't, have you?"

"Does anyone else know about the boy?" Lee asked. It seemed strange to say Stu's son, so he didn't.

Wingate shook his head. "No one. Even with all the ties I have to our government through the Department of Defense, they would never allow me to put together a project like this. It would open too many old wounds, both here and in other countries. We don't exactly sit on the pinnacle of popularity around the world anymore." Lee watched his father shift uncomfortably on the weight bench. "There are others I could hire for this assignment, but I asked you to head this operation because I feel it means as much to you as it does to me. Vietnam took Stu away from us, Lee. It's only fitting that it return to us his son."

"Has the boy been told someone will be coming for him?"

"Taggert has taken care of all that. The boy is ready to come home."

"Yes, sir."

"Taggert will leave word for you and your men at your drop point. I was told he will then inform you where your meeting place will be. His rescue operations are not unknown to the Vietnamese, and he takes a greater chance with every one he attempts."

Lee still listened to his father, but the professional soldier in him was already making lists of things he would need for a mission of this nature. To live off the land in hostile territory—and to make contact with a mobile group evading capture, as well—would take some finesse. If only there was more time to prepare...

As if sensing what was on his mind, his father said, "I would have told you sooner, Lee, but I already feel as if I'm taking a chance. As you've noticed, I maintain a large security force, but how many of them are truly loyal to me and how many also work for the government, I can't say. Your McKay is one of the few overt acts the Defense Department has made."

"I understand. One thing I've noticed in my business is that things have a way of working themselves out as long as you keep a clear head and let your experience guide you. Time is never a true ally. At best it becomes an encumbrance to your opposition."

Wingate pushed himself to his feet. "Your plane will be leaving tomorrow morning. Will that give you enough time to make arrangements with your men?"

"Yes, but I'll need a secure line."

"That's one thing I can't guarantee around here."

Lee smiled. "It's okay. I felt like a drive tonight anyway."

"Don't bother with trying to get weapons together. I've already made arrangements with a man in Saint Martin. You'll also have a room for the night while you wait for the rest of your men. There will be a jet at their disposal. Here's the pilot's name. I've used him before for discreet operations."

Lee took the folded piece of paper without looking at it. His emotions were still a confused maze within him and he couldn't help but wonder what his father would have done if he had declined the mission. Was there someone else? He felt sure that there was. His father had never been a man to put all his eggs in one basket. Why him, though, after all the years of hurt and neglect?

"Is there something on your mind?" Wingate asked.

Lee looked into his father's eyes. "Why me?"

Wingate spoke without hesitation. "You've surely got the experience. And, as I've said, you've got a personal stake in this, too. That's something an outsider wouldn't have. They might not stay when the going got rough. I can trust you, too, when I can't trust many people around me. None of them who could pull off an assignment like this."

"How could you be sure I would go?"

"Because I knew you wouldn't want to let me down. You never have."

Lee nodded, as he knew he was expected to, keeping his thoughts to himself.

"Was there anything else?"

"If there is, sir, I'll let you know."

"Good enough. Once you leave the country, I won't be able to help you. My influence doesn't extend into any of the Communist Bloc countries, except in a few selected areas. I would suggest that you and your men not use anything that

would give away your identities. Even the men in Saint
Martin won't know who you are or where you're going. The
pilot will have instructions on your rendezvous point, but
not why you're going."

"I understand."

Wingate nodded and the look he gave Lee was both stern
and evaluating. "It's been a long time, Lee, and I've always been a gruff man. I'm afraid I don't have all the words
for what I feel in my heart."

"I know," Lee said. He watched his father turn and go,
feeling more complete than he had in years.

3

Mack Bolan cradled the phone in his cupped palm so that the whipping hot Oklahoma winds wouldn't interfere with his conversation. Hal Brognola was on the other end, and neither man had a lot to say. Bolan had communicated his feelings that something was going on that no one knew about. The sudden trip to Will Rogers airport further supported those feelings. Even the regular security men had been taken off guard by the sudden change in Wingate's plans. Yet the sleek Lear jet waiting on Lee Wingate had been ready and fueled when they arrived.

From his place at the outside phone booth, the Executioner commanded a full view of the runway and the limousine where Wingate and his son still remained in conference. The driver, a tall black man Bolan had gotten to know over the past few days, stood casually at the front of the car. Two other vehicles, loaded with CIA security men from Wingate Munitions, flanked the bullet-proof limo like small fish surrounding a scavenger.

Bolan had ridden over in the limo, listening to the driver as he talked about his college days in basketball, while Wingate Sr. and Jr. rode in the back. Lee's face hadn't betrayed anything, but Bolan recognized the tension behind the mask—a sense of readiness for action that echoed in the soldier's own body language.

The Oklahoma sky was blue and filled with puffy white clouds, looking as if the heat choking the hot tarmac of the airport didn't exist at that level.

"I don't know, Striker," Brognola was saying. "I can get a guy down there from Justice to investigate the nature of the flight, but that's going to take some time."

"I don't think that's something we have a lot of," Bolan replied.

"Maybe it's nothing to worry about."

Bolan watched as the chauffeur took his jacket off and tipped his visor back. "If somebody wasn't worried, Hal, I wouldn't be here now."

"Yeah."

A jet took off from one of the runways farther out, the thunderous roar trailing in its wake like a fat balloon.

Bolan was dressed casually in a black sport coat and charcoal-gray slacks. The Beretta was snugged in leather under his left arm, while the AutoMag was safely cached inside a hollowed-out tape recorder he carried in his left hand. Clips for both weapons, as well as a combat knife, were concealed in specially tailored pockets in the jacket and slacks.

The back door of the limousine opened and Lee got out. He held something in his hand, but Bolan was too far away to make it out. Wingate got out, as well, giving some last-minute instructions to his son.

"Put a man on it, Hal," Bolan said, "and let me know what you find out. Give me a call later and I'll arrange to contact you back from a safe phone."

"Okay, but I think we're just getting edgy because everything has gone so well. In two days the blueprints for Wingate's addition to the SDI program will be on the Man's desk and we'll be out of the picture." Brognola broke the connection.

Bolan hung up the receiver and started back in the general direction of the limo. The men in the unmarked security cars had left the vehicles running, and he wondered if the engines would overheat before anyone moved.

Lee Wingate left his father's side and approached the Lear jet.

Why would the merc leave if he feared for his father's life? Bolan asked himself. And there was no doubt that the elder Wingate was sending him somewhere. Why? There was another facet of their relationship Bolan hadn't discovered—a goal they shared. Or one that Wingate had passed on to his son.

Just as Lee Wingate laid his hand on the railing of the steps leading up into the belly of the jet, the tortured sound of spinning tires shrieked into Bolan's ears.

Across the barren expanse of superhighway, through the shimmering waves of heat, Bolan could make out an attack force. Two sedans, with a motorcycle rider wedged between them, headed for the limousine on a path that would bring them right between the Lear and the big car.

A projectile flashed from the passenger side of the lead vehicle, and the unmarked security car to the limo's left exploded in a white-hot ball of flame. The men inside never had a chance.

"Get in the car," Bolan yelled to Wingate as he broke into a run, unleathering the Beretta as he moved. He snapped a 3-round burst at the car bearing the grenade launcher. The window on the passenger side starred, but he didn't think he had seriously injured anyone.

The remaining attack car slid to a halt in front of the Lear in an effort to block its passage. The motorcycle rider sped toward Lee Wingate, his body hunkered low over the handlebars.

The elder Wingate had managed to scramble back inside the limo, and for a moment the Executioner thought the munitions maker would be able to clear out of the attack grid—until he saw the chauffeur blown away by the passenger in the car blocking the jet. Only after the man's body jerked with the impact did he hear the Kalashnikov's familiar bark.

Lee Wingate had already drawn his pistol and was returning fire, ignoring the motorcyclist. Bullets from his .38 whined off the top of the sedan and drove the shooter to cover.

The remaining two security men pulled into the path of the car with the grenade launcher, blocking its approach to the limo. Screams of torn metal filled the air and the cars locked in a death embrace. The driver of the security car died instantly. One man stepped out of the damaged attack vehicle and pumped a clip from a Kalashnikov through the unopened window, spitting glass over both occupants. Before the security man could get clear, the attacker had changed clips and was firing again, sending him to the ground.

The motorcyclist had left the bike in a dive that tangled Lee Wingate and himself in the railing of the steps. The merc leader went down under the unexpected assault, was knocked through the railing and landed on the ground. Before he could recover, the rider had thrown himself on top and was drawing a combat knife from a sheath on his left arm.

Bolan dived for safety behind the bullet-proof limo as the shooter with the Kalashnikov started tracking him. Using the moment he had bought himself, he hefted the AutoMag he had recovered from the tape recorder shell and returned the Beretta to its shoulder holster. He ripped his tie off with his left hand and dumped the jacket so he could move quicker.

Rolling to his left side, Bolan looked under the limo and found the shooter's feet. Then he thrust the big .44 in front of him and squeezed off a shot that knocked the man down and took him out of the play.

Bolan pushed himself to his feet. As he passed by Wingate he paused long enough to slam the door shut after checking on the man, who was hunkered down in the back seat, reaching for something concealed in a door panel.

The side mirror by Bolan's head exploded as he looked over the top of the car. He felt the sharp sting of flying glass brush across his skin.

As he swung Big Thunder up in a two-handed grip, Bolan tracked onto the driver of the lead car. Russian, he realized as he looked into the man's eyes. The AutoMag bucked twice, once at the target's belt buckle and once dead center in the chest.

When the warrior glanced around the car he saw that the remaining two security men were down and maybe dead. Two Russians from the blocking car were moving toward the Lear jet. The motorcyclist had sliced a razor-sharp knife along Lee Wingate's jaw, and blood was running down the merc commander's neck. The .38 was just beyond his reach.

Bolan started to lock into target acquisition just as Lee flipped his adversary, making the shot impossible. He pulled up the big .44 and swung it toward the two approaching men. They caught sight of the big man and hustled back to their vehicle. The booming reports of the pistol sounded like thunderclaps. Glass scattered from the windows.

Bolan changed clips, letting the empty hit the ground at his feet. Why were they after the jet? There hadn't been a move made toward the limo since the initial confrontation. Was Lee Wingate their target rather than his father? Did it have something to do with his activities in South America instead of his father's part in the SDI program?

Bolan heard the limo door open. He flicked a backward glance over his shoulder and saw Stuart Wingate standing behind him with a Colt .45 in his fist. The older man's eyes were focused on his son's private battle instead of the chaos surrounding him.

"Get down," Bolan gritted between clenched teeth.

One of the Russians in the car opened a door and crouched behind it, drawing a bead on the elder Wingate.

Bolan raised the AutoMag and punched three rounds through the door, exploding the metal and turning the man's chest into a red ruin.

The leather-clad rider had freed himself from Lee and had taken a package from the younger Wingate's jacket. Bolan recognized it as the same package Lee had been holding when he got out of the limo.

The rider started up the ramp, drawing a pistol as he climbed the steps. Lee got to his feet and hurled himself up the steps after his assailant.

As the remaining Russian exposed himself long enough to take a bead on the merc colonel, Bolan found himself wondering again if the attack had been directed at the father or the son.

The first shot from the AutoMag caught the Russian in the shoulder and spun him around, leaving him wide open for the 240-grain round that took him between the eyes.

Lee Wingate caught up with the rider with a flying tackle that knocked the man against the railing. The rider jerked with the impact until Lee grabbed the man's belt buckle long enough to retrieve the package. Then he threw his attacker over the railing.

Lee looked at his father expectantly.

"Get out of here," Stuart Wingate roared.

Lee seemed hesitant.

"Williams," Wingate bellowed to his pilot. "You have your orders. Get him the hell out of here. Now."

The pilot nodded and climbed back inside the Lear. Lee tucked the package inside his shirt and followed.

The warrior stood, wondering if the target had been the man or the package. He changed clips in the AutoMag as he glanced at the carnage surrounding the limo. The wrecked car was still burning, hung heavily with thick black smoke. He could hear the sirens of fire and safety vehicles in the distance.

The Lear taxied off, lifting into the sky in a sudden blast of power.

Bolan moved to the motorcyclist's side. A crimson froth bubbled on the man's lips, the bright red a testament to arterial flow. Bolan knew the man wouldn't make it.

"American fool," the man breathed in Russian. He stared at Bolan with a pained grimace. "You lay down your life so willingly for one who has betrayed you and your country." Then he died.

Bolan headed toward Stuart Wingate while the Lear faded into the distance.

The munitions man took a cigarette from his pocket and lit it, watching Bolan carefully. "You don't shoot too badly for a public relations writer."

Bolan ignored the gibe. "They were waiting for you," he said. "They knew you were going to be here today."

Wingate nodded deliberately. "You'd think so, wouldn't you?" Then he got back inside the limo and closed the door, leaving Bolan to stand outside as the police surrounded them.

HE WALKED in the shadows of the night, claiming them as his own.

Dressed completely in black, and with the hafts of his knives covered in black tape, he had to be looked for in order to be seen, a phantom drifting soundlessly along the streets of Ho Chi Minh City. His Uzi was concealed beneath his long coat. Too many people were looking for him, and too many knew of his weakened condition.

But even a wounded panther kept its claws, though the knowledge didn't remove any of the fear that pumped through his veins. Even if the orders were not to shoot on sight his presence inspired that course of action.

Not many knew of his survival. He hadn't regained consciousness until several hours after the shooting. He'd come to in a funeral home, covered by a thin linen sheet. The bullet-proof vest Solly Taggert hadn't known about had been removed, of course, as had the pouch filled with gold coins.

He had awakened slowly, not aware of the pain that racked his body until it exploded in a sudden onslaught across his chest and head, leaving him breathless. Naked, he had forced himself from the cold morgue table, to stand on his feet despite the dizziness that threatened to make him vomit. He had breathed shallowly at first, to fight the nausea and to keep the fire raking across his chest to a minimum.

He had stumbled his way through the funeral home until he found the bathroom. The mirror revealed ravaged flesh over his eyes, bruised and torn from the bullet. He had felt new terror claw at him as he realized how close he'd come to being blinded.

He had found clothes in another room, covered with blood as his own must have been, although this victim had been much larger. His legs had been steadier when he walked out of the building.

That had been ten days ago, Pham pondered as he made his way through the city's darkness. He hunched his shoulders painfully, tucking the Uzi closer to his body as a government vehicle loaded with soldiers rumbled by. He had people in the Vietnamese government who knew him, who hired him at times for odd jobs for the country or for their own personal gain. But no friends. He had existed without those for a long time now.

As the military jeep passed, he raised his head again to check his surroundings. Still in the red-light district not far from the bar where Taggert had gunned him down, he walked the narrow and winding streets to the outer perimeter, where cheap living spaces could be rented with comparative safety.

The bruises still lingered on his chest, but that was a small price to pay. The bullet-proof vest had been like a second skin to him for years. Almost irreplaceable except in some of the higher priced black markets. He hadn't yet had the opportunity to procure another, and he was agitated about the upcoming confrontation.

More than anything else right now, Pham wanted revenge. To put Solly Taggert's head on a pole and leave it in front of the bar, mute testimony to what happened when people underestimated him.

There would be more stories to add to the ones he knew were already whispered in the barrooms. And in his business, Pham needed those stories to keep the amateurs off his back.

He paused at the street corner, noting the staggered groups of pedestrians moving from bar to brothel and back again.

His fingers strayed to the weapons concealed and strapped about his body, as if touching amulets of protection: the butt of the Uzi in his right hand; the throwing knives at his waist and in both boots; the .25 automatic strapped to his inner thigh just under his crotch; the 9 mm pistol on his left hip in a cross draw.

What had Taggert discovered? It was a question that had loomed large in his mind as he struggled with fever and infection those first few days. Taggert was not a risk taker unless the payoff was there to make it worthwhile.

Whatever it was, Pham had decided while he was convalescing, it had to be big. Solly Taggert wouldn't have tried to take him out if it wasn't. Pham knew for a fact that Taggert was afraid of him, had seen it in the American's eyes as they sat across the table from each other. So Taggert was taking chances of a magnitude he'd never taken before. Perhaps the wrath of the Vietnamese army could not extend across borders, but Pham's vengeance knew no boundaries, geographically or temporally. And Taggert had known that when he pulled the trigger.

Pham had a lot at stake already, too. His reputation for one, which tied in closely with his personal safety. The girl who had taken care of him and nursed him back to health for some of the gold he'd taken from one of his emergency hiding places in the city now rested in a shallow grave outside the city. He hadn't wanted to take a chance that he'd talked while the fever raged.

Now that he felt almost whole once more, he stalked the night again, a cold, one-eyed panther looking for his next kill.

Pham knew more about Taggert than the American knew of the Vietnamese. He knew the places the big ex-soldier liked to hang out when he was in town, he knew the women Taggert would ask for when he visited the brothel. And he knew the men Taggert would use on a big assignment.

He had found out that two of them had already left the city. Pham had learned that Taggert had stopped by one man's house while Greenberg recruited the other. He had picked his prey wisely. Hershel Gant, the man he was going to visit tonight, was one of Taggert's favorite mercs. Gant was a British commando in his fifties who had lived in and around the Orient for more than thirty years. He was an explosives expert while he was on the job, a transient drunk when he wasn't. It had taken Pham two days to find the old soldier. The boy Pham had paid for the information had reported to him less than an hour ago.

Pham made another corner that wound him more tightly into the maze of run-down apartments.

As he passed through an alley furtive movements overhead caused him to spin abruptly and shove his shoulders against the wall to brace himself as he brought the Uzi up to bear. Just before his finger tightened against the trigger, he saw the young couple overhead, limned as one entity by the moonlight.

The Uzi slid under the coat again as Pham cursed himself silently, angry that he was so easily spooked since his brush with death. Perhaps now was the time to get out of his current way of life. Start something new. Or perhaps do nothing at all. Maybe Taggert's operation could provide the means to that end.

The shadows swallowed him again as he made himself a part of the walls he followed. Within minutes he reached his destination: an apartment building where, according to the information he had been able to garner, Gant lived alone on the second floor.

Pham walked boldly through the building and climbed the stairs. There were a few curious stares from the tenants in the hallways, but no one challenged him. He kept his head averted so that the eye patch and the bandage, which he had concealed under a black scarf, weren't visible.

Halting at the door, Pham noted the light spilling from the crack at his feet and wondered how best to handle the situation. He felt sweat trickle down his spine. If Taggert had already picked up two of his men, chances were that he had been in contact with the rest of the group.

The Vietnamese knuckled his left hand and rapped on the door, calling, "Gant." He listened intently, hearing the soft sigh of springs as someone slid from the bed. "Gant," he repeated.

"Who is it?"

"Taggert sent me."

"What the hell does he want?"

Pham was poised on a knife edge of indecision, knowing his next move had to be chosen with care. If Taggert hadn't already talked to the man . . .

"The rendezvous point has been changed."

"Good bleedin' Christ. On an operation as big as this you'd hope that bugger would have everything set up nice and proper."

The door creaked open and Gant stepped into view. He was a barrel-chested man with sandy hair and a walrus mustache that pointed upward with the fierceness of a bull's horns. He stood an easy six foot six and carried a good 280 pounds. A solid man, Pham realized, one who wasn't slowed by his bulk.

Gant was naked except for a pair of boxer shorts. His massive chest was covered with tattoos and rust-colored hair that looked like shingle nails.

"What's the matter with the blighter?" Gant asked as he waved Pham in. "Gettin' a wee bit nervous, is he? I told him this job was a little more than he was used to handling."

Pham made no move to step inside. Instead he moved his jacket aside and raised the Uzi.

"What the hell is this?" Gant flared.

Pham kept his voice soft, full of menace. "Move back, or I'll kill you."

Gant's eyes narrowed, but he stepped backward, keeping his hands in view.

Pham followed him inside and shut the door. "The bed," he ordered, waving the snout of the Uzi.

"Taggert said you were dead," Gant said as he backed toward the bed.

"Maybe I was," Pham replied. "It's been said that I have been before."

A grin split the big man's homely face. "Judgin' from that scratch on your head, Taggert wasn't wrong by much."

Pham remained silent until Gant reached the bed. "Sit."

The Briton sat, keeping a cordial look on his face, but light from the low-wattage overhead bulb reflected from the sheen of perspiration on his forehead.

"Solly has a new interest," Pham said as he took a straight-backed chair from its place by the window and sat on it backward. "One that he has recruited you for. I want to know what it is."

Gant shrugged. "Go ask him."

"I hold your life in my hands, fat man."

"You're getting shortchanged, you little slant-eyed bastard."

Pham slowly reached under the jacket and brought out a skinning knife. The blade gleamed under the light. He let the barrel of the Uzi rest on the back of the chair. "I'll get the information one way or another."

"You ain't gettin' anything here," Gant snarled. He rocked back on the bed and shot out a big foot, striking the chair high and hard.

The move was suicidal, and Pham barely restrained himself from pulling the trigger. The force of the kick jarred him from the chair and caused new waves of pain to erupt from his bruised ribs. He went over backward, losing the Uzi in the process. Before he had a chance to get to his feet and regain the weapon, the big man was on him.

Gant nearly crushed the smaller man when he landed on him, and Pham couldn't restrain a cry of pain. Desperately the Vietnamese turned the knife over in his hand and shoved it toward Gant's face. The edge scored a cheek, drawing blood.

The big man grabbed for the skinning knife before Pham had a chance to use it again. The fingers of both big hands locked around Pham's wrist and forced it upward. Pham went with the motion, letting Gant pull him into position, then hooked the fingers of his right hand in Gant's crotch. He squeezed. Hard.

With a bellow of rage and pain, Gant rolled off the smaller man. Pham got to his feet before his opponent recovered, then lifted his left leg in a vicious roundhouse kick that collided with the man's nose. Blood spurted and joined the earlier flow that had been drawn with the knife. Pham stayed at arm's length as the two men circled each other in the small apartment.

Gant's blows were for the most part ineffective and drained the man's energy quickly. Pham let him swing, dodging most of them with little difficulty.

"Goddamn wog," Gant swore. "Stand still and fight."

Pham loosed another flurry of blows, but this time the big man got lucky and snared his left wrist. But before Gant had a chance to exert leverage, Pham whirled inward, turning backward to strike his adversary in the throat with his right elbow. He repeated the blow twice more before Gant let go of his arm and crumpled to the floor.

The Vietnamese staggered to the chair and used it for support while he gathered the Uzi and the knife. He watched dispassionately as Gant wheezed and coughed in an effort to regain his breath.

He advanced on Gant. The big man tried to force himself to his feet and couldn't make it.

Without warning Pham lifted the knife and made two neat slices on the backs of Gant's legs, hamstringing the man. Then he started asking questions. Within minutes he knew about Stuart Wingate's grandson and Taggert's plan to sell the boy back for three million dollars.

Eight minutes later, Gant was dead and Pham had faded back into the night.

LEE WINGATE GRABBED the edges of the Lear's hatch and pulled himself through. Williams had already buckled himself in, and the jet was rolling down the runway. A voice on the radio kept ordering Williams to stay grounded.

The pilot adjusted his mike on the headphone hookup and responded, "Negative, Control. Those sons of bitches down there mean business, and we seem to be the target." Then he cut the radio off and threw the headphones to one side.

Lee glanced out the window at the burning wreckage of the security car, at the bodies surrounding his father's limo. For a moment he felt a pang of guilt as he realized he couldn't remember the chauffeur's name. An island of the living among the dead, he thought as he looked at the limo. He studied the dark-clad figure of McKay, noting the big silver pistol the man held in his right fist. Black seemed to suit the guy. Just where did McKay fit into all of this?

"Pull up a chair and have a sit, kid," the pilot told him. "Ain't every day you get shot at."

Lee smiled slightly. It was easier for him to remember the days he hadn't been shot at.

He slid into the copilot's seat and buckled the harness, snugging the .38 Colt Government Model under the waistband of his pants after putting in a new clip. A spare clip went into his front pants pocket.

When he looked up he noticed the pilot was watching him.

"You act like a guy used to handling guns," Williams said. "You serve in Nam?"

"No."

"I did. Two tours in gunships. Had all the shooting and killing I wanted back then."

Lee gazed at the blue sky that had opened up ahead of them, white clouds disappearing before the first tendril could embrace them.

"Guess if that big guy hadn't come on like he did, we'd all be dead now," Williams speculated. "At least we would have been in a lot of trouble. They seemed more interested in taking us out than your daddy."

Lee considered that, replaying in his mind everything that had happened. He hadn't noticed it at first, but he had to admit the attack had been geared toward the jet. Toward him. He snapped his eyes open again and reached inside his shirt for the package his father had given to him.

It was thin and flat, about the size of an old 45 record. His father had told him it contained access codes to a Swiss account with three million dollars and Solly Taggert's name on it.

Were they after the package? Or were they after him? The man who had attacked him was Russian. How did the Russians fit into this?

He turned the package over in his fingers and put it away. Riddles. He had never been any good at riddles. Stu had, though. Lee had always been more of a doer than a thinker. Even the planning he did while in a firefight resulted from looking at a situation and deciding what he needed to *do* to tilt the odds in his favor. He didn't need riddles now.

Williams stuck a package of Red Man chewing tobacco in front of him. Lee shook his head.

The pilot shrugged and hooked a jawful from the package with a forefinger. He took a stained Texaco mug from under the seat and placed it between his knees.

"You're not one for small talk, are you?"

"No," Lee replied. Then he pushed himself up to retreat to the back of the Lear and get some sleep while he still felt safe. There was no telling what was waiting for him once he was back on the ground.

As BOLAN STEPPED from the shower he heard the phone ringing. He grabbed a towel from the rack as he passed it and draped his body.

The motel room he was staying in was on the north side of Oklahoma City. The second-story view took in the rest of the motel and the swimming pool below. It was dark now and a few lights at the pool's bottom pierced the inky blackness of the starless night.

He had spent most of the afternoon going over the story of the attack with the Oklahoma City Police Department. Stuart Wingate had been exempt from going downtown due to his governmental connections, so Bolan had gotten the third degree. The McKay identity held up under close scrutiny, including the gun permits for the modified Beretta and the AutoMag.

When he returned to the Wingate home, his bags had been packed and the housekeeper told him a room had been arranged at a nearby motel. He was told Wingate was busy and couldn't talk to him, but that Wingate had his room number and would be in touch. Having no other options at the moment, Bolan had gathered his bags and gone to a motel—not the one the housekeeper had suggested. Thoughts about what the dying Russian had said stayed in his mind.

By 4:00 p.m. he was registered at the motel, had another rental car so Wingate wouldn't recognize it if he decided to go back unannounced and had talked to Brognola again, this time to tell him about the Russians. The big Fed had broken the connection to let the intel from the attack filter in through his office, as he knew it would. Bolan had gone to eat and had taken a shower when he got back.

He picked the phone up, expecting to hear Brognola's rough voice. Instead it was a stranger whose voice was a full octave higher. "If you know what's good for you, McKay, you'll get the hell out of this town." Then the line went dead.

Bolan finished toweling off and pulled on a pair of jeans, wondering why Wingate went to the trouble of finding out where he was staying. Why did he feel the need to threaten him?

It had to have something to do with that package, though he didn't know what it contained, he knew the Russians were after it instead of Wingate. They had, in fact, known that such a package existed.

And nobody, Bolan thought grimly, on the good guys' side had been aware of it.

He cleaned his weapons while waiting for Brognola to call. He wanted to go back to the Wingate home to see if he could discover anything from that end. Wingate was hiding something, that was certain. Bolan knew enough about the security system to pass through—maybe not easily, but he could do it.

When he finished with the hardware, he pulled the couch to a secure spot against the wall and took a nap. The

AutoMag was a heavy bulk on his chest, a reminder that unfriendly forces knew where he was.

When he woke, the phone was ringing and his left arm had gone to sleep under his head.

4

"Striker?" Brognola said.

Bolan grunted an affirmative and looked at his watch: 2:13 a.m. "You're working late, Hal."

"Everybody's working late on this one. You'd think somebody had taken a potshot at the President himself," the big Fed grumbled.

"Only this isn't quite the same."

"No. Not when I told a couple of people what the Russian said to you. Stuart Wingate has been a golden boy around Wonderland for a long time, dating back to JFK's time. The old hierarchy doesn't want to see anything happen to him. Some of the younger guys want to know what the hell is going on."

"And what are you telling them?"

"I tell them what you told me."

Bolan bent at the waist, stretching muscles cramped from hanging over the couch at both ends. Old wounds pulled at ligaments, creating twitches in different muscle groups. He moved the curtain over the patio window and looked at the pool. Fewer lights were on now, and the darkness was all-enveloping. "What does Wingate have to say about it?"

"He says he was as shocked as everybody about the attack."

Bolan let the curtain drop back into place. He left the lights off in case someone was watching his room. "He probably was. What does he say about his son's disappearance?"

"Said his son had a trip to make."

"And couldn't be bothered with hanging around long enough to fill out a statement about the attack."

"Right."

"Did you get any kind of flight plan on the jet?"

"There was one filed...."

"But it never reached its destination point."

"Bingo."

"And Wingate doesn't have anything to say about that either."

"No."

Bolan sat on the couch, wishing he had something cold to drink. "What have we got on the pilot?"

"His name is Scotty Williams. He's been in Wingate's employ since 1978."

"A company man."

"Yeah."

"Did the Bear turn up an address on the guy?"

"Yeah." Brognola seemed hesitant.

"Something wrong, Hal?"

"This is going to have to be handled with kid gloves, Striker. Wingate has to cover a few gray areas right now, but he still carries a lot of weight up on the Hill."

"Which is why I'm not going directly to the source and finding out why a dying Russian agent told me Wingate was betraying his country. Something smells, Hal. To turn over all the rocks on this end I've got to have somewhere to start prying. For now Stuart Wingate is out and his son has disappeared. As close as Wingate was playing this one, I'd be willing to bet the only one left who knows where that jet ended up is the pilot."

Brognola's voice was tired. "I know, dammit, I know. The Man wants you to stay on top of this one, too. Even if things get a little out of control. This is coming on the end of a lot of other bad press, and he wants it cleaned up as soon as possible.''

"I'll keep the profile as low as possible," Bolan said. It was one thing, he thought, to go after someone you knew was dirty. There weren't any compunctions, no higher court the guy could go running to. But when someone as powerful and influential as Stuart Wingate tried to hide his dirty laundry, things became too complex. If you played by the rules.

"What have you got on the pilot?"

There was a pause at the other end, then the sound of shuffling papers. "Williams, Scott," Brognola began. He covered it all in military jargon Bolan remembered well. Two tours in Vietnam, helicopter gunships, Purple Heart, civilian jobs from 1970 till he landed the position with Wingate Munitions. No criminal activity. One ex-wife and three kids, one now in college. And a home address.

Bolan copied the address on a sheet of hotel stationery.

"The CIA and Department of Defense are breathing hot and heavy on this one," Brognola said. "They're going to be covering this guy with a fine-tooth comb. You're going to have to be careful not to trip over them."

"I'll be there and gone before they realize I'm not part of the same team."

"If I get anything, how am I supposed to get in touch with you?"

"I'll check in from time to time. Once I get started on this thing it could move pretty fast. If Wingate couldn't keep it from the Russians it proves there's a leak somewhere. It's up to me to find it."

Bolan said goodbye and hung up. He took a pastel pink sport shirt from his bag and put it on, tucking it into a pair of black pants. The shoulder rig and the Beretta went under a white lightweight jacket. White runners and wrap-around black sunglasses completed the ensemble. A womanizer, the file had said. He checked the mirror in the bathroom and was satisfied he looked the part he chose to play. Just an old friend, he thought to himself.

"I'M TRYING TO FIND Scotty," Bolan told the girl behind the security desk at Williams's apartment building. He gave her a wide, winning smile because she looked young enough to be impressed by it.

She was blond and pretty, and Bolan would have bet she knew most of the men who lived in the building—the single ones, like pilot Scotty Williams, would have made sure they introduced themselves.

"Scotty's not in right now," she said. She looked genuinely forlorn about the idea that Bolan had wasted a trip to see an old friend.

"That's what I get for not calling ahead first," Bolan said. "But I wanted it to be a surprise. We haven't seen each other for years. Do you know when he's going to be back? If it's only going to be a little while I'll go get a couple of drinks around the corner and check back later."

"He'll probably be gone for a few days. He told me last night he was planning on a week layover the next time his boss sent him out."

"Did he say where he was going to be? Maybe I could give him a call."

The girl shook her head. "Sorry."

Bolan waved it away. "It's okay. We'll get together when we can. I'll just go upstairs and leave a note saying I was by."

He turned from the desk and made his way to the elevator bank. He fluttered his fingers to the smiling girl as the doors closed. A week? Why a week? Unless Williams was going to be the pilot for Lee Wingate's ultimate destination. Or to make sure Williams wasn't around to be answering a lot of questions.

The elevator rose silently to the fifth floor, and the doors opened onto a hallway that was quiet and empty. Bolan walked to Williams's door as if he were expected, removed a small case from an inside jacket pocket and shook out a lock pick. It was a skill he had developed during his urban warfare, necessary in his kind of life.

He inserted the lock pick and gently probed, glancing over his shoulder toward the elevators. The red arrow pointing up let him know someone had taken an elevator from a lower floor. The numbers slowly winked on and off as the elevator climbed. When it flashed 4, it stopped. And the lock sprang.

Putting the lock pick away, Bolan gripped the Beretta in the breakaway holster and leaned against the door hard enough to swing it slowly open.

The apartment light was on, revealing a modestly furnished room. A bachelor's home with "off-the-rack" contemporary furniture except for the big-screen television against the far wall, where giant images of Hawkeye Pierce and B. J. Hunnicutt loomed like kindly spirits. The coffee table had a glass center, as did the two end tables. The only difference was that a canned Coke sat on the coffee table. A gray film circled the bottom of the can, and perspiration slid down the red sides.

Okay, Bolan thought, one guy. But who? There were too many sides already involved to be guessing with any success. The Russians were interested, the CIA and FBI were interested, Wingate was running his own game and not telling anyone what the rules were. And himself. With none of them knowing if they were even playing at the same table.

Bolan eased into the apartment, shutting the door behind him, making sure the sound of the lock engaging was loud enough to be heard. He flattened against the wall, bringing the barrel of the Beretta up to cheek level.

The room had a hallway next to the big-screen television, which Bolan assumed led to the bedroom. Careful to make no sound on the thick carpet, the big man took up a position near the corner. He slowly raised both arms above his shoulders, making sure the light from the lamps didn't cast any shadows past the end of the wall. Then he waited.

A hesitant shadow crawled around the corner of the wall and Bolan watched it lengthen and thin out. A moment later it became the barrel of a snub-nosed, large-caliber handgun.

The gun froze for a moment, as if unsure it could be seen. The guy holding it dropped down, moving to his hands and knees, Bolan guessed from the jerkiness of the movements. Then the gunner threw himself around the corner in an all-or-nothing play, scrambling to a kneeling position with both hands on the pistol grip.

Bolan stepped forward, measured the distance between himself and the man dressed in a sport shirt and designer jeans, planted his left foot and kicked out before his target had the opportunity to react to the sudden threat.

The kick landed with snapping force, popping the big man's head back and sending the pistol flying.

Bolan moved on his quarry before the other man could do anything about getting up from the floor. He laid the silenced barrel of the Beretta on the guy's nose, sliding it down to his mustache before applying pressure to keep the man's head on the floor.

"Don't move until I tell you to," Bolan growled. The man remained silent, his eyes fixed on the gun. Bolan lifted his gaze from his prisoner and scanned the rest of the small apartment for any sign of a backup. Satisfied, he returned his attention to the man at his feet.

STUART WINGATE SAT in the back of the big armored car and stared through the bullet-proof glass at the cemetery, emotions swirling inside him. Night had fallen and lay quietly over the dormant graves like a soft smoke. Against the darkness, the trees over the headstone that held his gaze seemed two-dimensional, a child's paper cutout.

It was a peaceful grave site, he'd always told himself. Set apart from many of the others by the trees. He'd spent a lot of time there during the years since Stu's death.

Ahead of him, on the other side of the glass partition, the driver kept checking the rearview mirror and the road for signs of other travelers. Behind him was another car filled with CIA security men. Since the attack that morning, their number had trebled. The section chief had tried to talk him out of the late visit, but Wingate had remained adamant. After all, he had asked, he wasn't a prisoner, was he?

Maybe later, he told his pale reflection in the dark glass, but not now.

He unlocked the door and pushed it open, sensing the movement of the security man on the opposite side of the big car. "Wait here," he ordered, his voice quiet and contained, leaving the man no options.

Wingate stepped out in the muggy night air and started up the small pebbled rise leading to the grave. He heard doors slam shut behind him as the CIA men abandoned their car to keep him under their protection. He ignored them and the call the section chief made to him. Running footsteps pounded toward him until the agent marched abreast.

"Do you think this is wise, sir?" the section chief asked.

Wingate pressed his fists deeper in the robe he wore over his nightclothes, knotting the silk in his grip. "I'm going to visit my son's grave."

The section chief stepped in front of him, effectively blocking the path.

Wingate stopped and stared at the man. The CIA man was young, barely past thirty. This was probably his first big assignment. He was slim and dapper, with innocence overlaying a lethal core, which Wingate could actually feel. He'd seen the Ingram MAC-10 shoulder rigging the chief had strapped on at the mansion as they got ready to leave.

"I really must object," the chief said. Then added, "Sir."

"Object all you want to," Wingate replied. "Put it in a letter and tell your control that I wouldn't follow orders."

The section chief looked uncomfortable. He had already transcended the normal boundaries of his job as he saw it.

"Young man," Wingate said in a level voice that belied the anger he felt, "I'm going to give you a very simple choice. You can get the hell out of my way, or you can stand there while I blow your brains all over the trees behind you." He took the .45 from the robe pocket and pointed it at the section chief's forehead.

The man spread his arms away from his body.

Wingate kept him transfixed there while he made a small circle around him. Once past, he turned his back on the man and walked on, keeping the .45 in his hand beside him. Its heavy weight against his thigh felt alien.

There would be no more government work, he realized as he came to a stop in front of the marble headstone. Maybe no more munitions work at all. But it didn't matter. He had planned on getting out of any personal ties with the munitions factories the day he had verified the existence of his grandson. There would be no time.

Wingate knelt and traced the gold letters on the headstone with the fingers of his left hand.

It's been so long, son. I found myself counting the years after I got that call about your son and was surprised at how few there have been compared to the loneliness I've felt. I still miss you so very much.

Unshed tears burned at his eyes, and he felt ashamed when he remembered the times he'd chastised his son for crying. A man didn't cry, he'd said, then learned that fathers did.

They'll be calling me a traitor for what I've done, Stu. They'll say I betrayed our country. And maybe I have. But I think we were betrayed first. It cost both of us our lives.

The marble felt warm in his hand and it made him feel stronger, as if the one-way communication between them was more sure this night.

I'll take care of the boy. I'll raise him right, the way you would've wanted him to be. I won't be back here again, son, so this is my goodbye. I'll miss this place and the closeness I've always felt to you, but I know you'll understand. I'm sorry you never got the chance to be buried here.

He stood erect then, letting the tears run silently down his face. He dropped the .45 on top of the gravestone and turned to go.

"ARENT YOU THE GUY from the airport this morning?" the man asked Bolan.

The Executioner kept the Beretta trained on the guy while he circled to the patio doors across from the small dinette. He looped the cords from the curtains in his hands and pulled on them, testing their strength. He took a pocket-knife from his pants pocket and cut two five-foot lengths from the cord, then threw them to the man on the floor.

"Tie your feet together," Bolan commanded.

The man tried an easy smile. "Hey, look, you don't have to do this. We're on the same side. I'm CIA. My ID's in my jacket pocket."

Bolan had already figured that, but it didn't matter. Too many questions were coming up that he didn't have explanations for. Such as, why would the CIA be watching Williams's apartment? Unless they wanted to prevent anyone else from finding out anything about the pilot. No, they definitely weren't allies.

"Tie your feet together," Bolan repeated. "Just like back in spy school because I'll be checking for style and originality."

The smile dropped from the man's lips. He started to say something, but the grim look on Bolan's face stopped him cold. He grabbed for the cord angrily.

"Slowly," Bolan advised. "You've already made me nervous once tonight. There's no reason to be stupid about this. Use both strands, I want it doubled."

"I don't know who you are," the agent said, "but you're buying into a lot of trouble."

"Don't let it worry you," the Executioner replied. "I've got a big credit line." He moved the curtains aside and peered outside. "You got a backup on this little baby-sitting operation?"

"Go to hell," the agent snarled.

Bolan looked back at the man, noting the tautness of the cords and the knots. He went to the other side of the curtains and repeated the operation. With a fistful of cord, Bolan stepped back to the man sitting on the floor. "Hands out," he ordered.

The agent didn't move.

"Want to take a chance on a concussion? You're going to be here all night as it is. Or until your buddies check up on you or your relief comes. I don't have a lot of time."

The man shoved his hands forward and Bolan tied them tightly together, using the slack length to knot them into the cord at his feet.

"Who are you?" the agent asked. "This morning it looked like we were working on the same side."

"I only play my side," Bolan growled.

"What the hell are you talking about?"

Bolan ignored the agent and took a chair from the small dinette, lodging it under the doorknob.

"Who put you into this operation?" the agent asked.

Bolan didn't break his stride as he walked past the guy to the bedroom. "Keep the questions coming and you're going to end up modeling a gag."

He holstered the Beretta and flipped on the light. A king-size waterbed filled the room, a small wet bar occupied a corner and the closet was filled with styles that were echoes from the first season of *Miami Vice*—pastels and loose cuts.

Overhead he was reflected in sixteen sections of mirror centered over the bed. It definitely fit the playboy style Kurtzman's computers had turned up.

The warrior crossed the room and opened the small nightstand next to the bed, shuffling through stacks of porno magazines, an assortment of X-rated videos and color snapshots. He finally found the phone under the edge of the bed, sitting on top of the address book he was looking for. He thumbed through it patiently, looking for something that might stand out and give him some type of clue. Most of the entries were two-syllable names of women: Marci, Cindi, Shari, Lulu. And stars. Bolan figured this was the book Williams showed friends, like a grandmother's brag book. He flipped the useless address book to the center of the bed.

How much time, he wondered as he scanned the bathroom, did Wingate give Williams to set the flight up?

He rummaged through the medicine chest and found a small vial of cocaine in the back.

A day or two at least, he decided as he dumped the contents of the vial in the toilet and flushed.

Williams would have made some phone calls to set up refueling routes and emergency plans, but he doubted the pilot would have used his home phone. Still, it was worth a try.

He returned to the bedroom and lifted the phone. Remembering the CIA agent he had tied up in the front room, he unscrewed the mouthpiece and checked inside. He then replaced the mouthpiece without disturbing the bug he'd found inside and set it down.

Brognola would be able to get the phone records. It would take time, but he could get them.

He ignored the stony gaze the trussed up agent gave him as he examined the kitchen. On the wall, above the small closet where the trash was kept, Bolan found a calendar with handwriting neatly penciled in on different days. Most of the entries were mundane items pertaining to domestic affairs around the apartment.

But on the previous day Williams had made a note to call Terri.

Excitement filled him as he went back to the bedroom. He picked up the address book and started thumbing through the pages again. He found listings for five Terris, four of which he discarded immediately. The fifth, Terri Quentin, lived in Saint Martin.

It wasn't much, but it was the only thing going right now and he needed some lead to follow. It fit the picture he had gotten of the pilot. Williams would have arranged companionship of some kind if he was expecting to do a few days underground.

Brognola could check the phone records to see if Williams had called Terri Quentin's number anytime during the past two days. But he was sure of it. The big Fed would also be able to get the woman's address, which the book was lacking.

In the living area Bolan knelt in front of the agent and started patting him down.

"So what the hell?" the agent asked. "You going to rob me, too?"

Bolan removed the man's wallet and plucked his ID card from it. He gave the guy a grim smile as he stood. "No," he said, "I'm just going to join your side. For a little while. These cards beat the hell out of American Express."

He left the agent still trying to think of something to say. In the hallway he closed the door again and placed the ID card in his own wallet over the McKay credentials.

On his way down in the elevator Bolan thought it all over. The CIA knew more about the Wingate situation than Brognola did. Which meant they knew more than the President and weren't bothering to inform the Man about what was really going on.

It had bothered Bolan from the start when he was told an agent had broken deep cover to bring the plot to hit Wingate to the attention of the CIA. And the cryptic words the dying Russian had said. The KGB knew, too.

And Lee Wingate's disappearance, was that known about beforehand?

Probably not, he guessed. The attack at the airport had been totally unexpected. Men had died there. Good men. Maybe someone in the inner command circle had known, but the knowledge was certainly limited.

What had been the CIA's motive, though? Why choose to go it alone? Unless the information stopped at a certain level.

Bolan had no real respect for the Central Intelligence Agency since the Farnsworth affair. They had already proved themselves to be too easily accessible to plants. His pairing with Don Albright a while back had been a welcome relief from the normal work he saw in the Agency. The whole operation of the CIA had become too political, even up to the time of the Iran/Contra hearings.

He checked the CIA ID in his wallet just before the elevator let him out on the first floor. Just so he would know who he was.

The girl at the counter gave him a smile and said, "That must have been some letter."

Bolan shrugged. "Actually that wasn't why I went up there," he confided. He leaned across the counter to intensify the intimacy of the moment. "I need to know if Williams has had any messages the past two or three days."

The smile on the girl's face became brittle. "I'm afraid information like that is confidential, sir."

Bolan immediately picked up on the official tone in her voice. He reached inside his jacket and took out his wallet, letting her get a quick glimpse of the shoulder rigging. "It's okay," he told her. "I'm about as confidential as they come." He flipped the wallet open mechanically, as if he'd been doing it all his life. He let her read the letters, keeping his forefinger over the agent's photograph.

"I'm sorry, Mr. Keenan, you should have told me who you were."

"Call me Gil." Bolan gave her an easy smile. "I couldn't. It wasn't necessary before. Like I said, I'm confidential."

The girl nodded and reached under the counter. "We don't usually keep messages at the desk, but the management made an exception in Scotty's case and a few of the others who are in and out all the time." She paged through a small notebook with Williams's name on it. Once she found her place she passed the book over for Bolan's inspection.

There were only a handful of entries over the past three days. But yesterday a notation had been made that Terri returned his call.

Bolan handed the book back and said thanks.

A look of concern was on the girl's face. "Is Scotty in any kind of trouble?"

"Not yet," Bolan said truthfully. He turned from the counter and started for the door. Two men in dark suits came through it before he could clear the foyer. He kept on walking, hoping they wouldn't notice him. Their purposeful strides and the way they looked around immediately told him they were Gil Keenan's backup.

Bolan watched as they stood together in a moment of conference, looking like a matched pair of Dobermans. The Executioner broke into a run when one of them pointed him out to the other and started reaching under his jacket.

"Hey, buddy," one of them yelled. "Hold it right there."

Ignoring the command, Bolan slammed into the fire-exit door and went on through, forcing himself up the stairs two at a time. He'd made the second landing before they came crashing through after him.

Bullets cracked, spitting and spinning from the handrails to whine off the concrete walls.

Unlimbering the Beretta, he flicked it to 3-shot mode and returned fire in order to slow them down. Concrete dust showered them from the walls just above their heads. He watched in satisfaction as they dived to the floor, then returned his attention to the stairs.

The warrior didn't head for the basement because he knew other agents would have been positioned there, a group who would be monitoring the operation and the phone in Williams's room. He'd left his rental car parked out by the street on the east side, away from the front door. There was a back entrance to the apartment building, but he knew the Company men would have covered that by now.

At the third floor he left the fire escape and crawled through a window and into the hallway. A party had evidently broken up, as the way was blocked by a cluster of people telling one another goodbye.

Raising the Beretta so they could plainly see it, Bolan rushed through the first opening he got as the party goers spread out before him. Their screams drowned out any chance he had of hearing the pursuing Company men.

At the end of the hallway was a large plate-glass window and the blackness of night beyond. The map inside the soldier's head told him this was the window he wanted.

Coming to a halt at the window, Bolan peered down at the large pool area, which he had noticed during his soft probe earlier.

It was big enough and close enough, he thought as he studied the pool, with nothing but the straight side of the building overlooking it. And deserted except for a handful of couples engaged in conversation around it. But was it deep enough?

He threw a glance over his shoulder and saw the party goers still in a state of panic. The matched pair of agents was forcing its way through the mob.

Holstering the Beretta, Bolan shrugged out of his jacket and dropped it to the floor, pausing only briefly to remove his wallet. There was nothing left in his clothing that would lead anyone to his McKay identity. And he intended to be out of the state within the hour.

He knelt and picked up a potted fern that weighed nearly a hundred pounds. Shots ricocheted from the wall beside him as he threw the plant through the window. Allowing only a second for the flying glass to shatter out of his way, he followed it down into the night.

5

Lee Wingate picked up the tail almost immediately, despite the pulsing nightlife that ran in an alternating current around him. The soft glow of neon lights from the buildings surrounding the street spilled inside the cab, highlighting Scotty Williams's face in pinks, blues and greens.

Shifting in the seat, Lee moved so he'd have easier access to the .38 in his belt. The pilot never seemed to notice. From the time they had left the hangar, the man had been talking. If Lee had had his way, he and the pilot would have parted company as soon as they hit the ground. But that wasn't the way his father had arranged things. Williams held the hotel reservations and the cash flow Lee would need to set the rescue operation into full swing. Part of him argued that his father had made the arrangements to protect him, but another part suggested his father didn't trust him to follow his instructions.

There had been no one behind them at the airstrip, Lee was sure. Whoever was driving the tan French sports car behind them had picked the cab up en route.

He looked in the rearview mirror and studied the cabbie's reflection, seeing nothing more than a fortyish man with swarthy features and a hooked nose. Saint Martin was an island of mixed ancestry, so it was hard to pinpoint the man's nationality.

Williams was recounting one of his endless stories about a feminine conquest when he stopped abruptly and looked at Lee. "What's wrong with you, kid? You been tense ever since we set down. We're living in the lap of luxury for the next few days at the boss's expense. You're supposed to be in a holiday mood."

Lee ignored him, watching the cabbie. The man looked in the mirror, then cut his eyes away sharply when Lee stared back at him. The merc leader's inner alarm went from a soft buzz to a loud jangle. He reached his hand inside his jacket and closed his fist around the cold comfort of his pistol.

His voice was a whisper as he spoke to the pilot. "Is this the way to the hotel where we're supposed to stay?"

Williams looked at him curiously for a moment then checked the street signs. He shook his head. "You can probably get there from here," he said, "but it's longer. This takes you down by the tourist harbor."

Terrific. Lee slid the gun free of leather, keeping it out of the cabbie's sight. Williams was about to say something, but Lee froze him with a stare. Lightly Lee tapped the small package his father had given him to make sure it was still taped to his stomach under his shirt.

Feigning tiredness, Lee let his head loll back on the seat, turning so he could see the trailing car through hooded lids and still keep the driver in view.

Gradually the traffic thinned until it was a trickle. The road wound down to the harbor, where moored boats and ships rocked in their berths on one side, while restaurants, tourist attractions and motels lined the opposite side of the road.

It was now or never, Lee told himself. They were already deep within the territory the enemy had picked for a confrontation. But who was out to get him? Someone from his past? KGB? Or someone from the affair he was involved in now? Maybe Stu's son was just a story someone invented to get at the three million dollars.

He didn't know. All he was sure of was that whoever was following the cab was putting the lid on a box that he might not get out of.

Leaning forward, the merc tapped on the back of the cabbie's seat and said, "Pull over. I'm going to be sick."

The man didn't respond at first, as if he didn't know what to do.

"Pull over, dammit," Lee ordered and faked a dry heave.

When the cab pulled to a stop at the side of the road, Lee fumbled with the door lock, using up enough time to force the tailing car to pull over, as well. When it rolled to a stop only thirty feet behind the cab, Lee could make out at least three men inside.

Williams shifted on the seat, for the first time recognizing the other car for what it was. Lee felt a little better because now he was sure the pilot wasn't in on the surveillance.

Leaning heavily on the side of the cab, the merc left the door open and bent nearly double, keeping up the pretense of illness. Then he dropped to one knee without warning and brought up the pistol, arms extended stiffly in front of him.

He emptied the clip, drilling slugs into the front tires and across the grille, hoping to cripple the vehicle. He didn't want to hurt anybody. Not until he knew the identity of the players.

With the echoes of the shots still reverberating in his ears, Lee flung himself into the cab. Ignoring Williams, he dropped the empty clip and rammed home his last one. The cabdriver was halfway out the door when he heard the snap of the action.

"Inside, buddy," Lee commanded as he prodded the man with the barrel of the .38. Behind him he could hear car doors slamming. "Put it in gear and get us the hell out of here, now."

The cabbie obeyed, laying rubber as the vehicle shot from the side of the road, swerving in front of oncoming traffic.

"Who are you with?" Lee asked.

"Nobody," the cabbie replied. "I don't know what the hell is going on."

"No," Lee corrected in a hard voice. "*I* don't know what the hell is going on. I think you know a lot. Turn right here."

The cabbie hesitated until Lee pressed the pistol into his neck again.

The road they were traveling took them closer to the docks. There were fewer lights, yet the darkness seemed more friendly.

Lee could feel his heart beating frantically inside his chest, with the same type of adrenaline rush he had during firefights in the South American jungles.

"Are you KGB?" Lee asked.

The cabbie shook his head.

"Were they going to kill us?"

"I don't know nothin' about nothin'," the man said stubbornly.

"I can fix it so that's true."

The cabbie looked up, catching Lee's gaze in the rearview mirror. The man's eyes were watery. "Look, I—"

Lee put the gun behind the man's ear, so he could see it clearly in the mirror. "Don't say anything that isn't the truth."

The cabbie swallowed hard.

"Look, kid," Williams said, "let's not go off half-cocked here. We could already be in deep shit for shooting up that car."

"You want to get out and go it on your own? There's the door. Otherwise shut up and let me handle this."

The seat creaked as Williams settled back.

Lee glanced in the rearview mirror, angling so he could see the road behind them. How long, he wondered, before they got another car and came after them? If *he* was going to tail someone, he would make sure he didn't lose them even if something like this happened.

Lee said, "They've got the car wired, too, haven't they?"

The cabbie didn't say anything.

"I've been around," Lee told the man. "Didn't they tell you guys that?"

"I ain't nobody, man. They just hired me to drive the cab."

Lee considered, staring at the face in the mirror. He didn't buy it. Someone had gone to a lot of trouble to set this up. "Pull over here," he ordered.

The man froze for a moment before pulling to the side of the road.

"Leave the car running and get out."

Lee mirrored the driver's movements, almost out of reach behind the window divider when the man made a grab for something on the steering column. Throwing himself back inside the car, Lee grabbed a fistful of the man's hair and slammed him face first into the steering wheel, then pulled back heavily.

Bright blood streamed from the man's mouth.

"If you try something intelligent like that again," Lee snarled, "I'm going to shoot you. Now get out of the car. Keep your hands on your head."

Centering the .38 on the man's stomach, Lee inched around the open door and reached under the steering wheel. His hand came in contact with hard metal, and he found the grip and jerked the weapon free. It was a Virginian Dragoon .44 Magnum revolver.

"You always drive with one of these?" Lee asked. "Or were you planning on going bear hunting after you got off tonight?"

The driver licked his lips, and the merc leader could almost taste the salty blood, as well. "Look . . ."

"No, you look. I don't have time to dance around with you. Who are you working for?"

The man closed his eyes.

Lee raked the hammer back on the .44. "If I use this on one of your legs, you can kiss corrective surgery goodbye."

"I'm CIA."

"What was going to happen tonight?"

The man opened his eyes, as if sensing a reprieve. "Nothing. We just had orders to hold you until someone got here to pick you up."

"How did you know I was coming?"

"I didn't know, honest. We didn't get anything from the other end. Just orders."

Which still didn't help Lee figure out where the trouble was coming from. His past. Or his father's. Or why the CIA would try to pick him up. Unless they wanted the operation kept very quiet.

Maybe the guy had more information, Lee thought, but he didn't have time to try to dig for it. Reinforcements would soon be moving into place around them. Without saying anything he slid into the driver's seat. "You got any extra ammo for this bazooka?"

The man nodded. "The glove compartment."

For a long moment Lee stared at the CIA agent over the barrel of the .44, letting him feel how easy it would be to simply squeeze the trigger. Then he let the hammer down slowly. "Tell your buddies to stay away from me."

He dropped the cab into gear and sped off, not knowing where he was going but glad to put this place behind him. He touched the package under his shirt.

Looking in the rearview mirror, he studied the pilot's white face. "You got any friends on the island who could put us up for a few hours and keep quiet about it?"

Williams seemed hesitant about answering. "Yeah, but she's not going to be happy about it."

"What about the money?"

"It's in a safe-deposit box. I can pick it up first thing in the morning."

Lee shook his head. "Get it tonight. Use my father's name. Whoever is holding the cash will jump if you threaten to call my father. I don't want to take any more chances of getting caught out in the open."

"Okay."

Lee drove in silence, taking random turns through the darkened streets until he found a deserted pier in front of a warehouse.

"Get out of the car," he told Williams as he came to a stop on the wooden pier with the nose of the cab pointed out to the ocean.

"Let me get my bags out of the back."

"No. You're going to leave them there. For all we know the driver put a tracer on one of them when he put them in back. We don't have time to look for it."

"I've got a lot of money tied up in those clothes."

Lee looked over the back of the seat. "Those guys were supposedly CIA, Williams. They didn't try to pick us up at the airport, which tells me they didn't want anyone to know what happened to us. If they had a legitimate reason for taking us into custody, they would have taken us before we ever left Oklahoma City. They were waiting on us, remember?"

Lee opened the glove compartment and pulled out a box of .44 hollowpoints. He dropped the box into a jacket pocket, hit the accelerator briefly and rolled out of the cab.

He landed badly on his left elbow and felt shooting pains spiral up his arm. Lee looked up in time to see the cab go spilling over the edge of the pier to be swallowed up by the ocean.

Trapped in a hostile land with no one to rely on, Lee thought as he turned and walked toward Williams. The .44 felt heavy on his hip. In a way it was almost like coming home.

THE HEAT OF THE MIDDAY SUN beat down on Solly Taggert's back as he made his way through the winding alleys.
The Beretta rode comfortably on his hip, concealed by the
lightweight jacket he wore. He had been forced to wait until late in the day to pay a visit to Gant because he hadn't
wanted to take the chance that the big Briton was still
sleeping off a drunk. He was a surly, unpredictable brute
when he woke, especially if someone else did the waking.
Still, the man was more than worth the trouble involved because of his skill with explosives.

The stairs groaned under Taggert's weight, and he wondered how they ever managed to stand up under Gant.

A crowd had gathered in front of Gant's door by the time
Taggert got there, but the ex-soldier didn't see any official
uniforms so he pressed forward, shoving his way through
the people. There were a few muffled curses as he forced his
way to the open door, but no one tried to stop him.

He could smell the blood from the hallway even before he
saw Gant's body.

"Shit," he muttered as he walked through the doorway.
He knelt beside the big man's body, noting the hamstring
cuts and the slashes across Gant's face and chest, which he
felt sure had been made by someone asking questions. One
of Gant's thumbs had been amputated and was lying beside
his head.

Taggert stood and looked around the room. Gant didn't
have much. All the money he had ever put his hands on had
gone for women and rotgut whiskey. There was nothing of
value in the room.

Who would have gotten information this way? Taggert
wondered as he stared down at the corpse again. He noticed the broken nose and facial bruises for the first time.
Checking Gant's hands, he found patches of skin scraped
from the knuckles. Gant had been in a fight, he realized. But
with whom? There weren't many people who could subdue
the man once he'd gotten his steam built up.

Taggert was sure there had been only one assailant. Otherwise the room would have been demolished. And he was sure that whoever it had been had discovered what he'd come to find out. At least part of it. The room hadn't been searched.

One person, he repeated to himself. One person who had known something and had wanted to know more. One person who had been tough enough to take out Gant barehanded and callous enough to cut him.

A chill spread down his spine as he considered the possibilities. Someone was onto the operation. Not someone official, yet, but someone who had tumbled to it.

He forced himself away from the body and directed a question to an old woman standing in front of the crowd at the door. "What do you know about this?"

She shook her head and spread her hands helplessly. "Nothing. The man's body was found but moments ago."

"Someone had to hear something," Taggert persisted. "There was a fight in here and a man was killed."

The crowd started to break up and drift away as he stared at them.

Cursing silently, Taggert knelt by the body again and lifted the mattress from the bed. Underneath was a money belt. There wasn't much in it, but Taggert took what there was.

When he left the room the hallway was deserted.

Taggert took the stairs two at a time until he reached the alley. Police would arrive in moments to take care of the body and start asking questions. He didn't want to be around when they did because they sometimes operated like the guy who had questioned Gant. He headed back down the alley, watching for signs of pursuit. He didn't doubt for a moment that Gant's murder tied into the Wingate operation.

"Hey, soldier," a voice called behind him.

Taggert turned, his hand resting on the butt of his automatic. A young Vietnamese girl was leaning out a window on a second-story landing. She glanced over her shoulder to make sure no one was listening to her.

"I have information, soldier. About your dead friend."

"What about him?"

"Money talks, soldier. Bullshit walks. I learned that from you Yankees."

Taggert took a small pouch from his pocket and dropped two gold coins inside, then shook it so she could hear it clink together. "Enough?" he asked.

She shook her head. "What I know is very dangerous for me. After I tell you I will have to leave the city for a while."

"You're not getting any more."

"Not even if it could mean your life, American?"

Taggert hesitated. He had never rolled over for con games and he didn't plan to start now. Still, it was a small price to pay if the information was good. He added more coins until the young woman nodded.

"It had better be very dangerous to you."

"It is very dangerous to you, too."

"Who killed the man?"

"The night tiger," she answered simply.

Taggert shook his head. "That doesn't mean shit to me, honey."

She bit her lip nervously, as if afraid to say the name aloud. "One-eye," she said.

A cold dread filled Taggert's belly. "Who?"

"You know him as Pham. I saw him go into your friend's room last night, but he didn't see me." She started to shut the window, to lock out any further questions. Instead the glass panes shattered, spearing her hands. Her face dissolved into a crimson pulp and she fell out of sight.

Solly Taggert threw himself to the ground before he even heard the first shots ring deafeningly around him. Dust kicked up at his feet as the sniper searched for him. There wasn't any doubt about who the man was.

Even if Taggert thought he had killed him.

6

Bolan plummeted through the night air toward the pool. He fanned his arms away from his body, searching for balance as he fell. It hadn't been the best of dives. He'd had to double over as he propelled himself from the window to avoid the shots from the agents' guns. And if he hit the water wrong, it would be like going head-to-head with a brick wall.

Pulling his body into a ball, he tucked his knees into his chest until he had his feet under him, then extended his legs to lessen the shock. Even if he survived the jump, he was going to have to be mobile to complete his escape.

When he hit the water he was enveloped in a sudden inky blackness. He curbed the immediate impulse to break for the surface, holding himself underwater instead. Through the water, the building's third floor was just a haze. The warrior knew that the agents leaning out the broken window wouldn't be able to see much. But they'd be able to detect any sudden motion that broke the pool's surface.

Holding his breath and denying the pained outcry for oxygen buried in his lungs, Bolan slid free of the shoulder harness and pulled off the pink shirt, holding it in a balled fist to lessen its visibility.

Sensation returned to him in a rush when he broke the surface and took his first deep breath. The cold air ate at him with icy fangs, making his skin seem sizes too small.

The two agents hung out the window, searching the pool area with their eyes and guns. One of them was speaking into a walkie-talkie. Below and around them windows of the other rooms had been opened, spilling light from the building. There were other faces looking for him, too, Bolan realized, belonging to people who would also bring attention to his escape. He knew he'd never pull off an inconspicuous departure, but whatever he did would have to be bloodless. Bolan had worked with other government branches off and on in his war, coming across some good men and some bad. Right now there was no way to judge these. They were operating on someone else's intel, and the warrior didn't know what they had been told.

How many men? Evidently someone was heavily involved in the operation and didn't care about the manpower. How high were the stakes?

He reached for the Beretta, pushing himself back down in the water so he wouldn't reveal himself above the edge of the pool. Flicking the toggle to single shot, he opened fire and placed a row of shots just below the broken window, driving the agents back inside.

Then the Executioner had his hands on the edge of the pool and was pulling himself up onto the rough concrete. His shoes slipped under him for a moment as he drove his legs hard to get going.

Shouts broke out as the hotel populace noticed his position in an escalating wave. A shot spun off the concrete, but far to his right.

Changing course abruptly, Bolan vaulted a deck set, scattering chairs and overturning the table as he made his way to the wooden privacy fence surrounding the pool area. More shots were seeking him out now, closing in. He didn't look over his shoulder, concentrating instead on the eight-foot-high obstacle he was bearing down on.

The sound of running feet came from behind and Bolan knew he wouldn't get another chance. Even if they didn't kill him, it would take hours before Brognola could mesh the gears of justice to free him. And those hours couldn't be spared. Too many people were interested in the operation, in Lee Wingate's disappearance.

He hit the fence running. Without breaking stride or losing momentum, he planted a foot on the wooden slats and threw himself upward, arms groping for the top. Shots shook and shattered the planks around him, the vibrations soaking into his body.

"Take the son of a bitch alive!" a harsh Southern voice ordered.

Bolan flung the shoulder harness over the fence but maintained his hold on it, letting its weight help lever him over the top. He kept a low profile as he went over, scraping a layer of skin from his chest and abdomen as he slithered across.

He landed on his feet in a crouch, spotting the rental car only a few yards away. He sprinted for the vehicle and crawled inside, slinging the harness into the passenger seat. He gunned the engine and pulled out onto the street, leaving the lights off so that no one could get a glimpse of his license plates. Several checks for a tail revealed nothing, and he let the flow of the city sweep him into its welcome embrace.

He drove automatically, weaving through the late-night traffic at a speed only a little above the limit. Reaching over the seat, he popped the latches on his single suitcase and fished out a can of first-aid spray and a gray T-shirt that read Oklahoma State University Cowboys. He applied the spray liberally, feeling it sting before a numbing coolness spread over his abrasions. Then he slipped the shirt on.

He followed the streets in a vague pattern, working gradually to an access to Interstate 35 and on to Will Rogers airport. He was sure he hadn't been spotted but didn't want to take any unnecessary chances.

Whoever was covering the operation was doing a damn good job of it, and worked with more information than either Bolan or Brognola had. He believed that the control for the CIA operation knew everything there was to know about Lee Wingate's quest. Where would the line be drawn, though? Sure, someone back at Williams's had said he was to be taken alive, but that hadn't seemed the case at first. Those men were shooting to kill.

He checked his watch and found the time to be only a few minutes after midnight. Brognola would probably still be at his office. If not, Bolan had his home number.

Switching to the exit lane, the warrior pulled off the interstate onto the NW Twenty-third exit and found a pay phone across the street from a Long John Silver's Seafood Shoppe. As he waited for the connection to be made to Wonderland, he watched a large guy leave the pickup window. Going home, Bolan told himself, and pushed the thought out of his mind. Home was wherever he happened to find himself when it was time to sleep. It had been that way for longer than he cared to remember.

The head Fed picked up the phone on the fourth ring. His voice sounded tired and groggy when he answered.

"How are things at your end?" Bolan asked.

"Too quiet. There still hasn't been any word about Lee Wingate. How are things there?"

"Puzzling," Bolan replied, then recounted the night's events. "I've got a name here and an ID number. Maybe you can have it checked and find out who the control is on this operation." He gave Brognola the information, spelling Keenan's name.

"This will probably take a while, Striker. It's after one in the morning here and I'll have to wake up a few people before I can get any information on this."

Bolan watched the uneven flow of traffic in the street. Standing as he was in the shadows surrounding the pay phone, he was hard to see. A black-and-white police car passed by, and he saw the brake lights flare briefly as the officer gave him the once-over. Had a call gone out already? But the police car rolled on.

"That's no problem, Hal. Once you do find someone who knows something, I don't think the guy will be volunteering any information too soon."

Brognola's heavy sigh hissed through the phone. "Probably not, Striker. Half the time I don't think this government of ours was set up with a system of checks and balances. Stalemates are more along the lines of what really goes on. I'd have loved to have been to one congressional meeting in the early days of this country. Just to find out if convenience was ever an issue."

"How soon can you have a plane to Saint Martin ready?"

"Give me an hour for that. It will take at least that long to open up domestic channels to allow a nonchartered flight in. Also to get clearance for the guns. We're on pretty good terms with the government down there, and I know a guy in the State Department who owes me a favor or two. He'll bitch for a little while but he'll get the job done. What name are you going to be using?"

"Mike Belasko. I've got the ID with me and the Belasko name has a history with the government in case anyone starts asking questions."

"You think whoever is running the cover-up knows about the Saint Martin link?"

Bolan gingerly touched the abrasions on his chest and abdomen, feeling the dull pain spread across his ribs. It was a momentary pain, gone in seconds.

"I think so, Hal. The whole setup in the apartment smacked of a trap. I don't think they really thought they would intercept anyone looking for Lee Wingate, but it was designed that way. Whoever is running this wasn't expecting any outside interference, but he was prepared for it. I'm sure they want to keep a lid on this thing."

"I'll have the girl's address by then, too," Brognola said. "Is there anything else I can get for you?"

"See if the Bear can find out if Stuart Wingate has any contacts in Saint Martin. Somebody who's into free-lance operations. I'm beginning to think that destination was only a stopover for something else."

Brognola grunted an affirmative. "Where do you want the plane?"

"Will Rogers will be fine. Just have Mike Belasko paged when the pilot gets there."

"Right."

"I'll give you another call then and see what you've got." Bolan said goodbye and hung up the phone. He walked back to the rental and shrugged into the shoulder harness. A brown leather jacket covered up the hardware. Then he got in the car and made his way back to the interstate.

Anxiety rode his shoulder like a dark angel. Already two of the teams involved had a jump on him. Lee Wingate had already made good his escape from the people who had been watching him. Or had he? Sure, the KGB attack had thrown everyone off, but somehow it didn't scan that the CIA people watching him hadn't known where he was headed. Which meant there was probably a team waiting for him.

But why? Security reasons? Bolan couldn't buy that. Stuart Wingate had been involved in American politics too long to roll over for money. Besides, he had enough of his own. What could anyone offer him that would make him betray his country? And Lee Wingate? He'd risked his life dozens of times fighting the Communists in South America. Bolan knew that from Kurtzman's reports. But something had happened. Was happening, Bolan corrected himself.

Bolan shoved the questions out of his mind as he made the turn leading to the airport. Questions and conjectures were only good when you had a picture or a possible scenario in mind. What was involved here lacked motivation.

Why the interest on the CIA's behalf and why Lee Wingate suddenly dropped from sight were going to have to wait until he had more to work with.

The glow from the speedometer created a greenish reflection on his face on the windshield. The dying words of the KGB agent stayed uppermost in his mind. If Stuart Wingate was betraying America, how would he convince his son he was doing the right thing? Lee Wingate was a soldier fighting for an ideal, and was the one person former Army Sergeant Mack Bolan could understand with every fiber of his being. Politicians and industrialists were another matter, possessing morals that drifted with the perceived consensus of the public, or Dow Jones fluctuations.

The warrior had a gut feeling that Lee Wingate didn't have all the pieces of the puzzle, either. He just hoped it didn't get the man killed. By one side or the other.

CARY ROLFE STRODE through the apartment building like a man used to being in command. Actually Rolfe had only been a CIA section chief for a little more than a year, and had only recently been given complete authority over his operations. He no longer had to seek approval from a superior.

He forced his way through the group surrounding the elevator, keeping his pistol firmly in his hand. The men he shoved to one side glared at him belligerently for a moment, but quickly looked away after catching sight of the ugly black automatic in his fist.

Company man Joe Howard was holding the elevator for him, spread-eagled between the doors, letting his suit coat gap open to reveal the MAC-10 slung around his neck. He gave Rolfe a quick nod and stepped back to allow him entrance. The crowd started to surge forward, but halted when Howard ordered them back, menace in his voice.

The doors slid quietly closed, shutting out the shouted demands for information and the rumbling undertones of the crowd's fears. Rolfe had overheard someone say that a half-dozen people lay dead in the hallways of the third floor.

Punching the five, Rolfe stood back and holstered the automatic on his hip, checking his image in the stainless-steel panel. He looked calm and confident, a boy executive with an important mission. With the full blond hair and china-blue eyes and a year-round tan he had to work at, Rolfe had always thought he'd have made a good Company liaison for the television networks. At six-two, he was slim, leanly muscled and looked good in a three-piece. Not hulking like Howard or possessing those threatening qualities of his. Yet he had chosen Howard to be his aide because of these very attributes. Partly because the man was competent and partly because he made a nice foil for Rolfe.

"How's Keenan?" Rolfe asked as he watched the numbered lights escalate in value.

"Shook up some but okay. Dahl and Robinson found him in the pilot's room all tied up."

Rolfe nodded and checked his reflection again. The tension he felt slowly building inside wasn't showing. Good. He had trouble believing that a situation he had had so much control over could have gone sour. He was waiting on word from the strike team he had stationed in Saint Martin to find out how the snatch on Lee Wingate had gone. If he could get his hands on the merc colonel, catch him with the evidence of Stuart Wingate's betrayal, he figured his career would skyrocket in the Agency.

"Did he identify his assailant?" Rolfe asked.

"Not a name, but he did say he recognized him as the guy who had been attached to Wingate to do the news story."

"The same man who took down the KGB force at the airport?"

"Yeah."

"We got anything on this McKay?"

"Nothing that didn't show up the first time around, Cary."

Rolfe nodded. Howard was the only man under him who had the liberty of addressing him by his given name. Howard wasn't too creative in the thinking department, but he was reliable when issued orders.

"Did we have any casualties in the halls? I heard somebody say people were down on the third floor."

Howard shook his head. "A few people who'd just come from a party pissed their pants, but nothing happened involving our guys or McKay."

The 5 lit up and the elevator doors rolled open. Rolfe strode out purposefully and Howard had a hard time keeping up with him.

Two more agents stood guard at Scotty Williams's door, though no weapons were in sight. Rolfe gave them a curt nod as he twisted the knob and walked inside.

Keenan sat on the couch, dabbing at his nose with a wet towel. Blood still oozed from one nostril.

Passing by him, Rolfe went to the window and looked down over the swimming pool. Police officers were on the scene, and it wouldn't be long before he was answering their questions instead of asking his own. Ten men on this part of the operation alone, he told himself, and still it had gone sour.

He flicked the curtain closed and returned to Keenan. "You okay?" he asked the agent. He had learned long ago that feigning interest in someone else's welfare helped to win that person over to his side immediately. Actually he felt an almost inarticulate rage at the agent for letting McKay escape. First the Russians had hit the airport, blowing his coverage all to hell. Now McKay was on the loose.

"Yeah, though I've got a headache as big as this room and I can't seem to get my nose to stop bleeding. But the nose doesn't surprise me. I've been an easy bleeder since I was a kid. Been a lot of years since I got hit in the nose, though."

Rolfe nodded, thrusting his hands in his pockets as he looked down at the agent. "You're sure about this guy's identity?"

"There's no question about it. The man's a pro. You saw the way he handled the action at the airport. He knows how to move. He took me out before I had a chance to do anything."

"How did he get in?"

"Picked the lock, I guess. Hell, I never even heard a thing till I heard the lock click open. Then I was busy trying to get behind something so he wouldn't see me. The only place handy was that wall in the dining room, and I was set up all wrong to take him quiet the way you wanted me to. Somehow he knew I was there, like he had some kind of radar or something that let him know he wasn't alone and told him where I was."

"Did he ask you any questions?"

"No."

"Then he acted like he knew what he was searching for."

"No, but he was looking for something because he gave this place a GI inspection."

"Did he find anything?"

"I don't know."

"Did you identify yourself?"

"Yes, sir. Like I told him, judging by his actions this morning at the airport, I figured he was on our side."

"What did he say?"

"Told me the only side he was on was his own. It was kind of weird, though, because before he left he took my ID. It seems to me that if he's some kind of government agent, he'd have ID of his own."

Rolfe raised his eyes to get Howard's attention. "Take care of that," he ordered and watched the big man go to the telephone.

"Did the guy get away?" Keenan asked.

"Yeah," Howard said as he dialed. "The bastard did a double gainer with a twist out of a third-floor window into the swimming pool and walked out of here before anyone even saw what kind of car he was driving or even if he was alone."

"I swear to God the guy's a pro," Keenan said to Rolfe.

And talented, too, Rolfe thought as he considered the lock on the apartment door. It wasn't an easy one to pick quickly. Williams had invested in a solid piece of work. "Have Johnson take you to the hospital and get checked over. Give me a call later and let me know what's going on."

The agent nodded and left.

How the hell had things gotten out of hand so quickly? And what the hell was someone like McKay doing in this operation?

A week ago Rolfe had had all the angles figured out in his plan to trap Stuart Wingate. He had known about the grandson in Vietnam, about the ransom demand and had pieced together Wingate's plans to use his son as a go-between. It had been Rolfe's idea to tag along behind Lee Wingate until the exposure would prove most beneficial to his career. At thirty-two he was already one of the youngest section heads to oversee a task force as large as the one he commanded. There had already been commendations, and his name was becoming well-known to the CIA's hierarchy. Other people were starting to come to him for advice, for help. He wasn't about to give all that up.

That was why he hadn't volunteered the information he had gleaned from the illegal tap on Wingate's phones, the demands for the Star Wars blueprints from that first call. From then on, Wingate had secured the lines and additional intel wasn't forthcoming. But the one call had been enough to let Rolfe know he was on to a good thing. He could still remember the sudden rush he got when he had listened to the tape.

No one knew about the blackmail except Cary Rolfe. He had placed the tap there himself more than a month ago when he'd been assigned to Wingate for security reasons, tapping into Wingate's lines from outside the house and changing the tapes himself daily. Wingate didn't get many calls, so it only took ten or fifteen minutes every day to scan the conversations.

Until the first blackmail call. Then Rolfe had listened to the conversations Wingate had had with his son's commanding officers in Vietnam and found out that the grandson really did exist.

It might have been easier to accept the reprimand he would have received for the illegal tap, especially in view of the fact that Wingate was going ahead and giving the plans up. But Rolfe didn't want to do that. For the first time since he'd been promoted, Rolfe had found out how attached he'd become to the power he had earned.

And sure, maybe the KGB raid at the airport had confused the issue, but it also gave him a freer hand to continue his search for Lee Wingate. And now McKay, too.

Rolfe had assigned a man to Williams since the beginning, knowing Wingate would rely on the pilot at least to some degree. Williams was easy to control, and Wingate knew it. And he didn't need to see the big picture to operate. It was enough that his employer told him to do something.

And maybe, Rolfe figured, maybe Wingate hadn't even bothered to tell his son everything. But so what? When it came down to it, Cary Rolfe was going to be the man of the hour and nobody was going to stop him. Not even McKay, no matter who he really was or who he was connected with.

Rolfe made his way to the bedroom. He looked through the closets first, shaking his head at the clothing he found there. He preferred quiet suits of good quality and cut. Bright colors made a man look like a popinjay on television....

The young CIA chief knew he had a Russian counterpart somewhere in the game. The KGB had to know of the grandson, or they wouldn't have attempted the strike today. So the pressure was on, but Rolfe was betting on himself in this one. It would have been easier, though, if there had only been two teams involved. Only him and the Soviets.

Abandoning the closet, he worked his way around the room, finding nothing. Just as he was about to switch the light off, he caught sight of the address book peeking out from under a pillow on the bed. He flipped through the pages and found Terri Quentin's name and phone number, the same Terri Quentin whom Williams had phoned only days ago to tell her about flying to Saint Martin on business.

Had McKay found out about the Saint Martin angle?

So far Rolfe had nothing on the island country other than the fact that Williams and Wingate had traveled there for a layover—he had assumed it was to put together a mission to Vietnam. Rolfe had planned to bring the entire blackmail attempt to a head in Saint Martin. The CIA force he had sent had instructions to capture Wingate and the pilot and hold them until the section chief got there.

Rolfe tapped the address book on his fingers as the thoughts tumbled through his head. Who was McKay working with? That was a key question. Rolfe felt sure it was some government agency because the guy had had an easy access to Wingate's home, and judging by how swiftly the man had found Williams's apartment, he possessed a good source of information, as well.

Irritated by these sudden complexities, Rolfe tossed the address book back onto the bed and returned to the living room.

Howard was finishing up with the phone when his boss walked into the room. "Floyd and Danners saw our man talking to the security guard, right?"

Howard nodded.

"Find out what he said."

Howard nodded again, took a small transceiver from his belt and keyed it up.

Rolfe peered out the darkened window as he took a silver cigarette case from inside his jacket pocket and shook one out. Below he could still see the winking lights of the police cars flashing red and blue shadows that shattered against the building and the figures standing in the street. A crowd had clustered around the cars and police officers were cordoning off the area.

A news van from a local television station slid to a stop in front of the building. Rolfe experienced his first thrill of anticipation of the night, drowning out the anxiety McKay's interference had generated.

Howard's voice interrupted his concentration as he put together the presentation he would give the newspeople—after letting them cool their heels for a certain amount of time, of course.

"The guy flashed Keenan's ID and asked to see the pilot's messages," Howard said.

"What were they?"

Rolfe listened, watching as a young woman debarked from the passenger side of the van and a man crawled out the back with a minicam slung over his shoulder. The cameraman was panning the crowd as the woman went directly to the police vehicles.

The CIA section chief wasn't surprised when he heard Terri Quentin's name. Okay, the assumption that McKay knew about the Saint Martin connection was no longer a guess. Rolfe put his cigarette out in a ceramic ashtray. "Tell Hennings to contact Yarborough and tell him he's got company headed his way," he instructed Howard. "Give him a description of McKay and tell him to take the guy alive, if he can, but to stop him no matter what. If you need anything, I'll be downstairs smoothing this over with the local guys.''

Rolfe didn't wait for Howard's reply. He passed through the door without a backward glance, telling the two men standing guard outside to let the police officers in but to refer all questions to him.

As he stood in the elevator waiting for the doors to close, Rolfe stared at the two agents who guarded the apartment door. The play had gotten a bit complex, and the offensive line had reacted late, but the call was a quarterback sneak and Cary Rolfe was about to break into full stride.

7

The airport receptionist gave Bolan a smile as he approached the desk. "Mr. Belasko?"

"Yes."

"There you go, sir." She indicated a phone at the end of the long desk.

"Thanks." Bolan lifted the receiver and punched the flashing extension light.

"Striker?"

"Yeah," Bolan replied as he looked around at the crowded area. "Let me call you right back, Hal. Gotta get some breathing room at this end."

"Sure." The phone clicked in Bolan's ear.

Moving to the bank of phones across the vast room, Bolan recited a calling-card number to the operator. After the connection was made, he asked, "What have you got?"

"You'll have a Lear jet at your disposal in less than—" there was silence as the man from Justice consulted his watch "—ten minutes. The pilot belongs to Tinker Air Force Base at your end, flies for the general but I got him for a loaner."

"Sounds good, Hal." Bolan looked through the plate-glass window at the complete darkness of night and the threat of rain. He had awakened instantly when the Belasko name had been called over the intercom. The twenty or so minutes of rest he had gotten in the thinly padded chair had helped, but he still felt hollow inside. The warrior could live without sleep when there was a firefight on, but the man demanded rest occasionally. "Did you turn up the address on the girl?"

Brognola read it off. "Aaron also telexed some maps to the Air Force base. You'll have to sort through them because I didn't see them, but he did say he sent some of the particular areas you'll be interested in."

"Tell the Bear thanks for me."

"Sure."

Bolan shifted against the phone hub when he felt his shoulder going numb. He watched the flow of strangers around him as people drifted from one end of the airport to the other. Old memories tugged at him when he saw a young Marine round a corner with his duffel bag over his shoulder, his face set tiredly, only to break into a sudden smile as a family group called out his name and rushed forward. The Marine hugged his mother and girlfriend at the same time, while his father stood by with a proud smile.

How long ago had it been, Bolan wondered, since he'd been met at an airport by his parents, brother and sister? His subconscious flooded his mind with details: the scent of sister Cindy's hair spray and perfume, his mother's seeming frailty as he hugged her a final time, the sound of pride in his father's voice as he said goodbye, the lingering taste of the mint candy he and Johnny had shared while waiting for the plane.

Tenderly he folded the memories and tucked them away.

"I also got a line on the guy jobbing the CIA operation down there," Brognola was saying. "His name is Cary Rolfe, and he's something of a rising star in the Agency's ranks. A hungry rising star, though, Striker. A contact told me Rolfe isn't above knocking over the table on a conventional setup and hotdogging it if he gets a hold of something substantial. He's drawn flack a few times from ex-controls over his operations, but nothing stuck because the end result outweighed the number of infractions Rolfe made

along the way. Rolfe was assigned to Wingate after our mole
came back with the intel about the Russian strike possibility.''

"Did you get a picture of this guy?" Bolan asked.

"Not yet. Do you think you'll need one?"

"Maybe. But I think we've already met."

"At the apartment building?"

"Yeah."

Brognola related what scanty information he had on
Rolfe, and Bolan filed it mentally, tagging the Dallas education when he learned of it, matching it with the Southern
drawl he'd heard.

"Rolfe *was* there tonight," Bolan stated when Brognola
had finished.

"You think he's following up on something his department doesn't know about?" Brognola asked.

"If it was something his department knew about," Bolan said, "I'm sure you would know about it by now. No,
the guy's keeping his cards to himself and he's got his crew
tearing at the leash, shutting down access to any information he has. I'd guess they're moving in the dark, too. But
he's definitely got them motivated. He's also my personal
pick for the guy who ordered the unauthorized taps on
Wingate's personal phones."

"I can't really step in at this point and have him back off,
not without compromising you. Just remember what I said,
Striker—this guy is a definite head case. He's been living on
the edge for a long time and there's no telling what his
snapping point is."

"Righto. What about a contact for Wingate in Saint
Martin?" Bolan heard papers being shuffled and waited. A
young couple had just rounded a corner and stood looking
over the assortment of travelers just disembarking from the
latest flight in. A five- or six-year-old boy with dark hair and
dark eyes stood behind them with his hands in his pockets.
He talked to his mother briefly and smiled when she gave

him some change. Then he sauntered over to the candy machine near the bank of phones. The look the boy gave the vending machine was one of intent concentration.

"That one was a little tougher. Evidently he's been doing business with a guy named Ernst Wessel, an international arms dealer. Kurtzman had trouble sorting out all the details. There were a lot of shipment orders and bills of lading to dig through before the name surfaced. Wessel has been an outlet for Wingate Munitions for a number of years, but it hasn't really been of much concern until now. It turns out Wessel has been operating his broker service under three or four dummy corporations all buying from Wingate. Kurtzman says it looked like Wingate might have set it up to get undeclared monies. The dummy corporations existed a few years, then they went broke, owing Wingate Munitions a substantial amount. Wingate wrote it off as a loss, of course, but Wessel does too much business to think he would rip Wingate off. Besides which, Wingate is still doing business with the man."

"Put a good man on Wingate, Hal. You can bet if he has one alternative source of income there will be others. He's got that safety net there for some reason. And things have never come apart around him like they have in the last day or so."

"A further word on Wessel, Striker. This guy isn't strictly on the up-and-up. Aaron tripped across the name a few times concerning the neo-Nazi party here in America and a few assassination attempts. Nothing definite enough to move on, but you can bet he's dirty. He's also the kind of guy who would know when and where to listen for information trickling through the international grapevine. And if Wingate sent his son down there, you can bet he knows something about what's going on. I can guarantee he won't like anyone poking around his place of business," Brognola concluded.

"No doubt."

"Call me as soon as you know something, Striker."

"Will do," Bolan said and hung up. Thoughts cascaded through his mind, his warrior's instincts jangling loudly. Sure, it was one thing to launder money for income tax purposes, but Wingate was doing enough domestic work not to have a need for any undeclared monies. So it had been put there as a safety. And now Wingate was risking exposure by soliciting Wessel's help. Wingate was working on something he couldn't get done through the normal channels of his government, a government that would give him anything he wanted within acceptable limits. He'd sent his son to do it for him, a son who was trained for war and dying.

Down the wall from Bolan, the boy pressed a button and the candy machine hummed. The look of expectation dropped from the youngster's face as the candy bar failed to come entirely free.

"Having trouble, little guy?" Bolan asked as he walked over. With the flat of his palm, he rocked the vending machine and the candy bar dropped from its slot.

The boy reached inside and took it, flashing Bolan a smile and a quick thanks before he ran back to his parents.

Bolan watched him go, feeling the hollowness inside turn into a vacuum, then went to catch the jet Brognola had arranged for him.

PHAM GAVE THE GUARD a harsh stare, not speaking until the man blinked uncomfortably several times and finally asked him to state his business.

"Tell Captain Thinh I need to talk to him," Pham said.

The guard drew himself up to his full height, clasping the AK-47 more closely to his chest. "He gave me orders he was not to be disturbed."

Letting his single eye roam up and down the hallway of the brothel, Pham saw that he was alone with the guard. He knew he presented an ominous figure to the young man, both intimidating and mysterious. He could almost see the thoughts in the guard's mind, wondering if this was a test of some sort. Thinh was noted for his unwavering discipline and was hard on any of his troops who failed to follow his orders to the letter, which was one of the main reasons Pham liked doing business with the captain. In all his dealings with Vietnamese officialdom, he had found men who maintained the word they gave at the time of the initial bargain few and far between. Most officers and political aspirants worked at dividing up sections of the country, while men like Thinh were content to work the middle ground. The captain paid less for services than some others, but he paid on time.

"Your captain will want to see me once he knows I am here."

The guard was very polite when he replied, "I'm sorry to inconvenience you, sir, but Captain Thinh left very strict orders that I was to let no one through."

Pham nodded curtly and turned around, making as if to leave.

The brothel was almost always empty this late in the afternoon. Over the railing of the upstairs hallway, the lower floor was open for Pham's gaze. It was an old house, one with a good reputation for employing women with exotic skills. It was part of a finer past, with polished teakwood floors and gaily patterned wallpaper covering the walls. Too pretty to suit Pham's taste, but fitting perfectly with Thinh's idea of himself. It was easy to imagine American soldiers tramping through the darkly lit halls as they had many years ago.

Inside, Pham was a tight coil. The confrontation with Solly Taggert had been one of the last things he had wanted to happen. Killing Gant and letting Taggert find the body had been a step in applying pressure on the American, to keep him off guard until Pham could seize the Star Wars plans for himself. But maybe the American would think Gant had only been tortured for information leading to

Taggert. Pham was confident Taggert would believe he had escaped the firefight in the alley through his own skill and not because he was intentionally missed.

But still, time was running out. If Taggert was going to seize the boy to trade him for the plans, he was going to do it soon. How long would Taggert hold the boy? Surely no longer than a day. It would be too hard moving through the jungle with him. No, the swap would take place soon. And every moment Pham spent trying to talk to a guard who was obviously in fear of his commanding officer was a moment he could not replace. Taggert would be on the run now, wondering what was going on, and Pham wanted to keep him like that—reacting instead of thinking.

Without warning Pham spun abruptly, lashing out with the booted heel of his right foot, catching the guard just below the neck with a driving force that propelled him against the door he had been guarding.

Wood cracked as the door splintered, and the guard fell through. The AK-47 made a tired bounce on the floor at Pham's feet. Stepping through the shattered frame, Pham kicked the guard in the temple when he tried to get back up. He went down and stayed down. With the fingers of his left hand, Pham looped the sling of the assault rifle over his shoulder and carried it inside the room.

The bedroom was small but palatial in its appointments. The furniture was handmade of rich woods—and decades old, having been passed down by affluent families at one time.

Once he was certain there would be no more interference from the guard, Pham faced the bed.

Thinh sat in the middle of the four-poster, looking out of place amid the ruffled curtains and lace. The captain was younger than Pham, almost half his age, in fact. His close-cropped black hair and smooth complexion contrasted sharply with the pastel sheets that were wrapped around his body. The only thing about Thinh that didn't look out of place was the pistol in his hands.

Pham looked coolly down the muzzle of the gun.

Thinh smiled. Beside him sat a naked girl who looked no older than fourteen. Pham looked her over appreciatively, noting the budding beauty of her figure and her high, perfectly shaped breasts. Her hair was pulled atop her head, giving a more delicate shadowing to her features. Pham could almost imagine the soft and secretive scents of her body as he gazed at her.

"Is he dead?" Thinh asked as he put the pistol away.

Pham looked at the unconscious guard and shook his head. Then he returned his gaze to the naked girl, who dropped her eyes and refused to look at him, though not trying to cover her body.

"You have something important to say to me?" Thinh asked.

"Yes."

Thinh reached into a drawer in the nightstand and withdrew a pack of cigarettes. "Something very interesting, I hope, because you've interrupted a most pleasant experience." He tapped the young girl under her chin with a forefinger, bringing her eyes level with his. He smiled at her warmly, but Pham noted that the cold brightness of a calculating killer never left the man's eyes. It was one of the reasons they were so compatible when circumstances brought them together. Thinh was a soldier who liked the grislier aspects of his work.

"A most profitable thing, as well," Pham said. "Profitable enough, even for the both of us."

Thinh sucked on the cigarette, creating a brightly glowing coal at its end for a brief moment. "I'd heard you were dead. Shot down in a street not far from where we are now. Was that part of the same business?"

Anger flared inside Pham. "That was another business. A part that later led to this."

"And what business is that?"

Pham smiled, thinly and without humor. "How would you like to be the captain who captured the plans for the United States' Strategic Defense system?"

Thinh sat up straighter and pushed the girl from him roughly. "Leave us," he ordered. "Have wine sent up immediately."

A hurt look filled the young girl's face as she stumbled and nearly fell. Pausing at a closet near the bed, she took out a one-piece silk pullover and put it on. She left the room without a backward glance.

Thinh stood and dressed quickly. "Where do I fit in this scheme of yours, Pham?"

Briefly Pham outlined the situation, starting with Taggert's request for information and unexpected attack, and ending with the torture sequence with Gant.

"Do you know where the boy is?" Thinh asked when he had finished.

"No."

"It's a shame. He would improve our position a thousandfold."

"It's not the boy we're after," Pham reminded him. "And if government forces held him, instead of Taggert, the American might not believe the story. No. My plan is to let Taggert have full run of his operation until the plans are in his hands, then take them. That I can accomplish on my own."

"And what part do I play?"

"You have Soviet contacts," Pham said. "I need someone to broker the plans for me. And I do not know for sure how many men the American munitions man will be sending. They will need to be allowed free passage through the area, which is under your command. It wouldn't do to have some idiot—like the one you had guarding your door—destroy them and the Star Wars plans."

"What if you lose Taggert before the ransom is paid?"

"That will not happen."

Thinh looked as if he wanted to say something further, but stopped when Pham's gaze hardened. "What do I get out of this?"

"Half," Pham promised.

Thinh paused in buckling his holster around his waist. "Half?"

"Half of whatever you get the Russians to pay." Pham offered him a mirthless grin. "The amount we will be getting will be much more than a wise man can spend in a lifetime. And it will ensure we have a loyalty to each other."

The girl reappeared, carrying a wine flask and two glasses on a wooden tray. Thinh took the flask and poured, then the girl set the tray on the nightstand and left.

"What do we do with the Americans afterward?" Thinh asked.

"I only mentioned they should be let *in* unharmed," Pham replied. "They don't have to be let out."

Thinh nodded and handed Pham a wineglass.

Pham took the wine, saluting Thinh. "To good hunting."

Thinh smiled and lifted his own glass in a salute. "And," he said, "to half."

8

Ernst Wessel's major place of operations was a warehouse on the north side of the island country, complete with docking facilities for boats and seaplanes.

Mack Bolan stood across the deserted street that dead-ended into the warehouse grounds and surveyed the building. He wore a trench coat with the collar turned up to help keep out the surprisingly chill night air rolling in from the ocean. Underneath he wore his combat blacksuit, slit pockets filled with extra magazines for the Beretta and AutoMag. The 93-R lay snugged in shoulder leather and the .44 rode the big warrior's right hip.

For the past twenty minutes he'd been watching the building. During that time he'd seen lights flicker through the windows, bouncing like hand-held lanterns as they wended their way through the bowels of the warehouse. Almost as if someone were on routine patrol.

Or someone were waiting for someone else.

A neo-Nazi supporter, Brognola had said, linked with recent assassination attempts.

Even if Lee Wingate had been scheduled for a clandestine meeting with Wessel tonight, what were the chances of his being the only one?

The Executioner studied his watch again. Twenty-five minutes had passed.

Behind and above the warehouse the moon was a shining silver disk that scattered a lambent grayness over the brackish seawater. The grounds between him and the warehouse were open, flat, and Bolan knew he would be exposed to anyone looking outside.

And he was sure someone was.

The drifting will-o'-the-wisp of yellow light had already told him that.

Turning on his heel, he followed the ragged fence line down to the ocean, staying in the pools of inky darkness cast by the abandoned buildings fleshing out the opposite side of the block.

Once at the ocean's edge, Bolan shrugged free of the trench coat and went through a final weapons check. Then he slipped quietly into the water. An invisible undertow sucked greedily at him, eager to hold him in its deadly embrace.

He swam to the loading dock with smooth, powerful strokes, hardly disturbing the water. The small lapping of the ocean against the wooden pilings connected to the warehouse covered any noise he might have made as he closed in on his target. Easing up out of the water, Bolan held himself under the dock while the combat suit drained of seawater.

Just as he was about to haul himself up on the dock, Bolan heard the scraping of a foot against one of the wooden planks. He froze, left hand holding on to one of the heavy timbers and right hand darting for the butt of the AutoMag.

The scraping repeated itself as the person overhead walked to the edge of the dock.

Expecting somebody, Bolan wondered, or just killing time? He chanced a quick look and saw the silhouette of a hardguy with an automatic.

Bolan waited a few heartbeats, pumping his lungs full of oxygen for the coming confrontation. Then, when the shadow turned around to reenter the warehouse, the Executioner swung lightly onto the dock. His right hand curled around the silenced Beretta and pulled it free of its holster.

In two strides he was on the unsuspecting guard.

Using the butt of the Beretta, he sideswiped the man's head, catching him before he could drop to the dock. Seizing the guy's shirt collar, Bolan dragged the unconscious man to one side of the warehouse and propped him up in a sitting position. Then he took the guard's weapons and dropped them into the ocean.

Sliding a Ka-bar from a sheath along his left calf, Bolan cut up the guard's shirt and bound him hand and foot. Another length served as a gag.

Satisfied, Bolan stood and padded to the back entrance of the warehouse. Using the keys he had removed from the guard's pocket, he let himself in.

He paused for a moment, waiting for his eyes to become accustomed to the deeper darkness where he now stood.

Out on the water he had just left behind, the Executioner registered a small cabin cruiser, rocking gently on the waves. Soft yellow light leaked onto the upper deck of the boat only to fall back down the short stairway leading into the hull. Riffs of music wafted on the air. But the boat could wait for now.

A narrow walkway led into a large area of the warehouse to Bolan's left. Opened crates lined the sheet-metal walls, and hand trucks stood at attention beside a set of double doors leading into more storage. The warehouse appeared to be built like Chinese boxes, with compartments and regions tucked securely inside one another. Bolan felt sure Wessel had other, more secret places to hide merchandise from time to time, as well—places he could use to hide monies and securities or anything else he didn't want confiscated in case of a raid, legal or illegal—

Laughter erupted from the cabin cruiser, muffled by the waves locked inside the dock. Two or three voices at least, Bolan decided before returning to his investigation of the warehouse. The double doors remained closed, and no light showed.

More laughing. The warehouse would have to be put off. The warrior couldn't afford not to find out what was happening on the cruiser.

Tucking the Beretta into its holster, Bolan made his way out of the warehouse, toward the motorboat.

Balancing on his toes, he waited where the boat was docked, preparing to coincide his movements with its gentle rocking, then slid noiselessly on board. The deck rose gently under his feet as he stopped in front of the companionway leading down. Crouching, Bolan listened intently, trying to gauge the numbers. The Beretta found a home in his right hand, and he inspected it briefly to make sure the silencer was secure.

"So whaddaya think?" a man's voice growled.

"I think you're too high," came the reply.

"Too high? Who the fuck do you think you're jerkin' around here? Man, I know the score. I been around a few times. I ain't no blushing bride for Chrissakes. You get a load of this guy, Billy? A real riot, whaddaya think?"

The reply was too low for Bolan to hear.

"Where's Wessel, Scrooge?" the first man demanded. "He'll give me a right deal for this shit. Man, I got kilos of this stuff, you know. This is good horse, man. Hey, Billy, I bet this clown wouldn't know good horse if it reached out and bit him on the ass, whaddaya think?"

"Mr. Wessel isn't here," the second man said. "He left instructions for me concerning your shipment. Explicit instructions. I can only make the offer he told me to make."

"Oh, yeah? Well what if the product was better than he thought it would be? Whaddaya think about that? Maybe you ought to get on the horn and give him a call. Tell him I said it ain't good enough this time. Me and Billy, we're taking all the chances. Everything we got is tied up in this boat of ours. We bring the horse here and trade it for guns and shit. Then it's up to us to make the best deal we can in them goddamned banana republics to get our cut of the money."

"Your cut of the money comes to quite a bit, though, doesn't it? Otherwise you wouldn't be coming here, right?"

Bolan had heard enough. Not only was Ernst Wessel involved in political assassinations, he was also into drug trafficking. There were no innocents at this meet, and the Executioner was about the declare the arms warehouse a hellzone. Maybe Wessel's man was lying about his boss not being in the building. Maybe the man was still in the warehouse. If not, the guy brokering the trade was at least close enough to the top to know where Wessel was.

Bolan moved swiftly down the companionway, keeping close to the wall. At the bottom he paused to look through the small opening left by the door.

Three men were revealed under the glow of the low-wattage bulb, matching the number of voices Bolan had overheard. Two black men sat on opposite ends of a worn gray couch, dressed in turtlenecks and jeans. The younger of the two sported a kelly-green watch cap, as well. Both were armed with pistols: Watch Cap had a chrome-finished revolver in a shoulder rigging, while the older man had a belly gun clipped to the front of his pants. The third stood to the right of the door, his back to Bolan. He wore slacks and a shirt and tie, looking like a clerk from behind the counter of a local department store.

Bolan cupped his left hand under his right and stepped into the door, elbowing it out of his way.

Wessel's stand-in froze into place, a stunned look etched into his features.

Watch Cap reacted faster than Bolan had expected, rolling from the couch to take advantage of the cover it offered, his pistol up and spitting lead.

Bolan tracked the 93-R toward the shooter, kicking out a 3-round burst that tore material and stuffing from the arms of the couch. Watch Cap ducked, and the chrome revolver disappeared from sight.

Backtracking to the other drug dealer, Bolan heard the sibilant hiss of a bullet spinning past his ear. He dropped the sights of the Beretta to throat level and stitched a burst just under the guy's chin.

The black man was thrown back against the wall forcefully, a red smear darkening the blond paneling behind him. He slid down the wall and remained still.

A hastily fired shot by the surviving gunner behind the couch caught Wessel's mouthpiece in the shoulder. The guy spun around and careened into Bolan.

Grabbing the injured man's shirt and stepping to one side, Bolan pulled hard on the guy, propelling him face first toward the companionway. The man fell hard and didn't get up.

The Executioner put two more bursts through the couch, knowing it wouldn't provide a proper defense against the 9 mm parabellum tumblers. The shooter stood in a last-ditch effort, shoulders locked behind the straight line of his outstretched arm, trying to make a smaller target. Crimson stained his lower abdomen in two places.

Bolan felt the wind of the bullet as it whipped past his face. He emptied the clip at near point-blank range, the rounds taking off the top of Watch Cap's head.

His ears still ringing from the concussion of the gunshots in the close confines of the cabin, the warrior made a quick inspection of the cabin and found it empty. When he got back to the companionway Wessel's man was trying to climb up the steps.

The soldier grabbed him by the belt and dragged him up the rest of the steps.

Up top, Bolan paused to scan the rest of the warehouse. Empty. So far no one had reacted to the sound of the gunshots. He turned his attention back to his prisoner.

Squatting before the guy, Bolan knew he looked terrifying. Behind the muzzle of the black Beretta, under the striped layers of combat camouflage, he felt sure Wessel's man would tell him everything he wanted to know.

The guy watched him with widened eyes, swallowing convulsively. His right hand was clutched over the wound in his shoulder.

"I'm shot," he said in a croaking voice. Somewhere along the way he had lost the cultured tones he had used in dealing with the two dead men below.

Bolan nodded. "And if you don't tell me what I want to know, I'm going to shoot you some more."

"Who are you?"

"Unimportant."

The man closed his eyes, and for a moment Bolan thought he had gone into shock. Then he reopened them to stare at Bolan.

"How many guards are there here?" Bolan asked.

"I'm going to bleed to death."

"Maybe. But not from that."

Bolan glanced up at the doors that led into the inner sanctum of the warehouse. It had only been minutes since the exchange of shots. Where were the security guards?

"How many guards?" He leveled the Beretta to a point directly in line with the man's nose.

"Six," the man gasped. "Six men."

"Is Wessel here?"

The man shook his head, lower lip trembling as he kept the pressure on his wounded shoulder.

"Where are the guards?"

"I don't know. Honest."

"They left you here to deal with these two alone?"

"They are . . . were . . . regular customers. We had no reason to expect trouble from them. Otherwise they would never have been allowed in. Mr. Wessel screens his clients very thoroughly."

A prickling sensation of unease skated across Bolan's back, making him feel naked and revealed. Someone watching?

Looking up, Bolan searched the ironwork above, scanning the shadow-shrouded frame and using his peripheral vision to its fullest. There. Movement above the double doors. A flickering of light on something metallic almost flush with the ceiling. Palming the Beretta with his left hand, he drew Big Thunder with his right and thumbed off the safety. The distance was almost sixty feet from the deck of the cabin cruiser to the steel supports over the door. The 9 mm would have been a serviceable weapon under the circumstances, but Bolan wanted the accuracy and power of the AutoMag.

"Get down," he whispered as he brought the .44 up to bear on the figure he could barely make out against the blackness of the ceiling. Wessel's man almost knocked him down as he bolted for the walkway.

Bolan started to go after him, then had to duck back quickly as automatic fire traced lightning across the floor in front of him. Splinters flew from the cabin cruiser, spinning against his exposed face and arms.

Wheeling to one side, he shoved the AutoMag in front of him again and squeezed the trigger three times in quick succession. One of the 240-grain hollowpoints scattered brief comets in its wake as it ricocheted from the support struts. The other two struck home.

With an anguished cry the sniper dropped his weapon and fell from the ceiling, arms windmilling as he landed twenty feet below.

Six guards, Wessel's man had said. Now only five remained.

Looking back at the double doors, Bolan saw that his escaped prisoner had already made his way inside. Aware that precious time was elapsing, Bolan holstered the Beretta and reached for a grenade attached to his combat harness, pulling the pin with his teeth. He lobbed the bomb overhand toward the doors, listening to it bound hollowly before thudding against its target.

"Oh, shit," someone screamed. "He just threw a god-damned gren—"

The explosion swallowed the rest of the word.

Without waiting for the sound to stop reverberating within the building, Bolan ripped another grenade free and dropped this one into the interior of the cabin cruiser.

Then he was gone, across the deck and sprinting for all he was worth.

The double doors of the warehouse had been blown almost entirely from their hinges, leaving a gaping hole surrounded by steel shards and broken brick.

"Where is he, dammit?" a voice bellowed.

"Christ, I don't know. I can't see for shit."

Smoke roiled from the exposed doorway and Bolan saw a figure just across the threshold. His prisoner? he wondered as he threw himself through the door. Two explosions came on his heels, providing further impetus to his dive, the first from the grenade on the boat, and the second as the cabin cruiser went up with a thunderous roar that seemed to become a live thing pursuing him. For a moment it looked as if a star had supernovaed inside the docking area.

The figure ahead of him turned out to be another security guard, dressed in black like the first one. Cradling a Mossberg 12-gauge pump, he dropped the barrel of the weapon toward Bolan just as the Executioner rolled over on the concrete floor and triggered a round. The warrior finished the roll before the dead man had time to fall, flinging himself to his feet and already hunting cover against one of the huge crates that were stacked throughout the warehouse.

He listened, willing himself to hear running footsteps that would tell him in what direction his quarry had fled.

Nothing. His ears were still ringing from the explosions.

He fished a spare clip from one of the pockets of the blacksuit and slammed it into the butt of the AutoMag.

Quietly he slid around the stack of crates, utilizing the gathered shadows as much as possible. His eyes searched the darkness overhead until he found the catwalk that had allowed the guards access to the docking area.

Leathering the .44, Bolan started climbing the stack in front of him, forcing his way up hand over hand. From there he could make his way to the catwalk that crisscrossed the length of the warehouse. When the warrior was halfway up the stack, a gunman walked onto the catwalk, carrying an M-16. Evidently the cabin cruiser had caught on fire. The man was limned in an orange-yellow glow.

Bolan drew and fired Big Thunder in one smooth motion, hugging his body in close to the crates so the recoil wouldn't tear him loose from his precarious hold. A foot-long muzzle-flash tracked toward the gunman and he jerked backward like a puppet on a string, hurling over the waist-high railing of the catwalk. Only the muffled thump of the body hitting the crates below came to Bolan's ears.

He gained the catwalk swiftly, feet already in motion.

How much time had already elapsed? Bolan wondered as he pounded across the unsteady surface. Had Wessel been notified?

He peered over the edge of the ironwork at the pooled shadows below, searching for his target. Small vibrations in the metal told him someone else had dropped onto the walkway. Slight tremors, but something that was instantly noticeable to his combat-honed senses.

Without breaking stride the Executioner dropped to one knee and spun around, bringing the AutoMag into target acquisition.

"Son of a bitch," one of the two men behind him yelled.

Bullets whined off the struts over Bolan's head. He emptied the AutoMag into them, taking out the gunner carrying the assault rifle just before he sustained any damage himself.

Five down, Bolan thought as he reloaded the .44 on the run. The catwalk danced crazily beneath him, giving him a feeling of weightlessness as he hung suspended twenty feet above the warehouse floor.

Bolan finally spotted the office, tucked neatly against the front wall. It was made of cinder blocks, a cube that he guessed held bills of lading and inventory. And a telephone.

As he watched, a light came on in the office and he saw Wessel's representative make a frantic dive for the telephone.

Choosing the quickest route to the office, Bolan leaped free of the walkway, dropping ten feet to the top of a crate, then flinging himself the remaining distance to the floor. He broke the force of his fall in a roll, coming immediately to his feet, Big Thunder still firmly in his hand.

A large plate-glass window in the office looked out over the warehouse floor. Bolan's first shot shattered it into a thousand gleaming shards that sprayed over the man on the other side. The next round exploded the base of the telephone, leaving Wessel's man holding the receiver with the cord ripped free.

The man dropped the receiver and made a try for the door.

"Don't," Bolan commanded. "Any more running and you'll be using both hands to stop the bleeding."

The man froze.

Bolan stepped through the wreckage that had once been a window, hearing the glass crunch delicately under his booted feet. He kept the .44 trained on the man. "Where's Wessel?"

The man clapped a hand back over his bloody shoulder. Tears ran down his face. He slumped against the door weakly and sank to a sitting position. "At his club."

"Where?"

He gave Bolan the address.

"How long will he be there?"

"I don't know. Sometimes he gambles all night."

Bolan glanced around the office, taking in the computer system in the corner; the bank of filing cabinets covered with broken glass; the expensive desk and chair set; and the handbooks on weapons in oak bookcases that lined the walls.

"Tell me about Stuart Wingate."

"What do you want to know?"

"He sent someone here earlier. I want to know why."

"No one I know of. The only dealings I've ever had with the man were over the phone. And then only if Mr. Wessel couldn't be reached."

Bolan tried a different tack, shifting around in the office so he could keep the warehouse under observation. Six guards, he had been told, and he knew five of them were down. Maybe the sixth had been caught in the backlash of the explosion in the docking area.

"There was an American in today, to see Wessel." Bolan described Lee Wingate.

The man nodded. "He was here only a few hours ago. He had a delivery to pick up."

"Did you talk to him?"

"No, Mr. Wessel did. He said this was a very important customer, one who required his personal attention. Lately he's been letting me take care of the operations here. I didn't understand it at the time, but if the man was from Stuart Wingate it all makes sense."

"Wessel never said anything about this man?"

"No."

"But he knew ahead of time he was coming?"

"Yes. I arranged for the supplies and ordnance myself almost a week ago."

Bolan turned the information over in his mind. A week. That gave Lee Wingate an even bigger lead than he had thought. Whatever had triggered the events of the past twenty-four hours had been working for at least a week. Maybe longer. But what was at the root of it? It didn't scan that Wingate was turning traitor. He could have passed information to the Russians or any other outside force a lot quicker than that. And he wouldn't have had to involve his son. No. There was something else, lurking just beneath the surface. Something that dealt with Stuart Wingate's emotional state, for sure.

Whatever it was, Bolan felt sure Wessel would know something of its nature—whether Wingate wanted him to know or not.

"What did the American pick up?" Bolan asked.

"Ordnance. That's what we deal in."

Bolan resisted the impulse to mention the heroin that had gone up in flames with the cabin cruiser. "What kind of ordnance?"

"Personal weapons, M-16s, side arms, K rations, uniforms, first-aid kits. Jungle attire and supplies for bush country."

"Supplies for how many men?"

The man shrugged, grimacing in pain as he turned pallid. "I'm not sure. Three, six men maybe. A small force that looked as if it wanted to pass undetected more than anything else. Certainly not prepared for an extended battle."

"How did he transport the delivery out of here?"

"He had a plane."

"What kind of plane?"

"A seaplane. They came in through the dock."

"Did you notice the pilot?"

"Not really. He was an Oriental. I think I've seen him in here before. I think Mr. Wessel uses him for deliveries from time to time, but I can't be sure. There are men, like Wingate, who speak and deal only with Mr. Wessel. I think he's one of those.''

Where was Williams? Bolan wondered. Or had he merely been a decoy, splitting whatever forces tried to tail Lee and the pilot? He knew a conventional force of investigative troops would have been stopped cold at the door of Wessel Armament—even if the island government had decided to cooperate with an American effort to find Lee Wingate.

So, what was the final destination?

Supplies for bush country, Wessel's man had said. South America wasn't that far away, but Lee Wingate already had an army waiting for him there. And a war, as well. Bolan kept flipping it around, looking at it from different angles but knew he didn't have enough facts to draw any conclusions. Yet.

He glanced at his watch, rolling back his sleeve to note the luminous numbers. Already he had been there too long. Investigators could be on their way now.

''Get up,'' he told his prisoner, gripping him by his uninjured shoulder. The man cried out in pain as he got to his feet. ''You're familiar with where things are kept?''

The man nodded.

''Why don't you show me something in your C-4 line? Nothing fancy. Just a good economy model.''

The guy started to ask questions but wisely bit his lip instead.

Bolan followed behind, aware that one guard remained unaccounted for and that more could arrive at any time if an alarm had been sounded. His prisoner wended his way through the stacks in a halting shuffle, as if having a hard time remembering where he was. Finally he came to a stop at an area marked Dangerous! Explosives! in three different languages in neon yellow paint.

"Stand over there," Bolan ordered. When the man did as commanded, he used the heavy-bladed Ka-bar to pry one of the small crates open. Inside, wrapped in thick greasy paper, were malleable sticks of C-4.

Holstering the AutoMag, Bolan removed two of the sticks and began warming them in his hands, shaping them into an oblong ball.

"What are you doing?" his prisoner asked.

Bolan ignored him, placing the C-4 ball back inside the crate. The explosive was safe to handle as long as a detonator wasn't attached and set off. He found one of those in another crate along the same wall.

"Wessel doesn't know it yet," Bolan said, "but he's going out of business tonight." He connected the detonator expertly.

"But you can't do that," the man protested.

"Sure I can," Bolan assured him. "I know all about this stuff. Used to read *Popular Science* when I was a kid." He set the time for ten minutes. With any kind of luck the explosion would rock the whole building into the sea.

He drew the .44 and motioned the man ahead of him. He was still miles behind Lee Wingate and the subterfuge Stuart Wingate was running, but Ernst Wessel was going to be a nice extra. Even if the man had enough money to rebuild his supplies and renew his contracts, tonight was going to cost him millions of dollars.

He stepped through the front door after his prisoner, pulling it closed behind him. Movement in the darkness ahead started him dodging to his right in an effort to get out of the line of fire. Bullets ripped into Wessel's man, slamming him back into Bolan, impeding any forward movement.

The Executioner got his hand on the doorknob and slipped the door open, falling back inside the warehouse with the corpse riding him. More shots knocked wooden chips from the door frame, coming closer as part of Bolan's mind returned to the C-4 and the minutes remaining until the explosion brought the entire structure down on top of them.

9

Kicking free of the dead man, Bolan pulled himself around the corner of the door and got to his feet.

The shooter rattled the walls with his weapon, creating a deafening chatter of thunder that eroded all hearing.

Checking his watch, Bolan found that only six minutes remained before the detonation. Fisting the AutoMag tightly, he sprinted for the other end of the warehouse, knowing that if he could elude the sniper the C-4 would take care of the man.

Bolan raced among the neatly organized stacks, careering through the aisles as he bounced from one area to another, avoiding the main aisle that led to the opposite end of the building. He used the catwalk overhead to chart his course.

It wasn't just getting out of the building, he knew. The explosion would set off concussive waves that could be physically damaging many yards outside the warehouse. He might not escape the deadly force even if he was in the water.

A hurried burst from his pursuer's M-16 chewed a crate's exterior into confetti just above Bolan's head. The Executioner doubled back down the aisle he had been traveling, sliding out of view, around the corner.

Three minutes left.

The pounding of booted feet let him know the remaining guard wasn't wasting any time trying to find him.

Perspiration trickled into Bolan's eyes, stinging until he blinked it out. The noise the guard had been making stopped abruptly.

Coming to a halt at the end of the aisle, Bolan scanned the area cautiously. Seconds ticked off in his head. From his new vantage point he could clearly see the double doors leading to the docking area, hanging on torn and twisted hinges. Tongues of bright flame danced all around the cabin cruiser, making a carpet of fire.

And the guard was behind him.

Less than two minutes remained. Not enough time to try to make it past the guard to the other end of the building.

Looking up, he saw the catwalk hanging suspended overhead. The small doors inset in the walls were open and Bolan saw no signs of flame there. Evidently the fire hadn't spread up the walls yet. He leathered the AutoMag and started climbing. Once he was on top he reached for the railing.

Bullets sparked from the underside of the catwalk, making hollow thumps as they speared into the metal.

Bolan ignored the sniper, hurling himself onto the catwalk. There was no time left for anything except escape. Even if he could spot the guard quickly, it would be too late to get away from the explosion.

The M-16 stuttered to a halt as the magazine ran dry.

Bolan took the catwalk at a dead run. Making sure the Beretta and Big Thunder were strapped securely into place, he threw himself through a small opening and into the docking area.

The heat was intense in the smaller building. Splayed shadows with ever-changing shapes paraded across the sheet-metal walls. The support strut Bolan clung to was almost hot enough to burn his fingers. Crawling out to a spot near the double doors that opened out to the sea, Bolan found there was no break in the fire that had spread across the water, feeding off the gasoline from the boat's ruptured tanks.

Grimly, knowing there was no time for anything else, the warrior lowered himself from the strut and hung by his fingertips. The flames whirled and licked under his feet, seemingly alive.

He dropped, covering his head and face as well as he could. For a moment he felt burning flames, then he was in the water and under the fire.

Bolan stroked for depth, staying as far under as he could. Unerringly he swam for the north, out to sea.

Moonlight filtered through the water as he neared the end of the dock, showing him the smooth bottom of the sea floor in green and gray relief. As he passed through the mortared walls that secured the foundation of the dock he saw electric eyes near the entrance and knew that somewhere an alarm was going off in the warehouse.

His lungs felt drained, but he refused to give in to the temptation to surface for more oxygen. The blast would be worse up there. It was better to remain underwater where the sea could cushion some of the effects.

When the warehouse erupted, he tried to relax, let his body go limp, moving with the force instead of trying to fight it. The concussion was worse than he expected, shoving against the sea floor and knocking the remaining breath from his lungs.

Then the world turned black.

LEE WINGATE SAT in the copilot's seat of the seaplane, scanning the horizon with a pair of binoculars from the ordnance he had picked up at Wessel Armament. Chan Wu sat beside him in the pilot's chair, the headphones slung carelessly over his shoulder. The seaplane bobbed gently with the swell of the ocean.

It seemed like another world out there, Lee thought as he gave his eyes a rest from the binoculars. Inside the cockpit everything seemed normal, stable. But outside there was nothing but the emptiness of the sea. Dawn had yet to break around them, but promissory fingers had started searing the eastern horizon. Back toward Saint Martin.

He'd been up most of the night with Scotty Williams gathering the money and the equipment from Wessel, checking it over as they loaded it onto the seaplane. His eyes felt gritty from the lack of sleep, and the smoke from Wu's Marlboro wasn't helping. An American rock station played on the radio, just under the threshold of being too loud.

Shifting in the cramped seat, Lee adjusted the military belt around his waist, keeping the .45 automatic within easy reach. He trusted Wu to a degree, as far as he could trust anyone who could be bought. He had to in order to carry out his mission, but he never really let his life rest in the hands of someone he didn't know inside and out.

Wu crushed his cigarette in an ashtray that had been glued on top of the control panel and leaned forward to survey the lightening sky. "Be morning soon," the pilot said unnecessarily.

Lee nodded, lifting the binoculars to his eyes.

"Going to get a lot easier to be spotted."

"I know. They'll be here soon."

Wu shrugged and reached to turn up the radio. "You like Whitney Houston?"

"Never heard of her," Lee said.

Wu shook his head in disbelief. "Man, she's the hottest thing in female music right now. Where you been?"

"The end of the world and back again."

"You ever been to Vietnam before?" Wu asked.

"No."

"That's the end of the world, man. Right where civilization stops and the jungle begins. You remember that line in the old *Star Trek* series, the one about where 'no man has gone before'?"

Lee nodded.

"Yeah, well, that's Vietnam, man. Nobody with any sense would go back there."

"I'm not going back."

Wu shook his head. "Can't understand why anybody would send an FNG into that country. Man, you got to know your shit when you start traipsing through that elephant grass. Otherwise you're going to end up as one dead son of a bitch in a hurry. Anybody else in your crew been there?"

"All of them."

"Yeah? Well, listen to what those guys got to say, bwana."

Lee rested the binoculars in his lap, rubbing his eyes until black spots spun crazily on the insides of his eyelids. "You've been there. Why are you going back?"

Wu grinned. "I'm not going to be where you guys are. I got a contact with a safehouse in Laos. I'll never set foot inside that country. And I warn you right now, you GI Joes better damn well be ready when I bring that chopper down at the pickup spot. Otherwise I leave your asses there. You paid for a one-time effort, not my life."

"Yeah," Lee said, "you made that perfectly clear a couple hours ago. You're a real peach."

"Best damn pilot you're going to get for the job, though. Wessel knew that when he hired me."

Lee shot the man a cool glance. "I guess we'll be seeing about that pretty soon now, won't we?"

Shaking his head, Wu turned back to the radio and started singing along with Whitney.

Turning back to the field glasses, Lee ignored the turmoil in his guts. He'd stopped wondering why the CIA was after him. As long as he could evade them they weren't important to his mission. And evading them was easy. He'd learned a long time ago how not to be where they expected him to show up. The CIA had been all over South America, some of the agents intent on taking *him* out.

A black speck appeared in the western sky. Lee switched off the radio and keyed up the mike. "Sky Drop, this is Safety Net, over."

"Safety Net, this is Sky Drop. You got tea ready, mate?" Sergeant Rick Phillips, Lee's second-in-command, sounded as unruffled as ever. The Briton never seemed to get excited about anything and seemed most at home in a firefight.

"You'll have to bring your own crumpets," Lee answered.

"Not a problem, mate, but we might have a slight difficulty with Briscoe. Lad had a wee bit much to drink. He might sink like a stone, you know."

"Give him a rubber duck before he jumps, Sky Drop."

"Right. We'll be there in minutes, mate, stand by. Sky Drop out."

"Tell McAlister to have a safe trip home," Lee replied. "And that he'll probably find some of our CIA buddies waiting on him at the airstrip. He can tell them everything about your departure. Safety Net out."

Lee hung up the mike and opened the door of the seaplane. He climbed out on the wing and watched the transport plane veer toward them. He wasn't worried about Jack Briscoe. The man had been a Navy SEAL, used to being dropped off anywhere at any time to deal with unknown forces. He was competent—extremely competent—despite the occasional heavy drinking he indulged in. A lot of forgetting to do, Lee remembered Briscoe telling him one night in a bar. The man had been talking about Vietnam.

Turning the bleak thoughts from his mind, Lee watched as three parachutes popped open overhead and started drifting toward the waiting plane. Even though the team for this operation was small, he wouldn't have had anyone else at his side.

FORCING HIMSELF to keep his mouth closed, Bolan pulled himself up through the inky black of the sea. Suddenly he burst in the open air, gasping for breath.

Glancing back over his shoulder, he saw the warehouse engulfed in flames, a reflection of the dawn coming up on his right.

He treaded water until his breathing was almost normal again, then struck out for shore. Emergency vehicles would be on the scene within minutes, and he didn't intend to be anywhere around.

His legs were shaky as he touched land and lurched toward where he had hidden the rental car. He stopped long enough to retrieve the trench coat from the beach and pull it on. Not only did it serve to conceal the weapons, but now it kept him warm, as well.

Once in the car he turned the heater on until he didn't have to clench his jaw to keep his teeth from chattering anymore. Using a courtesy pack of tissues, he cleaned his face as well as he could. He didn't think there was any permanent damage from the concussive shock, but he had an almost blinding headache that started just behind his eyes and went clear through the back of his head.

Pain was something he had dealt with before. Something he would always have to deal with. One kind or another.

He drove the speed limit, stopping only long enough to get Wessel's club's address from a street-corner phone booth. Something was about to break. With all the pressure he was putting on, it had to. And he felt Wessel was the key.

Bolan pulled the rental to a halt at the rear of the club and killed the engine. Business had to be good, he thought, remembering the dwarf palms and exotic flowers gracing the front of the building. The grandeur was echoed in the line of sleek automobiles parked around him.

Using the lock pick he carried in one of the pockets of the blacksuit, Bolan let himself into the back of the club, closing the door quickly. He found himself in a darkened hallway. Moving to the right, he discovered a door leading to a kitchen where a half-dozen chefs busily prepared different dishes. The aroma that wafted to Bolan's nostrils made the soldier realize it had been hours since he'd eaten anything.

He closed the door and proceeded along the hallway in the other direction. This time the door he opened revealed a staircase. Prior experience in other clubs, at least those run by other unsavory characters of American society, led Bolan to believe this would take him to an observation deck.

At the top of the stairs he hesitated, waiting until his eyes grew accustomed to the darkness that was necessary to keep secret the one-way glass overlooking the gaming floor.

Two men dressed in three-piece suits kept watch on the activity below them. Their carefully cut clothing hid the hardware Bolan was sure they were carrying. An automatic shotgun rested in a chair between them.

Bolan quietly drew the Beretta, thumbing it to single shot as he crept up the rest of the stairs. He kept the 93-R tucked in close to his right leg, hidden by the folds of the trench coat. In his left hand he carried Gil Keenan's wallet with the ID and badge exposed.

The two men heard him coming and reached for their guns.

Bolan stepped into the hallway as if he had every right to be there. He flashed Keenan's ID, then folded the wallet and put it inside the trench coat pocket.

"What are you doing here?" the man on the left demanded. He appeared to be the older of the two, with red-rimmed eyes and dark, swarthy skin. An acne problem years earlier had left permanent furrows.

"Security," Bolan replied obliquely as he kept walking toward them. He saw the younger man glance at his companion, almost as if seeking some sign of what to do.

Scar Face narrowed his eyes, and he kept his hand on the pistol under his jacket. "Who told you that you could come up here?"

"The manager. He said someone was going to make an attempt on Ernst Wessel's life. His warehouse has already been hit tonight."

"I told you I heard an explosion," the younger man told his mentor.

Bolan nodded.

"Why weren't we telephoned?" Scar Face asked.

"I'm telling you now," Bolan said. "At first no one knew where Wessel was. I've called for a backup squad to escort him to our offices." The Executioner came to a halt an arm's length away from the man. "Where is he?"

The older man never looked away. "Down there. At the roulette table. Who's trying to kill him?"

Bolan shrugged. "They don't know yet." Which was true. He made as if to get closer, to see for himself where the arms dealer was, taking the final step toward the guard. Without warning he struck out with his left hand, smashing knuckles into the hardguy's unprotected temple as the man struggled to bring his gun free of the jacket. He went down without a sound.

As the younger guard started for the shotgun, Bolan transfixed him with the silenced barrel of the Beretta. The guy's stare was frozen into place by the unwinking eye of the 9 mm.

"Sit down," Bolan commanded. The guard sat, holding his hands above his head. "Now, carefully, take the gun out and throw it away."

The automatic didn't even bounce on the plush carpet.

Kneeling, Bolan pulled a collapsible grappling hook from inside his blacksuit and used the attached nylon rope to tie up both men. "How many other guards are there?"

"Only one. A floor man who breaks up the fights that are sometimes started."

"Where is he now?"

"In the kitchen. He went on break a few minutes ago."

Bolan nodded. Then he gagged the two men with their handkerchiefs.

Returning to the one-way glass, Bolan looked down at the gambling area. There were ten tables in all, ranging from blackjack to craps to roulette. He had no trouble recognizing Ernst Wessel from the photos the Bear had telexed to Tinker Air Force Base. The arms dealer was fat, with a bald head and thick, petulant lips that made his face seem naked, as if it should be covered by a beard. He was dressed expensively, the cut of his suit clinging stylishly to his overly large frame. A young blonde hung on his arm, looking like a lost bit of innocence in a den of iniquity. Around the couple was a sea of people of differing ages and nationalities, but Wessel floated unbothered in the center of them.

Bolan pushed himself away from the glass. He padded noiselessly down the stairs, the Beretta riding inside one of the deep pockets of the trench coat, which he buttoned before he went through the kitchen door.

The floor guard was young, too. The man ate at a small table just behind the swinging door that led to the gambling area. His hair was stylishly long, leaking into the suit-coat collar in back, and a mustache curled across his upper lip. As soon as he spotted Bolan, he stood and drew his gun, holding it uncertainly. The chefs stopped work to see what would happen.

"Forget eating and come with me," Bolan ordered as he passed by the man. He halted at the swinging door and held it open, waiting for the guard. "I haven't got all night."

The man looked around at the chefs as if seeking advice.

"You heard the explosion earlier?" Bolan asked.

The man shrugged. "I didn't know for sure that it was one."

Bolan nodded. "Someone just destroyed Ernst Wessel's warehouse. I work for him. They called me out of bed to get

him out of here before someone tries to hit him. Now hurry
up, dammit, unless you want to start worrying about casualties here, too.''

The guard holstered the pistol and followed Bolan into the
excited crowd. ''What do you want me to do?''

Bolan stepped around a croupier who was raking dice
back for the next shooter. He stood taller than most of the
men in the room, so it was easy to keep Wessel spotted.
''Have someone bring Wessel's car to the front of the
building and leave it running. You know which car it is?''

The guard shook his head. ''I don't, but the valet will.''

''Good. Get the car there and keep everyone you don't
know out of the building. I've already warned the two men
upstairs. They're watching and will provide backup in case
we need it.''

The guard nodded. ''Who's behind the attack?''

Bolan answered truthfully. ''No one knows. They don't
pay me to guess.''

''Wessel doesn't know he's lost the warehouse yet?''

''No.''

''He'll have a heart attack.''

''Maybe,'' Bolan said, ''but it's better than going up with
the goods.''

''True. I'll see you in front.''

Less than a minute later Bolan stood at Wessel's side. The
fat man watched in rapt fascination as the wheel spun a blur
of red and black colors. When the ball dropped into slot red
six, Wessel murmured a curse. Bolan noticed the small stack
of chips in front of the man and figured it just wasn't Wessel's night.

Insinuating himself to the fat man's right, the Executioner whispered, ''Stuart Wingate sent me. There's been a
problem.''

Wessel nervously glanced over his shoulder. A line of
perspiration beaded his forehead. ''Who are you?''

''Somebody Wingate sent.''

Wessel narrowed his eyes. "I don't know you. I've never seen you before."

"You never met the guy Wingate sent to your warehouse tonight, either," Bolan said, hoping it was true. Lee was a professional soldier. It made sense that he would want to see for himself whatever it was that he was picking up from Wessel.

And Bolan was sure the arms dealer had never seen Lee Wingate before. Until the past few days, Stuart Wingate and his son had moved in entirely different worlds.

Wessel nodded, then turned to the blonde and excused himself. He fell into step beside Bolan, who made his way to the door.

"What's wrong?" Wessel asked.

"Not here," Bolan said. "You should know they've got this place under surveillance."

Outside, Bolan found the floor guard waiting by a Mercedes sedan with the door open.

"What's going on?" Wessel demanded. "That's my car."

Bolan moved in close and let the fat man feel the barrel of the Beretta. "Get in and slide over," the Executioner ordered.

Wessel did what he was told, huffing with the exertion of getting across the seat. Bolan flipped a salute to the floor guard and pulled out of the parking area.

"What the hell is going on?" Wessel demanded. Fear made his voice tremble. "Who are you?"

Ignoring the questions, Bolan guided the expensive car into the sparse flow of traffic. Behind him, only seconds after he had left the club, a pair of headlights flared into brightness and a small Toyota followed in his wake.

Tail, Bolan thought as he turned at the first right and saw the Toyota mirror his move.

He placed the Beretta under his right thigh and exerted enough pressure to pin it to the seat, within easy reach. How much time did he have? he wondered as he watched the car glide after him.

He gave his voice a cold, steel edge when he looked at Wessel. "We're going to talk," he told the arms dealer. "I'm going to ask questions, and you're going to answer them. I'm in a hurry and we're being followed, so I don't have time to put up with a lot of crap. Understand?"

Not waiting for the fat man to respond, Bolan took a left, not so quickly that his pursuers realized that he was onto them, but at just the right time to force the vehicle to get caught in the oncoming traffic.

The numbers were running down fast, but the warrior felt he had some of the big pieces in his fingers now—if he had the time to fit them in with what he already knew.

The Toyota made the turn and came after him, maintaining the same neutral distance.

10

"What's Stuart Wingate involved with?" Bolan asked.

Wessel didn't bother to reply, merely staring at the dark streets ahead of them.

Reaching across the seat with a big fist, Bolan grabbed the arms dealer by the lapels of his jacket. "I want to know what's going on, Wessel, and I think you know something. Somebody else must think you know something, too, because whoever is tailing us didn't follow me there. They were watching *you* tonight. I don't think they're just hanging around to help you count your winnings. I know Stuart Wingate sent his son down here to get ordnance from you, ordnance that's geared for a specific mission. I don't think you're the kind of guy who'd let something as mysterious as that pass under your nose without a pointed question or two. Even if Wingate didn't tell you everything, I think you found out somehow. I know a CIA section chief named Rolfe did, because he's been busy trying to cover everybody's ass on this deal. My bet is that those are his men behind us. Men he assigned to plug any leaks on your end. How does that sound so far? Maybe I should stop and let you try to talk your way out of this with them. But I think you stand a better chance with me."

Nervously Wessel wiped his mouth with a handkerchief. He craned his neck so that he could see into the rearview mirror.

Bolan took a right at a stoplight, barely coming to a full stop. The Toyota's driver didn't make a move but under the streetlight Bolan was able to see at least one more man in the car.

"Talk," Bolan ordered.

"Who are you with?" Wessel asked.

Bolan pulled the lapels hard, off-balancing the fat man, then slammed his head into the window on the passenger side. "I'm with me," the Executioner said, "and right now I'm with you. If you want to keep it that way, start talking. I can put most of it together myself, and if I have to, I can take my questions somewhere else."

Wessel wiped his mouth again, fear etched into his features.

Bolan cut into the inside lane, driving toward the neon lights of the center of civilization, hoping the men were under orders to keep force to a minimum in populated areas.

"He's being blackmailed," Wessel said.

"How?"

"His first son, the one who died in Vietnam, he left a son over there. Wingate didn't know about it until a week ago."

Bolan's stomach tightened. "How did you find out?"

"I have contacts everywhere. The man who's holding Stuart Wingate's grandson—Solly Taggert—brokered the exchange through one of my contacts. I had to pay a lot for that information. Wingate repaid me when I helped him check the story out."

"And it's true?"

"Yes."

"Lee Wingate is going to make the transaction?"

"Yes."

"And what's the price?" Bolan asked. The Toyota was still behind them, following at a leisurely pace.

"The Star Wars plans," Wessel said.

"And Wingate is going to go through with it?"

"Yes. He loved his first son more than life itself. I knew him before the boy died. He was much different then, full of dreams for the future, of political conquests to be won. He believes the grandson will enable him to reawaken some of those dreams."

Bolan juggled the facts in his mind. Where did Cary Rolfe fit in? The CIA section chief knew all of this already, Bolan was sure of that. The CIA guy's actions all reaffirmed that. But why hadn't he gone to his superiors with the story of Wingate's betrayal?

"How did Rolfe find out?" Bolan asked.

"I don't know," Wessel answered. "All I know is that he had a crew of men waiting for Lee when he got here."

Bolan considered the data he had on Lee Wingate, rebuilding the man in his mind from what he had observed and the information Kurtzman and Hal had given him. As Stuart Wingate's number two son, Bolan knew the merc colonel had an emotional trigger his father could pull. But to get him to betray the United States?

"Lee Wingate doesn't know he's carrying the plans, does he?" Bolan asked.

"No. Wingate told him Taggert was willing to settle for three million dollars. He believes he's carrying a microdisc with the numbers to a secret account in a Swiss bank."

"Where is Lee now?"

"On his way to Vietnam. He had to wait on his men, but they should have been here by now. He used a radio at my place to notify them of a parachute drop area."

Vietnam. Images blurred in Bolan's memory. Pictures of a stark reality he'd never truly put behind him, even though two trips back in the past year should have helped to excise the ghosts.

"Where's Lee supposed to meet with Taggert?" Bolan asked.

"At the cathedral on Tu Do Street in Ho Chi Minh City."

Bolan checked the mirror. The Toyota was still there. "How old is the boy?"

"Fifteen, sixteen. I'm not sure."

Vietnam. Still a war of innocents. And, yeah, Lee Wingate counted as one of them. But how did the lives of the boy and Lee Wingate stack up against the security of a nation? Maybe to someone like Cary Rolfe they didn't count as much. Or to someone like Ernst Wessel they could be assigned dollar signs, profit-and-loss value. But not to Bolan. Innocents deserved to be fought for, especially when they were unable to fight for themselves.

How much of a head start did Wingate have? The merc colonel had to guide a small team through the jungle. Even if they were all experienced men it would take time to avoid detection and achieve their destination.

More time than it would take one man who already knew his way around.

He glanced in the mirror again, spotting the Toyota. Easing his foot off the accelerator, the Executioner let the small car close the distance between them.

"Who is Taggert?" Bolan asked.

"A loser," Wessel replied. "My sources say he's been selling his services in Vietnam ever since the war, and those services have been varied and violent. This is the first really big thing he's been on to."

"How did he find out about the boy?"

Wessel wiped his mouth. "A fluke. Nothing more."

Bolan watched the Toyota cruise in closer, until he could almost see the driver's face.

"Why haven't you cut yourself in on this?" Bolan asked.

"It's a one-time operation," Wessel said. "And it draws too much heat to make the payoff satisfactory. This is something for a loser like Taggert—someone who has nothing to leave behind when he has to go into hiding after an operation like this. Look at the number of people involved already. I wouldn't have any part of something like this. Taggert is going to be running and looking over his shoulder for the rest of his life. If the Americans don't get him, the KGB will. Neither government can take the chance that he didn't duplicate the plans.''

''But you're already involved.''

''Only because I have no choice. Stuart Wingate knows a lot. Some of the deals I've made from time to time were, let us say, of a very delicate nature. And I have no doubt that he would whisper a few choice items in the right ears if I hadn't given the ordnance to his son. But even he can't push me past a certain point. I would've backed out earlier if I'd known the CIA knew about me. I'll have no problem washing my hands of this once it's over. Solly Taggert will set himself up as the trophy and I will make sure my contacts know of my limited involvement.''

Slowing the Mercedes to a stop, Bolan watched the Toyota stop behind him. He revved the engine, building up the RPM. ''You're also going to have to go into a new line of work,'' Bolan said. ''You lost your warehouse earlier.''

''What do you mean?''

''I mean it got blown all over the oceanfront tonight.'' Bolan glanced at the arms dealer, noticing the flare of the man's nostrils as he tried to restrain his anger. ''All over. I do good work.''

Slipping the car into reverse, Bolan floored the accelerator and popped the clutch before the driver of the Toyota could move.

The rear of the Mercedes crashed into the smaller car with enough force to push it backward a few feet. Bolan saw the driver's head jerk with the impact. Shifting smoothly and efficiently, the warrior pulled forward and then rammed the Toyota again. The clamor of tortured metal filled the inside of the Mercedes.

Satisfied he'd done enough damage to the pursuit car's steering to incapacitate it, Bolan pulled out across the intersection, ignoring the red light and the blaring horns of oncoming drivers.

Wessel sat in the passenger seat clinging to the dash and pressing against the back of his seat.

Bolan drove economically, taking the quickest route to the airport, where the Lear would be waiting and ready. He checked the mirror at regular intervals, but no one else was tailing him. Evidently the team hadn't expected him to take such aggressive action.

Halting the Mercedes at a corner several blocks from the airport, Bolan lifted the Beretta and pointed it at Wessel. The arms dealer covered his face with his arms, as if flesh and blood would shield him from the bullets. "Out," Bolan ordered.

Slowly, as if anticipating a bullet in his back at any moment, Wessel vacated the car and stood at the side of the street.

Extending the Beretta at arm's length and centering it between Wessel's eyes so the man could stare down the unforgiving barrel, Bolan said, "Make sure I never hear about you again."

Then he stepped on the accelerator and the car shot away from the curb.

Bolan holstered the Beretta, then rolled down his window, breathing deeply of the fresh air that came with the morning light now streaming over the island. His body ached from the confrontation at the warehouse, from the long hours he'd already logged in pursuit of Stuart Wingate's secret.

His thoughts turned to Lee Wingate and the boy, remembering how treacherous Vietnam could be. Neither Lee nor the boy deserved the danger Solly Taggert or Stuart Wingate had placed them in. Too many people knew about the swap to make any extraction a safe one. People tied tightly to Bolan's government, as well, who would hold no more compassion for the merc colonel or the boy than any of the others did.

Bolan knew Lee Wingate was fighting a losing battle going in. And he knew why. Stuart Wingate had used his son. No, sacrificed him, Bolan amended.

If events were allowed to play out by themselves, Bolan knew Lee Wingate and the boy would both end up dead. And the Star Wars blueprints would be in the hands of a very powerful enemy. Sure, the plans could be changed, altered, but technology during the past few years had advanced to the stage that hiding military hardware in space was almost an impossibility. The Star Wars program had given America an edge during the Soviet missile-building frenzy. It was irreplaceable in terms of strategic defense.

And what happened if a foreign power was able to tap into the codes and counter the firepower inherent in the system?

Bolan pushed the unthinkable away as he drove into the airport parking area. Lee Wingate and the boy, Bolan asked himself, or the Star Wars program? If it came down to a choice.

But the warrior knew there was no choice at all—he had to get them both, the plans and the people. But at the moment he wasn't sure how he could pull it off.

SITTING BEHIND the tinted rear window of the rented town car, Cary Rolfe watched as the local fire department struggled with the blaze that engulfed the warehouse. The three units on the scene were far from bringing the inferno under control. No one was anxious to get close to the structure because the ammunition was still going off occasionally. One bullet had already shattered the windshield of a nearby truck.

"What do you think, Joe?" Rolfe asked as he continued to stare out the rear window. "Think our guy was here?"

Joe Howard shrugged, tapping his fingers on the steering wheel. "I don't know, Cary, but whoever did this little number knew his stuff. I'll bet there isn't a goddamned stick left standing when they get that fire under control."

"It was him," Rolfe said with conviction. "You can almost feel him. Just remember the airport yesterday. McKay moved in while that Russian strike force was covering Wingate's whole security team and started taking them out. Yeah, this is something that guy could do."

"Still don't have a lead on who he's with?"

Rolfe shook his head. He removed a pair of sport sunglasses from the breast pocket of his jacket and put them on. Unlike Howard, the section chief had taken advantage of the flight to Saint Martin to freshen up and change clothes. Rolfe felt that a lot of times decisions were made on how a person appeared, and Cary Rolfe was never going to be picked over. In the tailored white suit, with his hair brushed back, he looked urbane. Like a guy you could trust, he had thought when he looked in the mirror on the plane.

"Has Robinson got anything out of the pilot yet?" Rolfe asked.

"No, and I don't think he will, either. The guy was at his girl's house. He wasn't going anywhere. He was just a gofer."

"Yes, well, we have to turn over every rock until we can come up with Lee Wingate. Tell Johnson to stay on him until further notice."

Howard nodded.

Rolfe opened the rear door and stepped out onto the street. He took a pair of binoculars from the seat, training them on the activity of the small boat on the sea north of the warehouse. "Call Danners and have him run a check at the airport for a plane that came in this morning from Oklahoma City. Tell him if nobody's interested in furthering foreign relations to just toss some money at one of the flight checkers. I want to know what name this guy was traveling under.''

Howard murmured an affirmative and reached for the phone mounted near the steering column.

Focusing the field glasses on the boat, Rolfe watched a handful of men gather on one side, pointing at something floating on the water. All he could see was a dark blur near the surface. Acrid smoke tickled his lungs, and he was glad he wasn't one of the firemen waiting to go inside the building.

Training the binoculars on the blur, Rolfe watched as one of the men on the boat reached down and tried to snag the object. Whatever it was, it was too heavy for him to lift from the water. One of his companions took a gaff from the stern and helped apply leverage. Gradually they managed to pry the thing from the sea.

A corpse, Rolfe realized as he saw an arm flop loosely onto one of the men. He zoomed in for a close-up before they got the body entirely on board. There wasn't much of a face left, but enough to let Rolfe know it wasn't McKay. The gaping head wound made him even more certain the destruction of the warehouse had been McKay's handiwork—aided by the hand cannon the man carried.

It had been bad enough when he'd been notified of Lee Wingate's escape from the crew assigned to him here on the island. But worse was that McKay had evidently made the tie-in between Ernst Wessel and Stuart Wingate. That information couldn't have been known until he had a check run on Wessel through his source in the States. The guy had good intel coming in from somewhere, but where? Who was backing him?

Irritation gnawed at Rolfe with tiny rat's teeth. But he didn't feel that the situation had gotten too far out of control, that it was beyond recovery. Whoever McKay really was, evidently the guy didn't have the kind of political pull to shut Rolfe out of the game. The CIA section chief took that as a positive. He was certain McKay knew how deeply he was involved in Wingate's cover-up, but no pressure had come out of Langley.

Which left Rolfe with plenty of room to maneuver. If he got the chance to act quickly enough.

Howard called to him from inside the car.

Rolfe clapped the lens cover back onto the binoculars. "Yeah?"

Howard tapped the small notebook he was holding. "I got a name and a flight destination from Danners."

"McKay?"

"That's not the name he's using now. Try Michael Belasko. That ring any bells?"

Rolfe thought for a moment but couldn't come up with anything other than vague, barely remembered comments. "Who is he?"

"I don't know much about him other than what I've heard, but the story goes that this Belasko guy is a free lance who works out of Justice from time to time. Usually when there's big doings going on. Way I've heard it, Belasko's pulled this country's fanny out of the fire more than once."

"So why haven't I heard of him? And what the hell is Justice doing involved anyway?"

"Guy keeps a low profile. Very seldom works with any partners. He goes in, does the job and gets the hell out. I don't think Justice is involved in any way operationally except for being a contact point for Belasko."

"We got any kind of address on him or point of origin?"

"No."

"What do we have?"

Howard looked back over the seat. "He favors a .44 AutoMag."

"Terrific."

"Guy's very professional, Cary."

Rolfe nodded toward the warehouse. "So's a goddamned claymore."

"Yeah."

"Where's he headed?"

"How does Dulles International sound?"

"Damn." Rolfe turned away from his second-in-command to watch the burning warehouse. So what was Belasko going to do now? he wondered. He tried to put himself in the guy's shoes but he didn't have enough on him. If he was just a talented battle broker, wouldn't it end here for him? Sure, if that was all there was to it. But judging from what had gone down at the munitions warehouse, Rolfe doubted it was going to be that simple. No, this Belasko didn't just take his work professionally. He took it personally, too.

Which left Rolfe in a position hard to defend to his superiors. There was no reason why he shouldn't have turned over everything he had found out about the blackmail attempt. His ass was hanging out on this one unless he could negate Belasko. Professionally. Or personally. He mechanically stroked the butt of the Dan Wesson .357 that was leathered beneath his left arm.

"Get us to the airport," Rolfe ordered. He watched the smoke from the burning warehouse recede behind them.

Professionally or personally, he thought. It didn't matter anymore.

BROGNOLA WAS WAITING when the Lear touched down at Dulles. The morning sun had just started to burn the chill out of the air, and activity around the runways had started to pick up. Security at Dulles was a top priority twenty-four hours a day, but Brognola's Justice credentials had allowed him to park on the field to wait for Bolan.

He put the car in gear as the Lear started its descent, and pulled up alongside the jet as the ramp touched the runway. Bolan was already outlined in the small door.

Brognola leaned across the seat and opened the door. "Good to see you, Striker."

Bolan nodded. "Hal."

He watched the Executioner walk the small distance between plane and car, noticing the man's careful sidelong glances. Like an animal, Brognola thought, hunter and hunted all in the same look. Again his mind was flooded with thoughts of the unfairness of Bolan's situation, dredged up from his subconscious, he was sure, where worry for the warrior never abated. Mack Bolan should have been a hero, not a man on a tightrope inching his way to his next heartbeat. He deserved more than he got out of his existence. Brognola refused to call it a life. Life was multidimensional. Not an endless tunnel.

Bolan got into the vehicle quietly, like a big cat. Brognola watched as the Executioner slipped the Beretta free of its leather and placed it on his lap.

"Expecting company?" Brognola asked as he put the car in motion.

"Lots of players in this one, Hal."

Brognola nodded. "I had Kurtzman tap into a couple of CIA lines to monitor Cary Rolfe's activity. You must have missed him by only minutes."

"Yeah, well, he must be running up a hell of an expense account. I had to trash one of his cars on the island."

"Want to talk about it?" Brognola studied the man closely, knowing he was one of a handful of people who would be able to recognize the fatigue Bolan was concealing. Those who'd followed the exploits of the Executioner thought he was some kind of machine, springs and steel instead of flesh and blood. Or a psychopath driven into fits of manic activity enabling him to do feats beyond the abilities of normal men. But Brognola knew better. Bolan was driven, all right, but he drove himself. And drove himself hard.

"Nothing to talk about, really. Rolfe's running interference but that hasn't gotten to be a problem. Yet. But I'm not sure how much he knows. He's made a lot of moves to stop

Lee Wingate and me. So far we've both managed to side-step him, but he could still foul things up. The easy part's over now, Hal. Things from this point on could get very messy."

"It already has gotten messy, Striker. I just found out Scotty Williams's body and the body of his girlfriend were found about an hour ago. They'd been tortured. My contact in Saint Martin figured I should know."

"Rolfe?"

"We think so."

The stony look on Bolan's face was unreadable, but Brognola knew the information had disturbed the big warrior.

"Got some coffee in the thermos," Brognola said. "Can't promise much because I made it myself before I left the office. You'll find a package of Styrofoam cups in the glove compartment."

Bolan found the package and poured two cups. "Did you get everything?"

"And then some. You can look through what Kurtzman and I were able to get and take what you need. There's a Harrier AV-8B set up to drop you near Ho Chi Minh City when you're ready to leave."

Bolan nodded and sipped the coffee.

"You want to tell me what this is all about now? I didn't have an answer for the Man when he asked me what Vietnam had to do with the Wingate thing."

Bolan did so with an economy of speech that left very little to question.

When he finished, Brognola took a stogie from his shirt pocket and stuck it in a corner of his mouth. "You don't think Lee Wingate knows what his father has done?"

Bolan shook his head. "It doesn't scan, Hal. Lee Wingate is a stand-up guy from his record and the way I read him. I've had to learn to make quick judgments of people. I trust my instincts. He has a blind spot where his father is concerned, but he's no traitor. His politics might not conform to the doctrine Washington is handing out, but how long has it been since mine have?''

"Yeah, well.'' But there was nothing for Brognola to say. He trusted Mack Bolan's instincts, too, and on one occasion it had saved his family's lives. He knew Bolan lived on the edge, knew that this had developed an affinity—in the man behind the Executioner's mask—for a deeper recognition of truth of self. Never trained to be a psychologist, Brognola had realized long ago that Bolan was a unique individual, a man destined to lead and learn. He belonged somewhere back in time, the Fed had told himself many times over. Bolan was an anachronism. A knight-errant without family arms. He operated from the very core of his soul, giving his own interpretation to the rights and wrongs of life around him. Wearily Brognola cast those thoughts from his mind and focused on the problem confronting them.

"You don't have to do this,'' Brognola said as he made the turn that would take them from the main highway to the area where the Harrier waited.

"There isn't anyone else to send, Hal,'' he said softly.

"Delta Force is trained to handle situations like this,'' Brognola protested. "If Phoenix Force wasn't tied up in Central America right now, we could send them in.''

Bolan shook his head and offered Brognola another cup of coffee.

Brognola waved it away, cigar in hand.

"This isn't a team mission, Hal. Consider: you've already got Americans involved in the kidnapping and ransoming of a boy who is half-Vietnamese. Several other Americans are en route now with intentions of going on foot into southern Vietnam to bring the boy back. You can't send in anyone with government sanction without causing an international incident. Lee Wingate and his men, if caught, will only be traceable back to their operations in South

America. You could say they're expendable. And in a way I am, too. I have no ties to our government, either.'' Bolan gave Brognola a grim smile. ''In fact, I've been publicly disowned a number of times.''

Reaching into his pocket, Brognola brought out a packet of antacid tablets and popped one into his mouth. They did little to relieve the sour taste bubbling up in the back of his throat. He sighed heavily. ''I know, dammit, I know. I just wish there was another way. More time, maybe. When was the last time you slept?''

Bolan grinned and bit into an apple. ''I've seen tougher times, Hal. When was the last time you had any sleep? I'll have a few hours on the way over.''

''So what's the game plan once you get over there?''

''I don't know yet,'' Bolan admitted. ''I'll have to play this one by ear for a while. There're too many variables involved.''

''What if Lee Wingate doesn't believe you about the Star Wars plans?''

''I don't expect him to. If things work out, Lee Wingate can run free with the boy and I'll take out the guys behind the blackmail.''

Brognola turned onto a dirt-and-gravel road, leading back through rolling hills with trees just beginning to show the touch of fall. They came upon the hidden airstrip almost as if by magic. The Harrier sat placidly on the tarmac, a sleek bird designed for cutting air and dealing death. Brognola didn't like the thought of ramming Bolan down the plane's throat and shooting him over to Vietnam.

''Godspeed, Mack. The Man has given a lot of thought about what's going to take place if the plans can't be recovered. He's already ordered the DOD boys to prepare an alternative plan that can go into effect in an hour's notice.'' He halted the car at the gate to the airstrip. ''Even if you get the plans and you get the chance to destroy them before anyone sees them, how do you plan to get out? Once you're dropped in, you're on your own."

"I've been making my way for a lot of years, Hal," the Executioner reminded him. "This won't be any different."

Brognola looked at his friend. "Yeah, it is, and you know it. This is Vietnam we're talking about. They put a price on your head over there."

"Like I said, this isn't a whole lot different, Hal."

Brognola thought about Bolan's last mission into Vietnam and tried to push the image of Bolan stranded alone in enemy country from his mind.

"How does the pilot feel about flying into hostile territory?" Bolan asked.

"Nelson came highly recommended," Brognola said as he glanced at the Harrier again. "I would have gotten Grimaldi if I had had the time. He's going to be pissed about being left out."

"Nelson?"

"He's good," Brognola said, "or I wouldn't let him fly you in."

"I know. You didn't have to tell me that."

"Your ordnance is already packed on the Harrier."

Bolan nodded. "I don't know what kind of arrangements Lee Wingate made, but I doubt they're anywhere as sophisticated as the Harrier. Hopefully, even knocking off his lead time, I'll end up with a couple hours head start on him."

"Just watch yourself over there." Brognola put the car back into gear and held it in place with the brake. "Kurtzman also broke into one of the CIA lines long enough to tap some of their files on the Agency's current Vietnam activities. There are a few deep-cover agents in place over there and a few who free-lance. With Rolfe's involvement in this I knew you wouldn't trust an agent, but the Bear got the name of a guy who operates around Ho Chi Minh City. His name is Matt Smiley. He ran a PBR for the Navy in the middle and late sixties. A lot of them were SEAL-trained. He might be a good man to have on your side if things get tight. Kurtzman bounced a message off to him this morning that he might be contacted for a very hush-hush scenario. The Bear used some of the code names he picked up in the search earlier. If Smiley asks, tell him Colonel Handley sends his regards. Your password is 'lightning bug.' Don't ask me why.''

"Thanks, Hal. Give my regards to Aaron when you see him.'' Bolan extended his hand and Brognola shook it, wondering for yet another time if this was the last he would see of his friend.

11

Taggert crouched silently in the jungle, thankful that the night was moonless, and watched the village. Raising his hand slowly, he slapped at a mosquito that had landed on his neck.

When Greenberg touched his shoulder he almost let loose a burst from his M-16. "Don't fucking sneak up on me like that," Taggert grated through clenched teeth.

Greenberg hunkered down behind him, almost invisible in the darkness. "Ease up, Sarge. This is going to be a cakewalk."

Angry with himself for being so close to losing his composure, Taggert focused his attention back on the village. He checked his watch and found it was almost midnight. Nobody had moved in the huts for almost an hour.

From his vantage point on a small hill overlooking the creek that ran in front of the village, Taggert could see most of the area, including the hut where Stuart Wingate's grandson lived with his maternal grandfather.

Too goddamned jumpy, Taggert told himself. The encounter with Pham had been totally unexpected, as if he'd come up on a fucking ghost or something. Images of the 5.56 mm tumblers kicking dust from the Vietnamese's chest kept playing in his mind over and over. The son of a bitch had been dead. Yet it had been Pham who had killed Gant. He hadn't told Greenberg or the others about Gant's death at Pham's hands, mostly because he knew some of them might pull out if they even suspected the man was still alive. He had just said somebody had killed the Briton while he was drunk, for the cash he had carried.

And Taggert had been looking over his shoulder ever since.

So far all he had seen were shadows.

"What's wrong with you, Sarge?" Greenberg asked.

Taggert looked at his companion, noticing the machete handle over the other man's shoulder. "I think I'm coming down with that goddamned malaria again. Fine fucking time for that, isn't it?"

"Yeah, well, you're going to be able to hang together. We got a rendezvous to make at 0700 hours. We gonna be rich men, Sarge."

Taggert forced himself to laugh and hoped he sounded less worried than he actually was. "If you keep that goddamned smile on your face like that, every one of those slopes in those huts is going to see you lit up like a Halloween jack-o'-lantern."

"That's the Sarge I'm used to," Greenberg whispered. "When you're ready to go in, let me know."

Taggert studied his watch again, smearing some of the blackface he wore out of his eyes. "Pass the word that we go in seven minutes from now."

Greenberg checked his own watch.

"Now," Taggert emphasized. "Mark."

The man nodded and moved into the darkness.

Soundlessly, Taggert thought, just like Pham would be if he was waiting out there. He couldn't resist looking over his shoulder again, shifting until his back was solidly against a tree bole. Goddamn. His guts felt like they were churning gravel, twisting sickeningly. Christ, but it would be good to put this hellhole behind him. As he sat there in the darkness Solly Taggert wished he knew what had kept him in Vietnam all these years, yet he really did know—it was because he seemed to have more control over his life here than he would have had in the States.

In his mind he saw Pham's body go twisting away again, staggering under the hail of bullets. Dead. The man had to be. But he wasn't. Taggert could remember the morning all too well: the girl's face vanishing; Pham's face behind the rifle, the telescopic sight covering one eye and the patch covering the other.

Taggert gripped the M-16 tighter, trying to force away images of the Vietnamese waiting for him somewhere in the jungle. He checked the M-16 again, touching the two magazines he had taped together for faster loading, and switched the selector to full-auto. His hands felt slippery on the stock.

If he ever got a clear shot at Pham again, he promised himself, he'd cut the bastard's head off just to make sure.

At the end of seven minutes he moved in, seeing four other shadows leaving the jungle with echoing movements, converging on the hut where the boy slept. Ellis and Meyer were at twelve- and six o'clock, in sniper positions to cover the team as they retreated. The jeeps had been left almost a mile away.

Taggert reached the door to the hut at the same time Greenberg did. He flattened himself to one side of the opening while the black man did the same on the other side. Holding the M-16 upright, Taggert looked at Greenberg and nodded.

Whirling suddenly, Taggert placed a big foot on the flimsy door and kicked hard, then spun back to his original position.

Greenberg dropped to one knee and covered the hut with his rifle.

Twisting his head to look around the open door, Taggert saw people moving in the blackness. "Don't move," he commanded in Vietnamese. "Don't move or we'll shoot." He waved the M-16 meaningfully.

Greenberg flicked a Kel-lite on, playing it over the interior of the hut.

There were four people inside: an old man with a wispy white beard, a woman who had to be his wife, a woman about half their ages and the boy.

Taggert took the Kel-lite from Greenberg and swept it over the boy. He was almost as tall as Taggert, already taller than the old man, lean and bronzed by the sun. He was a good-looking kid, Taggert supposed, with most of the features favoring his mother but with something else there, too. His frame was built a little broader than his mother's people, promising a bigger man when he'd finished growing. Then Taggert noticed the eyes. The folding of the eyelids wasn't nearly as pronounced as he'd expected. And they were blue.

Taking a step inside the hut, Taggert said, "Cover me." He slung the M-16 by its strap over his shoulder, leaving the barrel pointing down so he could quickly swivel it into an effective position if he had to. Reaching out slowly for the chain around the boy's neck, he turned the dog tags over so he could read them. Satisfied, he let them drop. The boy stood unmoving before him. "Thinks he's a brave kid, huh, Greenberg?"

"Fuckin' juvenile," he replied.

Taggert nodded. "Could be a problem, though. Get Jackson in here with the tranks." He leveled his assault rifle, covering his prisoner again as Greenberg left the hut.

"What do you want with us?" the old man asked in broken English. The old woman held on to him fearfully, keeping her eyes closed and crying silently.

Taggert ignored him, looking back at the boy. "What's your name, boy?" he asked in Vietnamese.

The boy looked at his grandfather, insolence burning deeply in the blue eyes. The old man nodded. The boy said, "I am Sang."

"Sang," Taggert repeated, wondering how Stuart Wingate would feel when he saw his grandson, if the man had even considered that the boy would look like he belonged more to Vietnam than he did to the United States.

Taggert indicated the dog tags. "Your father's?"

"They belonged to my mother," Sang replied in a voice that barely concealed his anger. "I have no father."

"Yeah, but you did have, kid, and that's important." Taggert switched to English. "You understand American talk, Sang? Maybe a little?"

"I have kept him here always," the old man interrupted in English. "He knows nothing of you people or of the city except what he has been told. We live in this village. We bother no one."

"Why are you here?" the younger woman asked in Vietnamese. "What do you want with us?"

"Tell her to sit down and shut up," Taggert told the old man.

The old man did as he was instructed, waving the woman against the wall of the hut. She started to object, but the man's voice grew hoarse and shrill and she did as she was told.

Greenberg reappeared with Jackson at his heels. Once inside, Jackson gave his M-16 to the black man and reached inside a pocket of his fatigues, producing a slim black bag filled with measured doses of drugs already set up in hypos.

"Now you, old man," Taggert ordered. "Up against the wall and take the old woman with you." He used the rifle to emphasize the command.

"What do you want with the boy?" the old man asked in English.

Sang's eyes moved warily from his grandfather to Taggert. His muscles flexed in his arms and legs as if trying to decide what to do.

Raising the M-16 to center on the old man's face, Taggert said in Vietnamese, "Sang, if you do not do exactly as

I tell you, I'm going to blow your grandfather's head off.
Do you understand?''

The boy nodded, holding back tears.

"Jackson."

The man responded immediately to Taggert's command,
holding one of the filled hypos in his right hand. "C'mon
kid," Jackson coaxed. "I'm actually pretty good at this
when I don't have to fight anybody. Been doing it to myself
for a lot of years now and *I* never complained. And this is
really good shit. The sarge don't believe in no halfway
measures when it comes to good drugs."

Sang lifted his hands to defend himself.

Jackson grinned, covering the needle behind his back.
"Don't fuck with me, kid. We don't have the time. And I
don't want to break anything if I don't have to." Jackson
moved in, only a few inches taller and a few pounds heavier
than the boy. He kept his left hand making small circles in
front of him.

"Tell him not to fight," Taggert ordered the old man.

The Vietnamese remained silent, holding his wife more
fiercely.

Taggert looked at the false smile on Jackson's face,
knowing that the little man was riding a high out himself.
Jackson was a killer when he was flying. Taggert knew from
experience. The man went in too hard, too fast to keep a
handle on the drug-instilled rage that filled him. A good
man to have on your side during a firefight, but someone
you'd have to kill to keep from coming back for your throat
again and again. From the glazed look in Jackson's eyes,
Taggert was sure the man had taken a hit just before the
penetration into the village.

Taggert started to tell the old man again to order Sang to
settle down, but it was too late. Jackson was already moving in.

The little man was fast with his hands and feet. It had saved him in a lot of close fighting in bars and in the jungle. Quiet, too. Almost as quiet as Greenberg in the brush.

Jackson feinted with his free hand, then shot his left leg out in a roundhouse kick. Sang moved, blocking the leg and twisting with the force, bringing his right hand up after the block and connecting solidly with Jackson's temple. Angered, Jackson dropped the hypodermic and brought both hands in front of him. He attacked the boy in a concentrated flurry of blows and kicks. Sang responded even more quickly, effectively sliding through the maze of force to score again with a kick that rocked Jackson's head and nearly knocked the man from his feet.

Before Taggert could move, Jackson ripped a knife free of his belt and threw himself at the boy, glittering steel fisted tightly. The boy dropped and rolled out of the way, wheeling below Jackson's arm to kick at the man's legs. Jackson went down backward and tried to rise immediately. Sang circled the man, keeping his arms loose and easy in front of him. Blue lightning flashed in the boy's eyes.

"Greenberg," Taggert said. Before Jackson had gained his feet the black man had stepped behind the boy and rattled his head with the butt of the M-16. The boy dropped with a groan, rolling over on his side.

Jackson threw himself on the unconscious boy, curling his fists into hammers and rained blows on Sang's unprotected face.

Taggert pushed the muzzle of his M-16 into the back of Jackson's neck and let the man hear him switch the fire-selector to single shot. "Get off of him now," Taggert ordered.

Jackson froze.

"I need him alive," Taggert said.

Jackson didn't get off Sang. "The bastard had it coming, Sarge. He had his choice. The little son of a bitch shouldn't have hit me."

Taggert pressed the muzzle more deeply into the man's neck. "I need him alive," he said, "more than I need you alive."

Slowly Jackson uncurled his hands and stood. His breath was ragged, and blood ran freely down the side of his face. The dark gleam in his black eyes told Taggert how much the drug was controlling the man. He knew he'd now have another reason to keep looking over his shoulder.

"I ought to kill you for pulling a gun on me." Jackson's voice was hoarse, almost extinguished by the fury that gripped him.

"Yeah," Taggert said with a grim smile on his face. He kept the M-16 trained on the little man. "I'm sure that thought would keep bouncing around in that small brain of yours. And it's one more complication I don't need tonight." He squeezed the trigger three times, Jackson's body jerking with the impacts.

Even then Jackson tried to get to Taggert as the drug in his system refused to let him die. He wrapped his hands around the barrel of the M-16 and tried to pull it away.

Taggert shot him four more times, shredding the man's chest, then kicked him away. Jackson shuddered once, then remained still.

Taggert swung his rifle toward the old man and the women against the wall. He emptied the rest of the clip and watched them fall, the old woman holding her husband even in death.

He turned back to the boy and saw Greenberg kneeling beside him. The black man had the drug kit in his hands and was priming a fresh hypo. Sang was still dazed from the rifle butt and groaned weakly as the needle was inserted none too gently into his arm.

"Definitely not going to be a neat operation," Greenberg said as he held the boy still while the drug took effect. Sang's arms flailed for a moment, moved less vigorously, finally came to a rest.

Taggert dropped to his knees beside the boy, touching his face with gentle fingers as he tried to determine the extent of the injuries. The kid's lower lip was split open almost the entire length and was swelling. A dark purple mouse had already appeared under his left eye. He was sure other evidence of the beating would show later.

"Nothing serious, Sarge," Greenberg observed. "But it's a good thing you stopped Jackson."

"Get him up and let's get the hell out of here."

Taggert moved back to the door, searching the village for any sign of movement. Meyer hailed him from a position forty feet away, giving him the all-clear. Changing clips in the M-16, Taggert nodded to Greenberg and followed the man into the jungle, knowing their backs would be covered by the others. Sang hung limply over the black man's shoulder as they threaded their way through the jungle.

A cold feeling ran up Taggert's spine. He knew it didn't have anything to do with what had happened back at the hut. He'd killed too many times for it to start bothering him now.

This was something new. An uncomfortable itch between his shoulder blades. A haunting, elusive fear that he had never felt before.

Branches broke behind him.

Splitting off behind Greenberg without saying a word, Taggert took up a post beside a tree, blending with the twisted shadows that traced the rough bark. He cradled the M-16 to his body, raising it to cheek level as the sound grew nearer, and applied pressure to the trigger.

He almost shot Meyer as the man came down the hill leading to the jeeps.

Shaking, Taggert jerked his finger from the trigger and sucked in deep breaths to ease his trembling. He studied the black sky overhead through the dense webbing of limbs. Closing his eyes to try to settle his nerves, Taggert saw Pham printed against the red of his inner eyelids.

He knew Pham was there, somewhere, watching and waiting. He was sure of it.

Angrily he pushed himself from the tree and followed his men down the hill, making use of as much cover as he could. It would all be over in a couple of hours, he told himself, before daybreak if everything went well.

Then he would be free of everything.

Including Pham.

MACK BOLAN HEARD black silk open with a sharp crack. The parachute harness jerked against his body and seemed to yank him back up into the moonless sky as his descent was slowed. He worked his hands into the chute straps and started to guide his drift. The backwash of the Harrier was a small and hollow thundering somewhere in the eastern skies. By craning his head a little he could see when the pilot kicked in the afterburners and sped for neutral airspace, staying well below radar detection.

Below him the jungle was a maze of shadows and hazy vegetation. A small stream ran through the hilly country under him to his right, a finger feeding into the Saigon River only a few miles away.

If the pilot's coordinates were correct, Bolan's drop point was only twelve or fifteen miles from Ho Chi Minh City.

And hours ahead of Lee Wingate and his crew, Bolan thought hopefully. There was no reason to think the merc commander could put his hands on something as sophisticated as the Harrier. The trip from the States had taken under six hours, with time out for refueling in Germany.

Relaxing his body for the coming impact, Bolan touched his equipment again to make sure everything was in place. Sheathed in a blacksuit, his face masked by combat cosmetics, the warrior felt he would only be seen if he wanted to be. The AutoMag rode his right hip, counterbalancing the Beretta tucked in the shoulder holster. For a long-range weapon he'd chosen Israel's Galil Model 332, chambered for a 7.62 x 51 mm cartridge. He'd used the Galil before and liked it for its countersniping abilities. The model Hal had secured for him came with a folding bipod and tritium night sights. In a waterproof pouch on his back were ordnance for a hard-punch assault if the situation called for one. The canvas pockets attached to the military belt he wore held extra magazines for his weapons. Other instruments of his trade, including knives and garrotes, were concealed in the slit pockets of the blacksuit.

And in a small pouch hung from his neck, Bolan carried a handful of marksman's medals, the one thing Brognola had objected to.

The marksman's medal had been the Executioner's signature in Vietnam and, briefly, in his fight against the Mafia in the earlier days.

It had been a signature both enemies had learned to fear and hate. The NVA had developed an almost superstitious fear of Bolan during the war. He and Pen-Team Able could fade and hit in a moment's notice, putting down an ambush that the Vietcong had organized for days, never leaving a sign going in or anything to mark their departure—except for the dead.

And the marksman's medals.

Sergeant Mack Bolan had recognized the fear he knew he'd generated in the enemy forces for the tool it was. Realistically, it was a force almost as powerful as any hard-punch weapon he'd ever carried into battle.

It was years later, but Bolan was betting the fear was still there in the government forces he might encounter, still a weapon he could employ when the opportunity presented itself. At the very least it could help him divert attention from Lee Wingate and his men.

But, as Brognola had said, God help him if he fell into enemy hands with the medals anywhere on his body.

Pushing the errant thoughts from his mind, Bolan estimated the distance remaining between him and the ground, knowing he was going to misjudge in the darkness.

The landing was hard, almost unexpected when his feet touched the ground, allowing him little time to try to roll away most of the force.

Moving quickly Bolan gathered the folds of the parachute and wrapped them around the bole of a tree, using stakes he'd cut from limbs to nail the black silk to the ground. There wasn't time to worry about burying the parachute, nor was it necessary. By the time it was discovered—if it ever was before the ever-creeping jungle claimed it for its own—Bolan knew he'd be miles away and the scenario would almost be played out.

He checked his compass against magnetic north, made sure his weapons were secure against being snagged by the vegetation, then headed out.

The warrior ran easily, lithely, a machine that fed on the labor involved to create new energy. As he made his way through the jungle, Bolan felt himself shrug off the final effects of the sleep he'd gotten in the Harrier, moving into a different frame of consciousness. His blood warmed in his veins, and he could feel the steady thumping inside his body. His breath came evenly, charging his lungs.

Even in the darkness Bolan could recognize the different vegetations around him, remember the color, texture, scent and taste of each, the humid odor of the land itself.

There had been no true home for the Executioner since the first retaliation against the Mob at Triangle Industrial Finance in Pittsfield. Sure, there had been a brief respite at Stony Man Farm, but that had been more of a way station than home.

But here he could feel it, the sense of belonging, almost a singing in his warrior's soul as his boots bit into the loamy earth and hurried him on his way.

12

Nothing stirred in the street below, and the everyday sounds of the families living below had quieted hours ago. A warm and humid wind wrapped itself around Pham, whipping his hair into his eye. Irritably he removed the black scarf from his neck and used it as a headband, knotting it carefully.

He sat at a table near the window, awaiting Taggert's return. The inner mechanisms of his Uzi were spread out carefully before him. Working patiently he oiled and reassembled the weapon, pausing from time to time to check the street. Thinh's men were scattered in other parts of the city, with orders to stay out of this section until called for. Thinh had told them nothing other than they were there to smash a budding black-market operation. That thought brought a smile to Pham because he was sure most of the captain's men would be convinced Thinh had only ordered the move to cut down on his competition.

Glancing at his watch, which lay beside the Uzi's hull, Pham saw that it was almost two o'clock. When would Taggert be back? According to Gant, Taggert had ordered the American task force to be in place by dawn to make the swap.

Pham had rented a room in a three-story structure that had once been a nightclub that catered to American GIs. From its one window he had a clear view of Tu Do Street and the cathedral of Our Lady of Peace. To the left, at the end of the street, was the old Presidential Palace. Going to the right would take a person by what was once the American Embassy.

Taggert had chosen a good place for the swap. The alleyways in that section of Ho Chi Minh City were torturous, sometimes trails through dirt, and covered with refuse and broken glass. A maze, really, that made pursuit difficult.

From there Taggert had the option of losing himself down in the wooden docks of the Saigon River to the south, or trying for Tan Son Nhut Air Base only a few miles away.

Gant hadn't known how Taggert had set up their escape if things went wrong. The big Briton had just taken it for granted that Taggert had arranged something. He'd always done so in the past.

Pham had completely reassembled the Uzi and slipped a full clip into place, easing the bolt down to load the first cartridge. He placed the weapon to one side and started cleaning the 9 mm pistol he wore at his belt. The small .25 belted near his crotch had been taken care of earlier.

He heard the apartment door open behind him as Thinh entered the room.

The army captain balanced on the edge of the table, well away from where Pham worked on the guns. He removed a pack of American cigarettes from his shirt pocket, took two out and offered one to Pham. Pham accepted the cigarette and the light the captain offered.

"Maybe the American has changed his plans," Thinh said as he took a Starlite scope from the window ledge and surveyed the cathedral. "Maybe you have made him too nervous to continue."

Pham shook his head, studying the Gothic spires at the end of the street. "He will be here. He has no chance of changing the arrangement he has put into motion. Gant told me Taggert worked through his contacts to set up the swap. There's been no time for him to designate a new place."

"Why do you think he chose the cathedral?" Thinh asked.

Still working in the darkness of the room, Pham stripped the 9 mm and laid the slide on the table, catching the spring automatically as the gun came apart in his hands. "Because it will give him the greatest chance of escape. There are many alleys there. Once he has his hands on the Star Wars plans, I don't think Solly will have any loyalty to anyone. Not even his own men. He didn't set this up to make sure everyone gets away free. He doesn't care about the Americans or the boy. Just think what will happen when your men hit the street and start flushing them out—mass confusion. Solly Taggert will then make his escape by whatever means he has of leaving the country."

Thinh took another drag off the cigarette. He looked at Pham with a mirthless smile. "An opportunistic plan," the captain said.

"Yes."

"But, even in this confusion, Taggert will not escape?"

"No," Pham replied calmly as he snapped the small automatic back together and looked down the empty road that led to the cathedral. "No, he won't escape from me."

IT BEGAN TO RAIN half an hour before Bolan reached the outskirts of Ho Chi Minh City, the warm, tropical rain he remembered from his tours of duty, the kind that could last for days if the conditions were right, making movement more strenuous and limiting vision. Or it could suddenly end, leaving only a few pools in its wake.

He took a black poncho from his bag and put it on to protect the Galil from the downpour, continuing on despite the uncomfortable weather. The AutoMag and the Beretta were safely snugged in leather.

It was almost four when Bolan came to a halt outside the city. He took up post in the brush a hundred yards from the dirt road that led into the city proper.

After a few minutes of waiting and watching, the warrior followed the shadows into the city, comparing what he saw to what he remembered, making sure he still had reference points he could go by.

Staying mainly in the alleys, Bolan walked through the narrow passageways with one hand on the Galil, hidden beneath the folds of the poncho. In the old days the city had been a sort of neutral zone, an area of safety for soldiers of both sides. It had been richer in those days, he realized as he walked through the streets. The small shops still existed but many of the nightclubs had vanished, along with the American money that had given them birth and life.

The cackle of chickens and the barking of dogs carried through the night now and then, but most of that was washed away in the rain. Few people were out at this time of night, and Bolan knew they would mind their own business.

On one of his sojourns through the alleys he'd found a coolie hat and put it on. It helped keep the rain out of his eyes and made his darkened face invisible to the occasional passerby.

Slowly, painfully conscious of the passing time, Bolan made his way to the docks.

By the time he reached the banks of the Saigon River, Bolan suspected Lee Wingate was walking into a trap. There had been a noticeable lack of guards on Tu Do Street, as well as on the main roads leading to that part of the city. The jaws of the trap? Bolan asked himself as he stared into the dark waters of the river. An old, fishy smell pervaded the worn timbers at his feet as the dock rocked gently with the swell of the river.

It was a logical area to meet Wingate, Bolan decided as he considered the options. The cathedral could be found easily, and the area was generally deserted at night.

The rain continued to pelt him, washing the paint from the warrior's face.

Maybe the whole blackmail thing was one big scam, Bolan found himself thinking. Then he dismissed that. Brognola had checked around. From what the big Fed had been able to uncover, Stuart Wingate did have a grandson in the country.

It would have been easier, Bolan thought as he squinted up into the cloud-blackened sky, if the boy hadn't existed. Then it would merely be a matter of finding Lee Wingate and convincing him of the boy's nonexistence.

Or of shattering the trap before the jaws ever got a chance to close.

Damn.

He thought about Stuart Wingate again, remembering the old man as he had seen him over the previous days. Cold and calculating, yeah, and ruthless. Bolan wondered if knowing what he'd sent his son to face would have meant anything to Wingate, then decided it wouldn't. The only thing the old man might feel toward Lee Wingate would be anger if the merc colonel couldn't pull the switch off and get the boy out of Vietnam in one piece.

Putting himself into motion, he started eastward along the dock, looking for Smiley's boat. He'd read the man's dossier while in the Harrier, committing what he needed to memory.

Smiley had gone to Vietnam in the late sixties compliments of Uncle Sam's Navy effort in the war. The man had been SEAL-trained and put in charge of a PBR. The patrol boats had been called the Brown Water Navy and usually went in for the really dirty jobs, both in and out of the water. They defused mine systems designed to hamper American movement, sent crews deep into the Mekong Delta area to flush out snipers and destroyed smugglers delivering arms to the Vietcong. Another facet of their job, Bolan remembered as he walked, had been public relations. A lot of times the PBRs had been used as floating hospitals for South Vietnamese who had been wounded in the war effort or were suffering from domestic diseases. And they regularly carried candies to pass out to children at ports where they stopped.

It was a tough job. Bolan had met a few of the men who manned the patrol boats and had been impressed with them. They were usually a rough lot, easily provoked into a fight and wired to stay until it was over.

Matt Smiley had turned in his resignation at the end of the war, choosing not to return home and to stay with his Vietnamese wife. Unofficial word had it that Smiley was responsible for getting some of the American POWs back after 1975, and that he regularly helped fund the Meo movement against the Communist government by dealing with the black market.

The fact that he had managed to survive this long was mute testimony to the man's abilities.

Shrugging his shoulders to keep the rain from running down his back, the Executioner walked easily down the docks, searching the boat names. Most were in Vietnamese. There were a few freighters in port, and sounds of voices drifted occasionally to Bolan's ears. The hulking ships dwarfed the smaller craft.

The warrior found the boat near the end of the dock. It was a small vessel, perfect for meandering around the delta area, Bolan realized, and outfitted with both diesel engines and sail. At the moment, the mast stood black above the deck, waving in the dark skies like an unsteady compass needle.

Without hesitating Bolan flicked the safety off the Galil and headed for the boat. He halted at the edge of the dock and checked to make sure no one was watching him.

"Hello," Bolan called softly in Vietnamese. He rapped on the hull with a knuckled fist then called out again.

A slight scraping noise barely reached the Executioner's ears, letting him know someone was working his way around the boat. He stepped back, ready to swivel the assault rifle into play if he had to.

A head poked up over the hull, peeking out from behind an old M-1 Garand. "What do you want?" the old man holding the rifle asked.

"I'm looking for Smiley," Bolan said.

The man was wearing a yellow slicker and a fishing hat gaily decorated with multicolored flies. "He's not here." The rifle barrel didn't waver from Bolan's midsection.

"Where can I find him?"

"Who are you?"

Bolan shrugged. "He doesn't know me."

"Maybe he doesn't want to know you," the old man replied. "Maybe you bring trouble with you."

Bolan shook his head. "I've got work for him."

The old man seemed to reconsider. Bolan had no doubt that if he made the wrong move the man would try to kill him. The man raised his face from the sights of the Garand and looked at Bolan more intently. The Executioner saw the man was Vietnamese and was even older than he'd judged. Nearly eighty if he was a day.

"You got word?" the old man asked.

Bolan told him, then repeated it in English.

The old man nodded. "Okay, Yank, I'll tell you where he is. But you better watch your ass because there are some soldier boys out tonight looking to be men before morning."

"I noticed," Bolan told him. "Thanks."

The old man lowered the M-1, hawked hoarsely and spit into the river, wiping his mouth with a sleeve. "That got anything to do with what you want with Smiley?"

"Maybe. I'm hoping he can answer that for me."

"He's at the Pink Parrot," the old man said. He gave the warrior directions, adding, "And make sure you tell him not to forget to bring me my bottle. You Westerners have no respect at all for the aged. Not even my own son-in-law." Then he vanished down behind the hull again.

Bolan grinned despite the pressure of the mission and started back through the rain, following the old man's directions.

THE PINK PARROT was a dive. Bolan spent a handful of minutes surveying the outside of the bar, which was a single-story building with a tin roof. A neon Budweiser sign from the war days sat unlit in one window. Three soldiers were huddled under a small doorway down the street, complaining about the rain. They never gave Bolan a second glance.

Once inside, he moved down the length of the wooden bar, shaking his head at the scar-faced bartender, drifting through the dozen or so patrons to the back tables.

Cigarette smoke curled toward the ceiling and vanished in the darkness beyond the low-wattage hanging lamps. If it had been any dimmer, Bolan thought, the patrons would have needed canes to get around. Out-of-date American Top 40 hits blared from overhead speakers.

Most of the men in the bar were Vietnamese, with one or two other nationalities, and two Americans that Bolan counted. Two more government soldiers sat at the end of the bar, watching a center table. They weren't drinking anything, which told Bolan they were under strict orders from a competent commander.

The object of their surveillance was Matt Smiley, who sat at the table with two other men.

Taking a position against the wall in a shadowed corner, Bolan leaned back with one hand on the Galil and watched Smiley.

The guy looked like his pictures, Bolan thought, but he had evidently changed a lot. The photos Brognola had given him in the dossier showed a younger man, but one who definitely looked more military, as well. His hair was longer now, falling down to his shoulders. And the dangling earring in his left ear wasn't regulation, either. Smiley was a big man, six-three or more, and weighed at least two hundred and fifty pounds.

The ex-Navy man had a smile on his face that looked almost childlike as he stared at the two men across the table from him. They were wearing army uniforms, as well, but no smiles. On the table before them was a deck of cards and handfuls of Vietnamese currency.

With a laugh Smiley raked in the money, and said, "You two guys sure you want to keep on playing?"

Bolan noticed that most of the money was in front of the big American while one of the Vietnamese had almost depleted his bankroll.

The soldier with the least money nodded tightly, not looking at anything but the cards as Smiley shuffled.

Bolan glanced at his watch. 5:10 a.m. It would be light in another hour. Where was Lee Wingate?

The playing cards almost looked like postage stamps in Smiley's big hands. The pasteboards whispered around the table and each man assembled his hand. Smiley raised his cards and ordered another beer from the bar, catching Bolan's eye for the first time. Without giving anything away, the big man nodded imperceptibly.

Smiley dealt replacement cards and Bolan watched the soldier nearest him count his money for the third time.

Grinning, Smiley kicked the bet up when it reached him. When he was called, he laid his cards faceup on the table. "Three kings and two queens," he announced proudly. "What do you guys have?"

The first soldier shook his head and threw his cards down.

"I told you he was cheating," the second man said.

"What the hell are you talking about?" Smiley demanded. The good-natured grin had vanished from his face, leaving a dark devil's visage. He leaned forward and put his arms on the table.

Bolan was intensely aware of the sudden silence in the bar, a live thing that had dropped from the ceiling to writhe on the table between the men. Everyone stood by expectantly, waiting to see what was going to happen.

The second soldier pulled a pistol and leveled it at Smiley. "I knew you were cheating." He laid his cards on the table and slowly tapped them apart, exposing a ten of hearts, two red aces—and a pair of kings, one of them a duplicate king of spades.

A mischievous grin replaced the anger on Smiley's face. His dark eyes almost vanished in the laugh wrinkles. "What the hell," the big man said. "It could happen to anybody." Then he gave the table a hard push and the soldier's pistol went off with an ear-splitting report.

When he saw Smiley's body go tumbling over backward, Bolan was sure his only contact in Ho Chi Minh City had just been killed.

13

Bolan ripped the poncho to one side, exposing the Galil. It might be a wasted effort, he thought fleetingly, but if Smiley was still alive, he needed him to stay that way.

He put a burst into the man with the pistol first, the 7.62 mm tumblers blowing the guy over onto his comrade. Pushing himself off the wall, Bolan stayed in the shadows of the room, shooting out the nearby lights in quick order. On his way over to where he half expected to find Smiley's body, he changed clips and shot the other poker player as the man struggled to bring his side arm into play.

"Nice shooting, Red Ryder." Smiley's voice praised from the floor.

Bolan looked down to find the man grinning up at him. "Matt Smiley," the big man said as he offered his hand.

"You hurt?" Bolan asked. The Executioner kicked over a nearby table and used it as a shield. People were scattering all over the bar, stampeding to the front door. The three soldiers had leaped behind the bar and were bringing their rifles up to bear. Bolan shot one of them in the face and raked fire from the Galil across the top of the bar, forcing the remaining two under cover.

"Nah. Knew the little son of a bitch would miss me at this range. Figured you'd step in about then and take him out." Smiley reached inside his jacket and brought out a 9 mm pistol. "You'd have had to take him out sooner or later anyway. He's part of Thinh's army, and you're going to have to go up against that gang before long. At least this way we've lowered the odds a little."

Bullets jarred the table Bolan was using as cover.

"There are three more soldiers just down the street," Bolan said as he returned fire.

"I guess that means you're ready to leave." Smiley squared up the sights on his pistol and dropped one of the soldiers as the guy tried to peek around the corner of the bar.

"I'd say we've about worn out our welcome here," the Executioner said dryly.

"Yeah, well, this was a crummy joint anyway. No class."

Bolan took out the last man as he tried to make the door.

Smiley stood and ran to the bar, looking over the stock, oblivious to the dead soldier hanging over the counter. Making a selection, he grabbed a bottle from one of the shelves, then headed for the back of the building. "I suppose you met my daddy-in-law, right? Had to make sure I brought him something back or that skinny old man would try to kick my ass."

Falling back behind the big man, Bolan kept the Galil at the ready, burning off a burst at the first head he saw peek around the corner. He didn't think he hit the guy, but the bullets chewed a handful of splinters from the door frame. There was a crashing noise as Smiley ripped the back door off its hinges, then Bolan was outside, following the man down a narrow, twisting alley.

FRUSTRATION CHAFED at Sang almost as much as the ropes binding his wrists behind his back. It seemed that every time he was able to get his fingers into position to work at the knots, the truck hit another bump. Then he became too busy trying to keep his face from scraping along the wooden bed. Crates, filled with rotting fruits and vegetables, shuddered together around him. Every now and then the tarp over the rear of the truck would bounce free and reveal the head-lights of the jeep following behind.

His captors still thought he was under the influence of the drug. The black American had checked him before he was loaded onto the fruit truck, slapping his cheeks lightly to test his reactions. Sang had moaned groggily and kept his eyes closed. Evidently there was some concern that the drugs might have been too strong.

Rolling over on his shoulder, Sang tried for the knots again, realizing his fingertips were going to sleep from the reduced circulation. It wouldn't be long until his fingers were too clumsy to be of any use.

He squeezed his eyes tightly to keep the tears from coming again. Over and over his mind played out his grandparents' and aunt's deaths, until he thought he was going to go numb inside.

They had been his only family since he was a child. His mother had died soon after his birth, leaving not even a memory to stir within him during dark nights. Still, his grandmother had made his mother live for him, telling him endless stories of the things she had done as a girl. His father was unknown to everyone. An American pilot, his grandfather had told him when he was a boy and curious about the matter. That's all anyone knew.

Sang had never tried to find out anything about his father. Grandfather had never let him go to Ho Chi Minh City, where ex-American servicemen were known to gather. And the pain involved for his grandparents had been too intense to suggest such a thing. It was enough after a while that they loved him. The dog tags were a gift they had given to him, coming from his mother. When he was small, he had traced the letters of the foreign name, trying to make his mouth form the sounds.

Now he wished Grandfather had allowed him to sate his youthful curiosity. Maybe it would have explained why this man Taggert had taken him from the village and killed his relatives. The knowledge could have saved their lives.

And maybe his, too, Sang thought as he fought to stay balanced through another bump.

He wished he knew more of what was going on. His grandfather hadn't told the truth when he told the American Sang knew no English. True, it wasn't enough to really hold a long conversation in the American tongue, but he could understand what the subject was. From what he had put together so far, he knew Taggert was hoping to offer him to someone for some sort of tribute. But he didn't know why. It wasn't easy to understand Americans, Grandmother had told him many times. They were a strange people and did many strange things, often making unimportant things become important. Sang had even heard the old woman say the Americans ate small children and made sacrifices to cruel gods. Whenever he had been truly bad as a child, Grandmother had told him it was the bad blood he carried, and she made him do extra prayers that night, warding himself against future evils.

But his mother had loved the American, his father. Otherwise she would have married someone else in the village after the man died in the prison camp. But she had given herself totally to her love, even after she knew it could never be. Often he had wondered what it would have been like if his father had survived the war.

His father had been a pilot. Stronger than the winds. That, as a child, had seemed to possess a power of its own. At those times he had been a little proud of the American blood that flowed in his veins, despite his grandmother's misgivings about his temperament. It made him special in the village.

But now Sang agreed with his grandmother's interpretation of the Americans, for he could see them for the barbarians they were. His people would never do something like this. He wished he knew Taggert's reasons for taking him away from the village, knowing, somehow, that it tied in with the two pieces of metal he wore around his neck.

It took him a moment to realize he couldn't feel his fingers anymore. The truck swayed suddenly, responding to a pothole the left side dropped into. Sang's head collided painfully with the bed, sending a shooting spiral of color through his mind.

Unable to mute the new frustration, Sang felt tears burn between his eyelids and roll hotly down his face. He wept in the darkness, his breath coming in broken gasps as he tried to be silent so no one would know he was crying. For the first time in his life he felt totally helpless and alone.

There would be a reckoning, he swore to himself, remembering the murder of his family. Maybe it would not happen for a long time, but the day would come. Taggert was just the instrument, a tool to be used. But whoever he was being taken to, Sang knew that was the man who had planned out his grandparents' deaths and the death of his aunt. And that man, he promised himself in the darkness of the truck, would suffer as he was suffering now.

Suddenly the truck came to a stop and the engine was switched off.

BOLAN FOLLOWED SMILEY, tucking the Galil under the poncho so no one in the buildings on either side of the alley could see it. So far there had been no signs of armed pursuit; only the wet pounding of their footsteps echoed hollowly after them.

Ahead of him, Bolan saw Smiley melt into the side of one of the buildings. The Executioner followed suit, ready to bring the Galil into play at a second's notice. The alley opened up onto a narrow street, empty except for the familiar whine of an approaching jeep's transmission.

Smiley glanced back to make sure Bolan was out of sight. The Executioner nodded imperceptibly, and Smiley raised the 9 mm pistol to a position near shoulder height, his left hand poised at the corner of the wall, ready to pull himself whichever way he needed to.

There were four soldiers in the jeep, the two in the back manning an M-60 machine gun and a searchlight. The yellow beam swept back and forth along the street, barely touching an area before moving on.

Bolan saw a small grin grow across Smiley's face.

"Thinh's boys," the big man said. "They'll do anything the captain tells them to, but they're a little short on brightness. Of course Thinh wouldn't have anyone with too much intelligence around him. I don't think anybody knows, exactly, how much black market activity he owns or is a part of in this city."

The jeep reached the end of the street and turned right.

"I was beginning to wonder if you were going to make it," Smiley said.

"I've had a busy day."

"Haven't we all. You wouldn't believe how much money I had to win off Thinh's army before I could come up with any information for you. Your control on this little operation wasn't exactly real informative when he flashed me. I knew something was up, but I wasn't too inclined to be real curious until I got orders. If you meet Captain Thinh and get to live afterward, you'll find out he's one shrewd son of a bitch. And he's not alone. He's working with Pham, a local cowboy. You got to watch out for him, too. He's a cold son of a bitch. He'd kill his own mother if the money was right and never give the old lady a chance."

Bolan shifted until he was on the other side of the alley, looking down the opposite end of the street from Smiley. "What have you been able to put together?"

Smiley rubbed at his chin. "Probably most of it. I found out there's a buyback going on involving a kid from a village near here. Supposed to be some high stakes involved if Thinh is taking a cut. And Pham don't play unless it's going to pay. We're talking high-dollar talent here, friend. How many you got in your group?''

"Just me."

Smiley shook his head. "You're kidding."

"No."

"You know how many guys you're going up against?"

"Not yet," Bolan replied.

"We took out four, maybe five just now. Figure at least another thirty or forty guys in Thinh's outfit if he didn't kick the ante up for this operation."

"I've been in tougher situations."

"Shit, man, so have I, but I damn sure don't like to see them come rolling around every so often."

"It could be worse," Bolan said.

Smiley grunted unbelievingly.

"This captain you mentioned could have the boy. As it stands now, the boy is still mobile and accessible. I'll just have to outfinesse Thinh."

"How many missions like this you been on, pal?"

"Enough to know what I'm talking about."

"You ever had one go bust?"

"Not totally."

"Well, buddy, you may be looking at your first one this morning." Smiley scanned the street again. "You also got to outfinesse Pham and Solly Taggert. Or are you people planning on paying Taggert the ransom?"

"No ransom," Bolan said.

"Taggert's not the type to give up a meal ticket easily, especially considering how much this one has cost him. I know Pham's interest in this thing is partly financial, but a lot of it's personal. Taggert tried to kill him a few days ago and Pham has to clear his business image."

Bolan turned all the players over in his head. If at all possible, it would have been in his best interests to let the bad guys square off against one another and step in to finish off whoever was left. He'd set up similar operations back in his Mafia War days. But in this instance it could very well result in the boy's death. And he couldn't let that possibility go unchallenged. Bolan's whole life had centered around preserving innocent blood—from initial conflicts in Vietnam to his home-front wars and beyond.

"How did you guys get involved in this?" Smiley asked.

"At the last minute," Bolan assured him.

"Why is this one so important? Kids have been sold back to the States before. What makes this one so special?"

Because he knew Smiley would be risking his life to stay in the operation, Bolan told him, holding nothing back. "I'm going to need a back door when this goes down," the Executioner said when he finished. He studied the man's impassive face, seeing the professional soldier surface in the gleam of Smiley's eyes.

"You got any ideas?"

"There's Tan Son Nhut Air Base," Bolan suggested. "You can bet Taggert has something set up for himself. I can't see him trying to get out of here by land or on the water. That leaves the air. I was thinking maybe you could commandeer whatever he has waiting. Can you fly?"

Smiley nodded. "Like an eagle, man, but that's going to leave you handling this end alone. The buyback team doesn't even know you're on their side, right?"

"Right."

"You go for long odds, don't you?"

Bolan favored him with a quick smile. "I've been known to stack a deck in my favor a time or two. And I've operated alone more times than I've worked with someone. If you want out, now's the time to say so."

"You must be one dedicated son of a bitch," Smiley said.

Bolan locked eyes with his companion. "Yeah," he replied simply, "I am."

"Terrific. I guess that means we're about the biggest pair of idiots this side of the Song Hong. I'm in. What kind of plan do you have in mind for this?"

"No real plan," Bolan answered, "but I'm going to get as much going on in other parts of the city as I can. Hit and git. Shake the army up so they don't know what to expect and hope to throw their timing off when the actual buy-back is being made. Then I'll see if I can be in some kind of position to cover for the boy and Wingate's force."

Smiley checked his watch. "You don't have a lot of time there. From what I learned from Thinh's boys, the thing is set for sometime shortly after dawn. Provided the American team gets here on time. And if you get too colorful with that kind of movement, you could end up scaring somebody off."

"There's no other way to do it," Bolan told him.

"Yeah, I know. You sure you want me at the airport? I might be more help here."

"I need the back door," Bolan said. "The only alternative is trying to pack it through the jungle and escape pursuit. We don't have the numbers for that. When we get out, it's got to be quick and clean. Chances are we won't be getting a second try."

"Do you know where Taggert's going to be with the boy?"

Bolan said yes and told him.

Smiley grunted and turned to survey the street again. "That area gives a man a lot of room to run when he's in a bind. I can buy that. Taggert's no idiot. The guy has lived in and around the city for a lot of years since the war, so he knows his way around. One thing you gotta know, though. Even if his ass is on the line, Taggert won't be looking for any handouts. You try to help him out of this and chances are he'll hand you your head and help himself to whatever you've got."

"He stays here," Bolan said.

Smiley nodded and holstered the 9 mm to keep it from the light rain. "You know your way around the city, or did you just put all this together from one night's stroll?"

"I've been here before."

"What about the air base? Can you make it there?"

Bolan nodded.

"If they had contacted me earlier, I might have been able to arrange something better. At least gotten us another man or two in here to help out." The big man sounded apologetic.

"There wasn't a lot of time available for anyone on this one," Bolan said.

"That doesn't make it a hell of a lot better knowing that, though, does it?" Smiley gave him a crooked grin. "You don't get an *E* for effort on an operation like this."

"Just make sure you watch your ass. When I need you, I want you to be there."

"When you need me," Smiley said, "you just look over your shoulder."

"Couldn't ask for anything better than that." Bolan reached out and took the man's hand.

"I guess I'll see you when I see you," Smiley said in farewell. Without another word he sprinted from the alley and vanished into the shadows draped across the street.

Bolan waited, pressed into the wall behind him, making sure no one spotted Smiley. Then he gave his weapons a final check, refamiliarizing himself with his war rigging before he went out to engage the enemy. Timing would be essential in his operation, and all movement would have to be automatic, on the heartbeat and by the numbers.

He touched the pouch of marksman's medals tied around his neck, knowing he would be reawakening old fears this morning, doling out terror to those who didn't go down under his guns. Maybe he couldn't take on Thinh's whole army by himself, but he could demoralize the hell out of the ones he didn't encounter.

A blitzkrieg of blood and thunder, the warrior thought as he walked down the streets of Ho Chi Minh City to do battle with an enemy he had fought years ago. A city that knew him, too, that had carried the Executioner's name on its lips for many years. Stories had been told in every bar in the city about an American who walked invisible and unheard through an enemy camp in the dead of night.

Now he was going to bring those legends back to poignant life for one more night. A blitz for sure, Bolan thought as he wended his way deeper into the heart of the city.

But a quiet blitz. For openers.

14

Mist flew in through the open bay of the cargo plane, lightly dusting the four men waiting just inside the belly of the craft. Lee Wingate peered through the darkness below, wishing the jungle didn't appear so formidable in the night. Dawn was only an hour or so away, but even that length of time seemed interminable. It wasn't just the jungle and the night shadows that bothered him, nor the fact that Vietnam seemed to have become a special part of the American culture that would never fade away.

Instead, it was the closeness he felt to his brother. Stu had died over here. The thought burned brightly in his mind, and he found himself dwelling on it often. The others had noticed his preoccupation, but they hadn't said anything. Briscoe had his own dark memories to keep him company, Phillips and Kelley had always been two to enjoy themselves no matter where they were or what the conditions.

Wiping the collected moisture from his face with a gloved hand, Lee turned from the cargo bay and inspected his crew once more. The jump site was only minutes away, and there could be no turning back once they left the plane. He hoped Wu had been successful in avoiding detection as the plane crossed over into the country from Laos.

Phillips and Kelley squatted down on the opposite side of the bay, engaged in one of Phillips's more colorful stories. It was probably one Kelley had already heard, but you'd never know it by the rapt attention on the younger man's face.

Sergeant Rick Phillips was British by birth and a warrior by trade. Lee didn't know for sure how old the man was—the stories he told often conflicted with his age—but Phillips had once told him of his training in the British commandos. The sergeant knew more about surviving off the land than any man in the group, and his knowledge had saved many lives over the years they'd been together. Phillips was a hard drinker, quick to laugh and a lover of group gatherings. Yet the man had always held a part of himself back, never revealing the personal side.

Even though he was dressed in the same dark gray uniform as the rest of the group, Pete Kelley looked like an unkempt scarecrow. His skinny build and sallow complexion belonged to an undernourished adolescent, and someone who didn't know him would have underestimated his age by fifteen years. But behind the easygoing manner was one of the last men you'd want to back into a corner. He'd been a door gunner in Vietnam and had lost a part of himself to the excitement and danger. Since leaving the service at the end of the war, Kelley had never held a job more than a few months at a time. Until he had signed on with Lee Wingate.

Lee wiped more mist from his face and looked at his watch. It was almost six. Wu had promised to drop them a few miles outside of Ho Chi Minh City, saying he was following a normal route used by acknowledged peddlers in the black market. The pilot hadn't volunteered how he'd come across the information, and Lee hadn't felt inclined to ask. He turned to his right to face Jack Briscoe, the last member of the team.

Briscoe sat in the center of the floor in a lotus position, dark eyes closed as he focused on some inner vision. His black hair blended in with the watch cap, bleeding down into the full beard he wore. Briscoe was heavily muscled, the

slabs and planes showing clearly through the thin fabric of
his uniform. The man had his own devils left over from the
war. The SEALs had been heavily involved in deep penetration during the war and had seen more one-on-one
atrocities than any other branch of service. They were often
at the front of the battle for days and weeks, cut off from
any friendly forces. Once, during a fever-induced delirium,
Lee had heard Briscoe call out to a colleague, warning the
man to stay away from a child Briscoe was sure was carrying a weapon. The rest had been garbled, but Lee was sure
Briscoe had lost a friend and killed the juvenile in self-
defense. But evidently he hadn't forgiven himself. Briscoe
was moody and intense, very good at what he did, but bur-
dened by whatever cross he bore. If the man had been less
talented, Lee wouldn't have asked him to come. But he knew
he couldn't afford to disregard the SEAL's experience, in
view of the situation they would be walking into.

Shifting the heavy parachute's weight more evenly on his
shoulders, Lee touched the package inside his shirt. Certain
the hard plastic container was still taped securely to his
chest, he checked his M-16 in the darkness, knowing he had
already done it a number of times before.

"'Twill be easier once we're on the ground," Phillips
shouted across the roaring wind of the open bay.

Lee looked at his sergeant and nodded, noticing the excited glint in the older man's eyes. "Yeah, I know."

"It's the waiting that really rags your ass," Kelley added.
His grin was boyish, as if the seriousness of the situation
hadn't touched him.

Unable to resist the irritability that fed on his nervous
system, Lee stood, holding on to the handrail beside the
opening. "This won't be easy," he said, locking eyes with
each man in turn. "You knew that when you came into this
operation. If anybody wants out, I want you to know I
wouldn't hold it against you. This isn't something we put
together ourselves. Everything we're working on, every-

thing we're working with, including the transportation, is something we were given. I don't know for sure whether the boy will be where I've been told, and I can't vouch for the pilot's guarantee that he'll be at the pickup point at the right time."

"The pilot I can guarantee," Briscoe promised with an evil look on his face. "We had a little chat while you were catching forty winks, Colonel. We reached an understanding."

"All right, then. We all knew what we were signing on for before we got on this crate. I just want you to know I appreciate the fact that you guys are standing by me in this."

Phillips waved it away. "If I knew you were going to get mushy on us, I might have sat this one out."

"We've been with you a long time now," Kelley said. "We've been through some shit now and then, but you always stood by us, too. It ain't like anybody here owes anybody anything. I think we all appreciate the chance for one more tour to kind of even things up a little. And if this kid wants out, I'm damn sure going to see that he gets the opportunity."

Lee looked at Briscoe.

"Don't look at me if you're looking for speeches, Colonel. I just came here to do a job. I'm in for the duration."

Lee nodded. He'd felt close to all of his men at one time or another, but never had the kinship seemed so strong. And never had he felt so close to Stu. It had been too many years since he'd come into so strong a feeling for Stu's presence. He'd never been able to draw as much out of the stone over his brother's empty grave as his father had. He'd never once been able to fool himself that Stu was anywhere near there. But here. That was something else again.

"Two minutes to jump," Wu's voice crackled over the aged speaker hanging toward the cabin of the cargo plane.

Lee watched as his men stood, making sure their gear was tightly strapped for the jump. Every one was a professional, had fought back-to-back long before this, but a nagging doubt haunted him. He'd learned long ago that an operation was never as pat as this one seemed to be. Something was bound to go wrong. Shrugging these negative thoughts aside, he pulled his parachute closer, flexing his shoulders until it seated to his satisfaction.

When the pilot called out the jump site, Phillips turned to the team and said, "See you on the ground, mates." Then the sergeant cradled his M-16 and stepped into the void beyond the cargo bay. Kelley was next, flipping Lee a mock salute as he fell through the opening.

Then, leaving Briscoe to cover the rear, Lee took his position and dropped into the sky, throwing his arms wide to help control his fall.

The jungle spun under him, a slow haze of dark green that looked alien through the mist filling his eyes. He ignored the tears that burned upward on his face, straining to see the two black mushrooms of Kelly's and Phillips's parachutes only yards away. Finally he found them, drifting lazily to his right, flitting shadows above the jungle. He watched the two men angle for the river flowing to the east, toward Ho Chi Minh City according to the maps Lee had studied in the plane.

Popping his chute, he felt it drag tightly against him for an instant, then suspend him between the shrouds. He guided his descent, intending to drop as close to Kelley and Phillips as possible, to keep the group together. They already had a fair hike ahead of them without having to find one another first.

Lee craned his neck and saw the dark blossom of Briscoe's parachute many yards above his own.

When he got close enough Lee saw Kelley and Phillips standing on the riverbank waiting for him. Their parachutes trailed over the ground behind them, and they made no move to conceal them.

Too late Lee saw the three men in the trees who were holding Kelley and Phillips at gunpoint. Lee tried to pull his .45 from the holster at his hip, but the ground rushed up, knocking the wind out of him before he had a chance to clear leather. As the merc colonel lay on the ground, one of the men jumped from the cover of the trees and kicked the pistol from his hand. The barrel of the guy's carbine was centered on his throat just above his Adam's apple.

Lee searched the sky, looking for Briscoe, hoping the man would see the enemy on the ground, wondering if there would be time for the ex-SEAL to do anything to avoid being captured, as well.

Briscoe's descent was taking him to the center of the slow flowing river. The other four men stepped from the trees, brandished their guns and yelled something. Lee couldn't understand the words, though the meaning was clear.

One of the men lifted his weapon and fired a couple of warning shots at Briscoe, then yelled at him again.

While more than twenty feet above the surface of the river, Briscoe released the parachute's harness and dropped into the water. He disappeared at once and didn't resurface.

Lee tried to get up before he remembered the carbine at his throat, then let himself be forced back into the wet sand.

"Bloody bastards were waiting on us, laddie," Phillips said apologetically. "Didn't see them until they were shoving their bloody rifles in my face."

"Are you guys all right?" Lee asked.

"Yeah, we're okay," Kelley replied.

Turning his head, Lee watched as the three other men started to search the waters of the river. Briscoe's parachute had landed on the surface and lay like some two-dimensional cloud, wavering in the current. The Vietnamese were talking, but Lee couldn't understand any of it. He hadn't realized how he'd be cut off from the land and the people without being able to speak the native language. It made him feel even more helpless.

Taking a deep breath to focus his energy, Lee knew he was going to have to try to get the upper hand on the man guarding him. None of them could afford to be taken alive in this country. The M-16 was wedged under him, the pistol was gone and he had no idea where it had fallen when he hit the ground. That left the commando knife tucked in a sheath inside his right boot. Even if he succeeded in getting his hand around the barrel of his captor's carbine, it would require a lot of twisting to get the knife and kill the man— even if he could do it before the men searching the river shot him down.

Where was Briscoe? he wondered, knowing the man hadn't drowned. Not with his training. SEALs were reputed to be half-man and half-fish.

Without warning, Briscoe erupted out of the river twenty yards from where he'd gone in, throwing water everywhere as he raised his assault rifle. Lee watched as the ex-SEAL sprayed hot death from his M-16, catching the three men at the riverbank flat-footed.

Then Lee was moving, swinging out with his left hand as he twisted away from the barrel of the carbine. He almost felt the impact of a bullet as it drove into the sand, kicking dirt up into his eyes. Blinded by the sand, Lee curled his fingers around the hilt of the knife and pulled it free, striking out for the man holding the rifle. With blurred vision he saw the blade slide home, spurring in between the man's ribs to reach and rend the heart beneath. A pained look filled the man's face and he fell heavily on top of Lee.

Lee pushed the dead man to one side and unslung the M-16. By the time he had it in his hands, Kelley and Phillips had taken care of their men, as well.

Flicking a glance over his shoulder, Lee saw Briscoe wading into shore with his M-16 held over his head. The ex-SEAL halted by the three bodies on the bank long enough to check them for vitals, then moved on into the underbrush.

Lee followed the bigger man's lead, sliding quietly through the wet vegetation. Ten minutes later, satisfied that the men they had already accounted for was the whole team, he returned to the riverbank. Phillips was just finishing dressing Kelley's left arm.

"How bad is it?" Lee asked as he walked toward them.

Phillips shook his head. "Not bad, mate. Bullet passed through. I packed it and bound it good and proper. She'll hold till we can do something with it."

Lee looked at Kelley's pallid face. "How does it feel?"

Kelley grinned. "Numb right now, but I'm sure I'll pay for it later."

"Where's Jack?" Phillips asked.

"Here," Briscoe answered as he stepped from the jungle, M-16 canted over one shoulder.

"Nice piece of work, mate. I'd already about given up on us all before you dropped into that river."

Briscoe grinned at the sergeant. "Couldn't have done it without you guys playing hostage and taking their minds off me."

"You're all heart, mate."

Lee retrieved his knife from the body, washed the blood off in the river, dried it on his leg and shoved it back in the sheath. When he looked back at his team they were waiting expectantly.

He pushed away the self-recrimination, locking it away until he had time to examine it. Already he had placed their lives in jeopardy by agreeing to go ahead with his father's plans without looking things over for himself. He wondered what else lay ahead, wishing he knew the right thing to do. Then he remembered his father's stern face, the challenge he'd read into every word his father had said. Right or wrong, he wanted this chance to prove himself in his father's eyes, to earn a respect he'd never had before. And there was the boy, as well, Stu's son. Lee knew he couldn't abandon him to whatever fate Solly Taggert had in store if the ransom demand wasn't met. He gripped his M-16 tightly and walked forward.

"I guess this means it might get rough from here on in," Kelley observed dryly. He didn't try to keep the boyish smile off his face.

"At least it won't be boring." Lee looked at the dead men. "What do you think of this welcoming party, Sergeant?"

Phillips rubbed his jaw with a big hand. "I'd say someone is expecting us, besides your man Taggert. These are army regulars, not some ragtag renegades. Take a look at the weapons they were carrying. Those are fairly new, not hand-me-downs from the war."

"That's what I figured, too." Lee turned from the corpses and looked at Briscoe's impassive face, the light rain nesting in the dark beard. "Jack, you want to take point?"

The big man nodded and vanished into the jungle, making almost no sound at all. Lee followed, letting Briscoe get ahead and set the pace. Raindrops dripped from the broadleafed trees around them, splattering onto the ground.

An image of Stu confined in a bamboo cage blossomed in Lee's mind and almost brought him to a stop. How long had his brother lived under those conditions? How could Stu have lived with no hope? Or had there been hope in the beginning? Wearily he shut that part of his mind off, focusing on his mission. Death already lay behind them, he thought as he scanned the foliage for Briscoe. How much of it lay ahead of them? And for whom?

THE OLD WOMAN SAT in the darkness and held her grandchildren. Silently she stared out the small crack she had left between the curtains. The grandchildren, two boys and a girl, held her knees tightly.

The house had little to offer other than a dry place to sleep under a tin roof. She had worked hard during the war years, she and her husband, making the best of everything they were fortunate enough to acquire. It had been a good home for their children, she told herself as she looked out at the lightening sky. And now it was a good home for her grandchildren. Her husband still worked in his shop, and though times were harder now, there was always enough rice to eat and patience for the grandchildren as she tried to teach them the old ways.

The Americans had changed much during the war. The young grew up with different ideals, hooked on things the Westerners had brought with them—Coca-Cola, clothes...and the drugs that had taken the children's mother away from them. They had never had a father and weren't even fathered by the same man. That was another thing the Americans had brought with them: their money. Enough money to buy her daughter's body time and time again. The old woman had wept with shame when she had found out what her daughter was doing with the American soldiers. And there were more tears when her daughter was found dead in an alley with her throat cut.

That act had only emphasized how unsafe the city had become since the North Vietnamese had taken over. It was bad enough without Thinh and his army being here. They were roaming Ho Chi Minh City freely tonight, creating havoc in homes as they pleased. Already a woman down the street had been raped in her own home by two soldiers.

Reaching out a thin and bony hand, the old woman touched the statue of Buddha sitting on the small table and prayed that the soldiers would return to their barracks. She wished her husband was at home.

"Grandmother, why are you afraid?" her granddaughter asked.

The old woman looked at the widely set brown eyes and smoothed the long black hair back out of the child's face.

She wished she had comforting words to tell the children but knew they would sense any falsehood on her part. They had been a part of her life ever since they were born.

"It's the soldiers, Vo," Hung, the older boy, said. "They are bad and grandmother is hoping they don't know we live here. We have to be quiet."

Hugging the little girl close, the old woman kissed her forehead and forced a smile. "Don't worry, little one. I won't let anything hurt you."

Smiling, the girl laid her head on the old woman's bosom and sucked her thumb contentedly.

"You have me here if you need me, Grandmother," Hung said.

She gazed at the boy and smiled gently. "I know, my little warrior, and I am glad you are here."

Counting the minutes as they passed, the old woman nearly went to sleep—until she saw one of Thinh's soldiers run into her yard. Even from that distance, with her bad eyesight, she could see the terror on the man's face. He ran wildly, ignoring the falling rain. Involuntarily she tightened her hold on the sleeping children.

The soldier vaulted a low fence and headed straight for her front door. He was being pursued by a man who was dressed in black and held a big silver pistol.

The soldier kicked in the door, shattering the old lock that held out the night. The noise woke the children and they started screaming. The old woman tried to quiet them so neither man would know they were inside, but it was no use.

The man in black leaped the fence and halted in front of the broken door only a few feet away. He was an American, the old woman saw, recognizing him for what he was despite the black tiger stripes he had painted on his face. The American raised the silver pistol.

The Vietnamese soldier raised his weapon to point at the old woman and the children. From behind the broken door the soldier shouted to his pursuer, "There is an old woman and children in here. If you do not leave I will kill them. Go away."

She saw the big American listen carefully as the soldier repeated his order. And she saw the foot-long tongue of flame leap from the barrel of the pistol before she heard the deafening reports. She knew she was dead then, and the children, too, because Thinh had encouraged his men to have no respect for lives other than their own. She was waiting for the bullets to rend and tear her flesh when she saw the soldier hurled away from the door.

Like the rag doll Vo often played with in the backyard, the soldier landed in an unmoving heap.

The American walked into the house, holding the silver pistol up and ready. He was a big man, filling the doorway, weapons slung about his body. Wordlessly he turned the soldier's body over to inspect the crimson-splashed chest. Assuring himself that his foe was really dead, the American stood again and holstered his weapon. His blue eyes held the fire of retribution, but there were other passions in there, as well. His voice was gentle when he spoke.

"Are you all right, little mother?" the big man asked in her language.

She nodded, afraid to trust her speech. Little Vo was still whimpering and holding on to her for dear life.

"I'm sorry this violence had to come into your home," the American whispered. "I wish there had been another way. So the children would not have had to witness this."

"They have seen worse," the old woman replied.

The American nodded and the old woman saw an old sadness flit across his face. "I'm sorry for that, too." Without another word, the man bent and picked the soldier up easily, carried him outside to the street and left him there.

Still watching, the old woman made herself get up to shut the door. She saw the American kneel down and go through the dead soldier's pockets, remove something. Then he turned and walked toward the house.

Gently he took one of her frail hands in his and handed her a pair of ornate mother-of-pearl combs. The old woman recognized them immediately as belonging to her neighbor's daughter. They had been a gift from her father only a year ago, and the girl had been very proud of them.

"Do you know who these belong to?" the American asked.

"Yes."

"I got there too late to help, but the men who hurt her are dead. Both of them. I can't replace the innocence she lost this night, but I know she probably placed much store by these. Please see that she gets them back."

"I will," the old woman promised.

"Thank you." He left her standing there and paused by the dead soldier long enough to take something from a pouch around his neck and drop it. The night accepted him back into its embrace and he was gone.

15

As the rising sun tried to fight its way through the morning cloud bank, Mack Bolan returned to the Our Lady of Peace Cathedral on Tu Do Street. Thinh's soldiers had started to look for him, dividing into patrols of four men each.

He trotted through the back alleys toward the cathedral, turning plans over in his mind. The situation was a bastard, he told himself as his eyes swept the narrow space between the walls. To manage an effective escape from the enemy force waiting for Lee Wingate, Bolan knew he'd have to risk the lives of Wingate and his men. And the boy. Otherwise everyone would be too spread out to help one another. If it weren't for the boy, he could have simply gone into the jungle until he found Wingate. But on the reverse side of that same coin, if it weren't for Lee Wingate's force, he could have concentrated on liberating the boy only. Some of them would die unless they were all very lucky.

How many men had he taken out? Twelve? Fourteen? Maybe a few more. He wasn't sure because he hadn't confirmed all the hits. There hadn't been time and in some of the situations he'd had to settle for only one or two men out of a small group. Still, the fear had been planted with each marksman's medal he left behind. He was sure the army captain was now feeling the pressure and reacting to it. And it might distract him from what was going down between Taggert and Lee Wingate.

The return fire from the soldiers had been sporadic at best, and Bolan knew they were under strict orders not to create a large disturbance. He figured the Vietnamese captain to be one savvy son of a bitch to exercise that kind of control over so large a group. Especially one that contained as many rogues as this one evidently did.

The memory of the raped mother and daughter still stung. Tracking down their attackers was a small luxury he had permitted himself. Part of him still loved this country, and always would. Good people were good people wherever they happened to be born. And in Mack Bolan's chosen line of work, it sometimes seemed there weren't enough good people to go around. Even then—like the women he'd arrived too late to help—many of them were damaged by the savages.

He kept the Galil under the poncho, cradling it in the crook of his left arm. The Beretta fit comfortably in his right hand, holding sudden death only a hiss away. The pistol worked better in twisting alleys. Easier and quicker to aim and—in 3-round burst mode—equally effective.

Choosing a building to the southeast of the cathedral, Bolan slung his weapons and jumped for the lower rung of the fire escape. The ladder pulled down and he went up slowly, senses alert to every noise coming from inside the apartments.

He reached the top and crouched below the edge of the building. Five stories down, the city was spread out before him. He could see the maze of small streets and alleys in the area, which were bare of pedestrians. He'd noticed earlier that the citizens had barricaded themselves inside their homes, guessing that it was Thinh's army that inspired such terror.

Bolan estimated the distance from his position to the steps of Our Lady of Peace to be almost four hundred yards. Uncovering the Galil, he adjusted the L-shaped "flipper" rear sight on the assault rifle to read 5, then swept the target area without letting the weapon show over the edge of the building. He wanted to get the feel of Taggert's chosen arena, find out any limitations he might have.

Satisfied, he retreated to a small greenhouse built atop the building, where most of the rain would be blocked off. The structure wasn't much, just a few two-by-fours and clear plastic, holding only a few tomato plants. He wouldn't be able to use it for cover once Thinh's troops discovered his sniping position after the shooting started. But that was okay. He hadn't planned on being a stationary target anyway.

He quickly fieldstripped the Galil and made sure all the working parts were free of any moisture that might hamper the action. He shifted the pouch containing the clips for the assault rifle to a forward position near his groin for easier access.

The warrior covered the Galil with the poncho, stood and made a circuit of the building. He'd chosen it earlier when he decided what strategy he was going to use. He knew he would be risking the lives of Lee Wingate and his men, but it was the only way to keep them from being pinned down by Thinh's troops and at the same time accomplish the mission's objectives.

Bolan was confident in his abilities. He'd proved them to others and himself time after time. Through the blitz, the Executioner had let Thinh and his force know who they were up against, letting their own fears find him in every shadow until they were no longer sure of an easy victory. He had posted warning with every body that the ante was going up on this operation.

The Saigon River was a long and muddy ribbon farther to the south. Other buildings, lower than the five-story structure he occupied, lined the south and east sides, only the width of an alley away.

Once he gave up the position on top of the building, Bolan knew he would be going into the battle blind. But he was

betting he could cause enough confusion before he had to
abandon it to keep an edge for himself.

Returning to the shelter offered by the greenhouse, Bolan reached into another pouch and arranged his grenades,
thinking of the jeep patrols he'd seen earlier. If possible, he
wanted to leave one intact to aid in his escape. But if he
couldn't have it, no one would.

He took out a granola bar from inside the blacksuit and
unwrapped it, savoring the almost bland taste. He hadn't
eaten in hours. As he crunched the bar Bolan saw a fruit
truck pull up to the steps of the cathedral and stop. Reaching for the small binoculars he carried at his web belt, he
uncapped them and focused on the truck.

Both men behind the mud-spattered windshield were
Americans. Looking down the street past the truck, Bolan
saw two jeeps roll to a stop a half block back. Two men sat
in each of the four-wheel-drive vehicles, shielded by the
canvas tops.

As he put the binoculars away Bolan wondered if Taggert was foolish enough to believe the swap was going to be
that easy. Or maybe the man was so interested in the payoff
that he was forgetting about the high stakes involved.

Dropping the poncho at his feet, Bolan took his position
at the edge of the building. He waited, wondering where he
would draw the line if things went sour and the good guys
started to die before everyone was in position.

Bolan closed his left eye and sighted in on the passenger
in the fruit truck.

PHAM COULDN'T HOLD BACK a smile when he saw Taggert
park the fruit truck in front of the cathedral. The night tiger,
he knew the city called him behind his back. One-eye. But
these names were given out of fear of him and the death he
could deal out. He knew the smile he wore would not fit
with this image. Still, it was forgivable, because this time the
prey was much larger than any he'd ever stalked before.

He stood at the window, wearing the headband he'd fashioned for himself, but now the Uzi hung around his neck by its strap.

"Solly," he breathed into the early-morning air. Carefully he touched the wound at his temple. He allowed himself his anger then, feeling it surge inside him, knowing it would be under his control when he confronted the American.

Pham was jerked from his reverie when the door opened behind him.

"We have trouble," Thinh announced.

"What?"

"The Americans arriving with the Star Wars plans met a small group of outlaws at the river. Luckily they escaped and only the outlaws died."

Pham watched as the captain walked to join him at the window to look at the cathedral, noticing how the man's eyes widened appreciatively at the sight of the truck.

"These 'outlaws' couldn't have been your men, could they?" Pham asked.

Thinh's face was carefully controlled when he turned to look at him. "No."

Pham ignored the lie, feeling the burning rage swell inside. He barely stopped himself from squeezing the trigger on the Uzi. "Good," he said in a neutral voice. "I'm glad that I was right about you not being so foolish as to risk everything in that manner. If those men hadn't been killed by the Americans, a stray bullet might have damaged the plans they carried."

"There is another American in the city, as well," Thinh said in a tight voice.

"There are many Americans here," Pham replied. "Many didn't go home after the war, by their own choice. People you have working for you in your black market."

"This one is different. He's moved quietly around the city for the past hour, killing my men."

Pham looked into Thinh's eyes. "This surprises you?"

Thinh glared back. "This American has been here before, a long time ago. I have no doubts that he's involved with Taggert and the approaching American force."

"How many men has this American killed?"

"Fifteen at last count.... I've given orders that my men are to be organized around the perimeter, with no one being alone. I was notified when Taggert began his return to the city."

Pham ignored the statement, knowing that only death would result if he challenged Thinh's intrusion into his watch over Solly Taggert. Right now he still needed the captain and his force.

"Why haven't your men killed this American?" Pham asked. "He's only one man, isn't he?"

"Yes. But not an ordinary man. My soldiers fear him even more than they fear me. It's only the fact that I will be here long after he's gone that keeps them under my control. Some of the young ones, though, wish to try their mettle against his."

Pham let a small smile trace his lips, thinking of Thinh's soldiers cowering from one man.

"I think you know this man, as well, Pham," Thinh continued. He held out a closed fist and slowly opened his fingers. There, lying in his palm, was the unforgettable sign of the American marksman.

A chill shuddered through Pham as he inspected the shiny medal, memories stirring around his mind. He made himself touch the medal, pluck it from Thinh's palm. It was hard, warmed by the captain's body heat.

"I know him," Pham admitted as he stared at the medal as if hypnotized. He forced himself to close his fingers over it, willed himself not to look at it again.

"It is the Executioner's sign," Thinh said. "Many of these trinkets were left with my dead soldiers. Why is he here now?"

Pham shook his head. "I don't know."

"The Americans must have sent him. It makes me wonder if the Star Wars plans are even anywhere near this city."

"If the Americans sent him, why would they send the other men, the ones who killed your 'outlaws'?"

Thinh said nothing.

"No, if he's here, he's operating independently. Or maybe he has returned for reasons of his own."

"He's still good at giving the quiet death," Thinh remarked as he walked to the door. "If you meet him tonight, it will be for the second time. Maybe you'll be able to recognize him. After all, he did leave you with one eye after he destroyed that ambush you set up during the war. Maybe he heard you were still alive and came back to finish the job. He may have escaped you all those years ago, but he will not escape me."

Pham didn't look at the captain as Thinh pulled the door shut behind him. He opened his white-knuckled fist and studied the marksman's medal. It lay there, a mute reminder of the man who had blinded him.

Angrily he turned to throw the medal out the window but found that he couldn't. If he possessed it, maybe it would bring him to its owner. Pham had felt their fates linked for a long time. He alone had survived the American's assault. He had once felt that he would be the one to destroy the Executioner and that was why the gods had let him live. But he'd never had the chance to cross weapons with the American again.

Now fate had intervened. He put the medal in his shirt pocket so he could feel it through the material. He looked out at the truck again, noting Taggert had gotten out from the passenger side and was walking to the rear of the vehicle.

Pham breathed a challenge, feeling the heat of the marksman's medal. "I am Death, Executioner, your death this morning. I will come for you from the shadows darker than the devil's heart, faster than the bullet that took my eye, creeping up to you on feet filled with tiger silence. I will be the last man you see.''

16

The whole city seemed eerie to Lee Wingate, like a scene out of a *Twilight Zone* episode. The streets were deserted, even though it was early morning. He felt there should have been more activity. They'd come into the city, encountered people on the wharf, and everything seemed normal until they reached Tu Do Street.

But maybe, he rationalized, the lack of activity was one of the main reasons Solly Taggert wanted the meet held here. At any rate, he didn't really have a choice.

Behind him, staggered in the alleys within hailing distance of one another, Phillips, Kelley and Briscoe awaited his orders. He waved for his second-in-command.

"I'm going in alone from here."

"If you say so, sir, but I'm not sure if that's a wise decision. Me and Briscoe feel that something's up."

Lee nodded. "I think so too, Sergeant, but we're not being given a hell of a lot of alternatives here. I'm going in."

Phillips gave him a tight-lipped nod. "As you will, sir." He released the hold on the rifle long enough to shake his commander's hand.

"Saying goodbye, Sergeant?" Lee asked softly.

"Just wishing you luck, Lee. We'll be here if you need us."

Lee nodded and turned to face the street, taking a deep breath to force the knot of anxiety from his stomach. He took the first step from the shadows, feeling exposed and vulnerable. Alone.

Shouldering the M-16 so the barrel pointed downward, Lee moved forward, keeping his eyes fixed on the battered fruit truck where the boy was supposed to be waiting. Your nephew, he corrected himself. Blood of your blood.

A man stepped away from the truck as Lee approached. He was big, broad shouldered and as battered looking as the vehicle. He gripped an M-16 in his right fist. Past his shoulder, Lee could see a black man sitting behind the wheel of the truck. The eyes of both men were wary and tired.

"Are you Taggert?" Lee asked as he came to a stop ten feet away. The area was open and desolate except for the truck. He glanced to his left and saw two jeeps idling in the distance.

The man nodded. "You got the package?"

"Yes." Lee tapped the rectangle over his chest.

"Let's see it."

Lee removed the package and held it out for inspection. Taggert took a step forward and the merc lifted his rifle, just short of actually pointing it at the man. Taggert froze.

"How do I know it's the real thing?" Taggert asked.

"How do I know you got the right boy?"

"He's still wearing his daddy's dog tags. How about your bonafides?"

Lee kept hold of the package. "It was your decision to make the deal. I figure if you thought Stuart Wingate would double-cross you, you'd never have tried to bargain with him."

"Let's see the package, tough guy."

"I want to see the boy first."

Taggert hesitated for a moment then walked to the back of the truck. The black man got out of the cab and followed. Lifting the tarp, Taggert moved to one side and tied it back.

A teenage boy lay inside, tied by ropes. His face was a map of black-and-blue bruises. Lee had to steel himself not to lash out in anger. "Must have been real excited about coming along, right?"

"Not our fault," Greenberg said. "Taggert killed the man who did this."

"I want the package now," Taggert growled.

Lee gave it to him. He wondered if the boy was conscious, but then saw the rise and fall of his chest. What could have forced his father to make a deal with animals like Taggert and his men? he ranted to himself as he studied the boy's abrasions. They didn't appear to be too severe—more colorful than anything.

Glancing at Taggert, Lee saw that the man was absorbed with the papers he'd pulled from the package, which contained a handful of computer disks, as well. Puzzled, Lee started to move closer, wanting to know what it was that he'd really delivered. A sick feeling in his stomach told him the price had been much higher than his father had told him.

Then the boy stirred, opening his eyes to look at Lee with unmasked hatred. For a moment the emotion surprised him so much that he didn't notice the color of the eyes. Blue. A blue that didn't seem to go with the skin color.

"What's his name?" Lee asked as he hurried forward to cut the boy's bonds.

"Sang," Taggert replied without looking up from the papers.

"I wouldn't cut those ropes if I was you," the black man said. "You might not be able to run him down again."

Kidnapped. The word tripped through Lee's mind. The boy's mother was dead, his father had told him. But the old man had also said the boy was ready to come home. Lee had forgotten that the boy already *had* a home—with his maternal grandparents.

Lee gently stroked the boy's hair, noting other similarities between him and Stu. The build, the intense look on his face despite the abrasions. Sang, he made himself remember. His name is Sang. He lifted the knife again to cut the ropes.

Something slammed into his left thigh and knocked him to the ground. Seconds later he heard the report of the gunshot. He tried to get back up, to free the boy so he wouldn't be hit by one of the flying bullets that filled the air, but his leg wouldn't hold him. Grimly he slipped his fingers over the edge of the truck bed and muscled his way to his feet, not knowing if he was going to be in time.

MACK BOLAN RODE the Galil hard, moving it repeatedly as he picked out new targets. He never saw which man fired the bullet that slammed Lee Wingate to the ground, but there were plenty of others for the Executioner to focus on.

At the truck, the black man and the guy he assumed was Solly Taggert had sprinted for the waiting jeeps, utilizing as much cover from the buildings around them as they could.

Two Viets ran for the fruit truck as Lee Wingate pulled himself up and inside. Bolan dropped both of them and they lay unmoving in the street. The Galil bucked repeatedly, thumping solidly into his shoulder as he squeezed the trigger. Spent casings tinkled tinnily against the building's edge.

Counting his shots, the warrior worked the rifle for all it was worth then switched the magazines quickly. There were fewer targets now as the soldiers kept undercover, and return fire was starting to chip away at the building, sending stone splinters flying toward his face.

A jeep manned by four soldiers careered around a corner just below him, heading for the fruit truck.

Where were Taggert and the Star Wars plans? He'd lost sight of the man during his assault on Thinh's forces. Bolan reached into his grenade bag, then pulled the pin on the baseball-shaped explosive. He counted off seconds before lobbing it into the street.

The grenade went off in midair only a few feet in front of the jeep. The explosion blew the soldier manning the big M-60 completely out of the vehicle and killed the driver instantly. Out of control, the jeep slammed into a nearby building. Several soldiers ran for new positions, fearing that the vehicle would explode, as well.

Standing above the edge of the building, Bolan lifted the Galil and poured a death stream into the fleeing men, working with the recoil to bring each new target into acquisition.

A bullet plucked at the web belt as another jeep-mounted machine gun wheeled into view. Bolan dropped, duck-walking to the opposite end of the building. He threw another grenade out into the street, knowing that the chances were slim that he'd hit anything, but also that he'd get a reaction nonetheless.

When the grenade detonated, Bolan abruptly stood again and raked the jeep with the Galil, sending 7.62 mm tumblers through both men. Slinging the assault rifle, he raced for the east edge of the building, hit the lip and hurled himself across the distance between buildings, windmilling his arms for more balance.

His feet thumped solidly on the rooftop, and he rolled to the edge of the building and spewed a full magazine across the fronts of the other buildings. Then he reloaded on the run, backtracking across the building to get a view of Lee Wingate's progress.

Silently he cursed Stuart Wingate for sending his son on a suicide mission. A head peered around a building near the cathedral. Ignoring the bullets that smashed into the building near him, Bolan sighted in on the head and squeezed the trigger, watching as it dissolved in a crimson spray. Shouted orders echoed below him and he risked a quick glance down, seeing a handful of soldiers rush through the front door of his building.

A man dressed in the same type of uniform as Lee Wingate sprinted across the open area in front of the cathedral, using the burned-out jeep as a partial cover. The merc was closing in on the abandoned fruit truck, but he was so intent on his goal that he didn't see the sniper on top of the cathedral.

Bolan raised the Galil to his shoulder and let his instincts guide him as he brought the sights to bear on the sniper. He released his breath slowly, squeezing the trigger with a velvet touch, spurring a second bullet on its way before the first had a chance to reach its intended target.

The sniper dropped his weapon and rolled lifelessly from the cathedral. The material of the uniform snagged on one of the Gothic spires, leaving the body suspended yards above the courtyard.

A scraping sound reached Bolan's ears, and he wheeled like a big cat, calm and dangerous.

Bullets ricocheted from the stonework around him. Only one of the three soldiers fully challenged the Executioner—the other two were only now bringing their weapons to bear.

Bolan fired from the hip. The initial burst ragged the front of the soldier's chest and blew him over the edge of the building. The second volley killed the remaining soldiers before they could get off a shot.

When Bolan looked back into the street, the merc had reached the fruit truck and had it moving. Bullets kicked into the tarp-covered sides. One of the rear tires had been punctured and the big vehicle listed to one side, but it was still mobile.

Slinging a leg over the edge of the building, Bolan lowered himself to a window and kicked the glass and frame out. Carefully he swung himself inside and dropped to the floor. He moved through the small apartment to the front door, the AutoMag probing the dark interior.

The warrior cracked open the door and looked into the hallway. Several of Thinh's soldiers were converging toward his position.

Shutting the door quietly, the warrior removed a grenade from the pouch as he backed away, pulled the pin and waited. As the door began to inch open, he rolled the grenade toward it and stepped around the corner into a small bedroom.

The thundering explosion almost deafened him despite his hands covering his ears. Before the smoke had a chance to settle, Bolan whipped around the corner on the attack. He bolted for the huge hole the grenade had blown in the wall, nearly stumbling over two men in the hallway. As they fired harmlessly into the wall behind him, Bolan took them out with two 240-grain mindbenders.

On the first floor Bolan avoided the main entrance, choosing to exit through an apartment instead.

He kicked the door open and raced past a young woman hiding behind her sofa, hoping she would remain there out of harm's way. Holding his arms in front of his face, the warrior launched himself through a window, landing on the ground amid a shower of broken glass. Blood trickled down his forehead and into his right eye. He staunched the flow with his forearm, letting the material of the blacksuit absorb the blood—soaking it up as it had so many times before.

Holstering Big Thunder, Bolan took the Galil in hand and charged down a small alley that would take him to the other side of the battlefield, wondering as he ran how many of Thinh's men were left.

When he reached the end of the alley Bolan spied two men wearing merc uniforms who were pinned down by enemy fire. A jeep was bearing down on their position, the big M-60 kicking a swath of death across the old automobile they had chosen for cover.

Knowing he was at the wrong angle for an effective hit, Bolan took one of his last grenades and yelled, catching the merc's attention. He tossed the grenade underhanded to the older man, who caught it deftly. "There's a good lad," the man said as he yanked the pin and lobbed the sphere toward the approaching jeep.

The grenade exploded inside the vehicle and turned it into a blazing inferno, forcing it off the road to land upside down. The younger merc with the bandage around his upper arm finished off the soldiers with a short burst.

The two men left their cover and joined the Executioner.

"You throwing this party, Yank?" the older man asked as he glanced around the corner.

Bolan gave him a wry grin. "Just helping out a little with the catering."

"Specialize in barbecues, do you?" The older man stuck out his hand. "Rick Phillips. This is Pete Kelley."

"Bolan."

"Pleased to meet you," Phillips said.

"You're with Lee Wingate?" Bolan asked.

"Yeah. At least we're supposed to be. I knew things didn't feel right, but I hardly expected anything of this sort."

"Where's Wingate now?"

"Don't really know. Briscoe ran to help get him out of the tight spot he was in, and I saw him get the truck to moving, but I don't know. About that time some of these bastards discovered me and Pete, and the bloody footrace was on. Thought we were goners for sure, I did, until you happened along."

"It's still not over."

Phillips grinned. "Ah, and you're a cheery soul, now ain't you?"

"That was some damn fine shooting," Kelley said. "Haven't seen too many men who could kick out that kind of fire rate with that much accuracy."

"Years of experience," Bolan replied as he craned his neck to glance around the killzone. The jeep still burned undisturbed and there were no soldiers in sight. "You ready to move?"

Phillips nodded.

Bolan took the point. But it was a busted play no matter how you looked at it. Lee Wingate's forces had been split in two. Wingate himself had been wounded, maybe seriously. Solly Taggert and the Star Wars plans had gone in another direction. What else could go wrong?

They followed the maze of alleys, spattering through the rainwater. Bolan expected to run into enemy troops at any moment, and held the Galil accordingly. He didn't expect what he found around the next corner: the fruit truck sat unmanned in the middle of the street.

The Executioner pulled up short, motioning Phillips and Kelley to do the same. Rain drizzled down his face as he surveyed the deserted street, wondering how far away Thinh and his troops could be. And where was Lee Wingate?

17

Matt Smiley sat in the cockpit of the cargo plane and almost managed to ignore the thumping that came from the payload area. He guessed it had started about five or ten minutes ago when the pilot of the plane regained consciousness.

It hadn't been hard to find the pilot or the plane Solly Taggert had arranged for the flight out of Tan Son Nhut. Smiley had built up a lot of confidants during his years in Vietnam, people behind the scenes, as well as the movers and shakers—people like the guy in the maintenance area who told him about Taggert's pilot.

It had been no challenge to walk up behind the unsuspecting man and send him off to dreamland with a hand as hard as knotted pine. Now, watching the rain fall outside the open hangar, he felt the boredom increase.

Smiley had always been a believer in *doing*, which was why he had joined up during the war and why he had stayed on after America pulled out. He knew he made a difference to the Meo tribesmen he had joined by marriage. Smiley and his boat worked the deltas and inlets in south Vietnam, hauling, transporting, whatever it took to get by. Occasionally he did things for the CIA people who were still in place around the country influencing policy-making whenever they could, quiet things that no one would ever link to Matt Smiley. In return the CIA paid him in gold. He took that gold and bought arms for the Vietnamese rebels still living in the highlands.

He loved the land, which tied him tightly to Vietnam's future, however rocky that ride might be. He recognized that love in his two sons, as well. They were eight and ten now, almost men by Meo standards. Smiley took great pride in them and in teaching them the skills he had taught himself in order to survive in the country. When he could he took them deep into the deltas for days and taught them to live off what nature provided, pointing out where nature had left a safe, dry spot.

There were fewer missions from the CIA, and it had been months since the last one. But Smiley didn't mind. Most of what the Company wanted done was dirty work. Smiley no longer did assassinations unless he was justified in his mind. Once he had been paid to kill a man he later found out was sympathetic to the MIA issue. If he had killed the man, CIA press peddlers were going to blame the Communist Vietnamese for the murder, saying they were trying to suppress evidence about the MIAs.

Smiley had turned the assignment down once he researched it for himself and confronted his control. The man had turned up dead a few weeks later anyway. The Communists were blamed for the murder but nothing really came of it. The Company had used Smiley less since then, but he'd partially made up for it by raising his rates. He would have liked to end the business relationship. Except the gold was good.

The hollow thumping from the cargo area began with renewed vigor.

Yeah, he supposed it was true: he and the CIA had become disenchanted with each other over the years. Which was one of the reasons he had staged the scene in the bar when he noticed the big guy walk in. That and the fact that he knew Thinh's troops would have noticed the guy anyway, and it would have boiled down to gunplay just the same. He'd been bored after spending hours to find out about Solly Taggert and the boy the man had kidnapped. And he'd been curious about the new CIA guy. He'd been the first agent to actively seek Smiley out. Most of them sat at the boat and waited for him to come rolling in.

When he had gleaned the information from Thinh's soldiers, Smiley knew this wasn't going to be a typical slit-your-throat-in-the-night mission.

What had surprised Smiley was that the guy had come in alone to pull the thing off. And Smiley got the impression that if the guy could have done it alone he would have. The way he'd come straight with him in the alley impressed Smiley, too. Usually the agents he dealt with never admitted to anything. Even when Smiley knew the guy had been responsible.

Smiley had wanted to stay and help, just for the opportunity to watch the big guy at work. The agent was all ice and reflex in the bar, and that was an improvisation. How would he perform against Thinh and his goon squad? One man against God knew how many soldiers.

Tired of sitting, Smiley finally left the cargo plane, stopping in the bay area long enough to slam his prisoner back into unconsciousness. The original pilot was a man Smiley knew from reputation. Real low-key scum. But he kept the plane up. Smiley knew because it was the first thing he'd checked after taking some banding from a trash can in the back of the hangar and tying the man up.

He came to a stop just inside the hangar doors and looked out over the small field. A handful of small winged craft dotted the tarmac, unmoving in the light rain. In the distance he could see a Vietnamese pilot in olive coveralls giving a helicopter a preflight check. The chopper was an old Huey, a relic from American involvement in the war, just as Smiley was. Still doing a job. It had been repainted in a dull mat finish, and Smiley guessed it was used a lot at night.

He looked at the sky over the city proper in time to see the first roiling cloud of black smoke curl upward.

Christ Almighty, Smiley thought as he pushed himself farther outside. He locked the hangar door behind him, using a lock he'd borrowed from his contact in the maintenance area. He had no doubts about who had caused the explosion that had rocked Ho Chi Minh City.

The guy had wanted a back door, Smiley remembered, but there was no guarantee he would ever make it that far.

"Hey, Matt," a voice called.

Turning to face the speaker, Smiley found one of the local mechanics holding out his hand. A marksman's medal lay in one greasy palm.

"You ever seen one of these before?" the mechanic asked. "Somebody brought in two or three just a few minutes ago. He said somebody's spent most of the night killing Thinh's—" The guy stopped suddenly, and Smiley knew he'd seen the black smoke over his shoulder.

Only this time when Smiley checked, there were two spirals. So, okay, the guy was serious about taking on Thinh's army and, yeah, he was seriously trained for it, but Matt Smiley didn't intend to be waiting to see how far the guy got.

As the mechanic ran back into the shop screaming out the news, Smiley reached for the automatic in his waistband and ran for the helicopter. The pilot heard him coming but it was too late. Smiley slammed into him, using his heavier weight and muscle to stun the guy against the metal skin of the helicopter.

Brushing the pilot aside, Smiley stepped into the cockpit and kicked the engine over, sliding an experienced hand into the yoke. The chopper moved at the direction of his wrist, cleaving the air with a thunderous roar. He rolled it toward the city as the pilot was just beginning to push himself up from the tarmac.

There couldn't be any doubt about the guy's identity, Smiley told himself as he kicked the chopper's turbine in the ass.

The Executioner.

Back here.

In Vietnam.

Fucking incredible.

LEE WINGATE COVERED the boy's body with his own. Loose crates of rotting fruits and vegetables slid freely on the worn wooden truck bed and he had to shove some away. Bullets ripped through the tarp, ricocheting from the metal struts that formed the covering's skeleton.

Sang fought beneath him, struggling to get free of the unwelcome weight and the partially severed rope strands.

Lee's body shook as the truck rumbled along at an increasingly fast pace. He felt the stickiness of his blood against the material of his pants. Christ, how bad was it? He hadn't had the time to examine the wound—he'd been too busy scrambling into the truck in an effort to free the boy.

"Take it easy," Lee whispered soothingly. He risked a glance back and saw a jeep burning in the center of the street. Who the hell had managed that? He knew Phillips and Kelley were in no position to grenade the vehicle. Briscoe had been too busy making it to the truck cab. For a moment he wondered if the CIA was still involved, wondered if he was going from the frying pan to the fire.

Rolling free of the boy, Lee discovered that he'd lost the knife somewhere under the sliding crates. He didn't have time to look for it now. He used the M-16 to lever himself to his feet, watching for any pursuit through the shredded tarp hanging down over the back of the truck.

The truck's transmission whined like an enraged banshee as Briscoe muscled it mercilessly.

Sang pulled the remaining rope from his arms and legs and started to stand up.

Lee motioned him down. "Do you speak English?" he asked.

The boy looked at him, the piercing blue of his eyes glaring from black-and-purple puffiness. "A little."

"Good because it's all I know."

The truck swerved abruptly around a corner and Lee felt the back end drift sickeningly. He grabbed one of the metal support struts overhead. "Stay low," he said. "There's less chance of getting hit by anything that way."

When Sang nodded, Lee turned his attention to his leg.

Luckily the bullet had gone through, and even though there was a lot of blood, it hadn't hit any major arteries. He tore sections from the bottom half of his shirt, making pads for the entry and exit wounds and three strips to bind them into place. He worked quickly, breathing in through his nose and out through his mouth in an effort to keep from passing out from the pain.

"You okay?" Lee asked as he tested the bandage.

"Yes."

"Did Taggert's men do that?" Lee indicated the facial bruises.

"One," Sang replied.

"What happened?"

Sang shrugged, and Lee was instantly reminded of Stu in the gesture, a younger Stu than the one who had died in Vietnam.

"Do you know who I am? Did Taggert tell you?"

"No."

"I'm your father's brother. My name is Lee. I've come to take you home with me." Lee wasn't ready for the look of pain and anguish that filled the boy's face.

"You sent Taggert for me?"

Lee nodded, not wanting to explain to the boy that he also had a grandfather he knew nothing of.

Standing with the assault rifle helping to support his weight, Lee wasn't ready when Sang suddenly leaped for him. The missing knife was in the boy's white-knuckled fist, and the bright blade slashed through the small distance separating them, seeking Lee's heart.

MACK BOLAN SPRINTED for the abandoned fruit truck, waiting for gunfire to erupt from the surrounding buildings. He was surprised when none came.

Where were they? he asked himself as he pressed up against the side of the truck and scanned the tops of the buildings around the street. The soldiers couldn't be that far away, and he was sure their departure hadn't gone unnoticed. He covered for Phillips as the sergeant barreled over to take up position on the other side of the truck. Kelley stayed in the alley.

Bolan reached up to move the tarp with the barrel of the Galil. Nothing moved inside. He stepped up on the rear bumper and examined the interior of the truck. Crates lay in broken heaps around the wooden flooring. A rotting odor assailed his sense of smell, forcing him to breathe shallowly to keep from gagging. Judging from the numerous white scars in the dark wood of the bed, the truck had been hit often and hard. Lee Wingate had been hit at least once, Bolan knew. Maybe more.

"Find anything?" Phillips asked as Bolan dropped to the muddy ground at the rear of the truck.

"Some blood. I saw Lee take a hit. He must've been bleeding pretty bad." Kneeling, the Executioner searched the ground for more blood, but the mud was too dark or Lee had had the time to fix some sort of pressure bandage for the wound. Bolan hoped it was the latter. The man wouldn't have been able to get far otherwise.

Advancing on the cab of the truck, the warrior looked inside. Only the torn and bare seats were there, covered with shiny glass from the shattered windshield. The keys were in the ignition and he tried them, thinking that the truck had quit and that was why Wingate and the others had left on foot. Bolan felt sure they'd left under their own power. Otherwise there would have been bodies around the truck. The merc commander wouldn't have gone willingly.

But why had Wingate elected to leave the truck? Bolan wondered as he tried to put himself in the man's shoes. With the leg wound as severe as it apparently was, Wingate would have wanted to put as much distance between himself and the advancing force as he could. There had to be some reason why they'd left the truck behind, but Bolan didn't have enough information now to guess at it.

"What now?" Phillips asked.

"We look," Bolan replied. "I've never left anybody behind before and I'm not going to start now." He gripped the Galil tightly and took advantage of the cover of the truck to check the streets again before going back to the alley.

The Executioner searched the options open to him, wondering if Wingate would have gone on down the street or ducked back in another alley in an effort to find the rest of his team. There was no way to know. It would be a seek-and-find operation. And you could damn well bet the numbers were running down fast as Thinh maneuvered his men back into position after the Executioner's initial introduction to hell.

He started to move out, ready to angle across the street toward what seemed to be the most logical avenue to pursue, when the heavy whup-whup of helicopter rotors cut through the air.

Fading back into the shelter of the alley, Bolan lifted the Galil skyward, bracing his arm against the building, waiting. His finger was poised on the trigger, ready to loose a burst as soon as the helicopter came into view.

The chopper drifted into the Executioner's line of fire like a cruising shark waiting for a kill. Breathing out slowly, the Executioner tightened his finger on the trigger.

SOLLY TAGGERT WATCHED his first jeep explode from a bazooka round as it drove into the waiting ambush. Two of his men had died instantly, consumed in a mass of flames. Thinh had stationed three jeeps at the site after they had rolled into town.

Taggert knew it had to be the Vietnamese captain because he was the only military official with this amount of pull in Ho Chi Minh City. He'd done business with Thinh before and knew the man had a cruel streak that ran core deep.

Evidently Pham had clued Thinh in on the swap for the Star Wars plans.

Taggert threw himself from his jeep when he saw the bazooka man raise his weapon again. Greenberg was right behind him. The swoosh of the bazooka missile wasn't loud, but the resulting detonation knocked him face first into the street.

He got up wiping the mud out of his eyes, running blindly across the street. He'd lost his M-16 somewhere along the way, but he didn't go back for it. Someone behind him was shouting orders in Vietnamese, and he heard one of the waiting jeeps mesh gears as it roared forward in pursuit.

Taggert ran for all he was worth, racing through a business area that eventually led to the jungle. For once he was glad of the creeping qualities of the foliage as it sought to devour the city. Now it wasn't threatening and imposing. It was his best friend.

His breath hammered to escape his lungs. He halted, debating on whether to wait for Greenberg to catch up. He knew his companion had escaped the explosion too, but where was he? Two would be better than one in the jungle against Thinh's forces. Especially if Greenberg had managed to hang on to his M-16.

How far was it to Tan Son Nhut Air Base on foot? Fifteen, twenty minutes? There was plenty of jungle between the city and the air base, plenty of places to hide along the way. Touching the package containing the Star Wars plans, Taggert felt immediately reassured. There would be money enough now. Once he was free of this goddamned country.

He edged farther down the street with his back to a building. Where the hell was Greenberg? Safety in numbers or no safety in numbers, he wasn't going to fuck around waiting for him much longer.

And where were Thinh's troops?

Maybe they thought he'd been blown up in the second jeep. Maybe they hadn't seen him get away.

Something thumped in front of him, causing him to dive back against the building. He looked, expecting a grenade, but found something totally unexpected.

Greenberg's head lay in the mud, his dulled eyes looking at Taggert with remembered pain. The neck was a mess of ragged slashes, mute testimony that it took a lot of effort to sever a spinal cord.

Taggert fought the sick feeling in his stomach as he tried to get a glimpse at who had thrown it. Pham stood above him on the roof of the single-story building across the narrow street. The golden sunrise was behind Pham, outlining him and turning all details to black shadows. Taggert recognized the machete in the Vietnamese's hand as the one Greenberg had carried.

Taggert whirled to run back the way he'd come as Pham leaped lithely to the ground in front of him, blocking access to the jungle.

Soldiers filled the street entrance ahead of Taggert, presenting him with a wall of automatic rifles.

Taggert went numb inside as he came to a halt yards away from the soldiers, realizing he was trapped between the buildings on either side. He turned to face Pham.

So close, Taggert told himself as he looked at the green jungle behind his nemesis. So goddamned close.

Pham dropped the machete and walked forward confidently, kicking Greenberg's head to one side as he passed.

"Beg, Solly," the Vietnamese said in a hoarse whisper. "Beg and maybe I'll let you live a little longer."

Taggert looked into the single black eye, his automatic a heavy drag at his waist. He was a dead man and he didn't try to fool himself about it. Even if Pham didn't kill him, Thinh's men would. He had to gamble that they wouldn't fire on him for fear of hitting the Star Wars plans and destroying them. It was slim, but it was a chance. He felt a little hope blossom inside him.

Pham kept advancing. "Give me the plans, Solly." He took a knife from a concealed sheath inside his clothing. The blade was long and thin, a stiletto that Pham held like a talon before him.

"You're going to have to get a lot closer than that to use your pigsticker," Taggert taunted. His fingers itched for the butt of his pistol. Not yet, he cautioned himself. "Are you sure you're man enough for the job?"

Pham gave him a thin-lipped smile that was devoid of humor. "You couldn't kill me from hiding, Solly. What makes you think you can when we're face-to-face?"

Taggert watched the stiletto dancing in the Vietnamese's talented fingers. Pham was within fifteen feet, and Taggert knew he couldn't miss.

"Give me the package, Solly," Pham ordered. "I saw you get the plans."

"Fuck you, asshole." Taggert's hand swept down for the pistol, feeling the sudden adrenal charge hit him as his fingers curled around the butt of the weapon. Pham's arm swiveled back to deliver the knife in an underhand throw. The 9 mm felt heavy and sluggish as it came up. Taggert wanted to duck, to move away, but he was committed to drawing the automatic. It came up slow and awkward, and as he lined up Pham's chest, the Vietnamese's right arm became a blur.

Taggert started to squeeze the trigger, waited for the recoil of the weapon to slam into his palm, expecting Pham to be knocked down instantly.

Instead strength left his arm as a burning sensation filled his throat. He tasted blood, tried to cry out but couldn't. He reached up and touched the handle of the stiletto buried under his Adam's apple.

He tried to squeeze the trigger but his hand lacked the strength. Then his fingers opened and the gun fell to the ground. He felt himself pitch forward and was dead before he hit the ground.

18

The American moved faster in his wounded condition than Sang had thought possible. The man's hand closed around Sang's wrist and prevented the knife from striking. Letting his anger fuel him, Sang tried to force the blade into the American who claimed he was his father's brother. Lies, an angry voice shouted inside him. It was all lies.

The man ordered him to stop, demanding an explanation for Sang's actions. The boy ignored him as hot tears ran down his face. He had to kill the man. For his family, the family that had never brought him any pain like he had experienced tonight.

"Killer," Sang screamed as he levered his body weight behind the knife and pressed the American to the floor. Then in English, "You are all killers. I hate you all."

Abruptly Lee shifted beneath him, throwing Sang off balance and taking the knife away. The boy rolled toward the edge of the truck bed, fear filling him as the American found the strength to stand and pursue him. He had no weapons left.

Sang looked over his shoulder, through the ripped tarp. The city waited. He had no friends there, but they were his people. Not like this American who claimed blood ties with him.

Feinting with his hands, Sang kicked out, shooting his left foot into the American's wounded leg, then turned and jumped from the truck as the big man went down.

He fell when he landed, sliding out of control for a moment in the wet mud. He pushed himself up and fled, choosing the first side street he came to. He wasn't sure if the American would come after him, but he didn't waste time glancing back to find out.

Pushing his body hard, Sang tried to keep his steps strong and sure as he ran. He didn't know where to go.

Without warning, arms reached from behind him and pulled him down. His head hit the ground hard and he felt his body go limp. Consciousness retreated, shying away thread by thread. But not before he recognized the uniform of the man who had captured him. A soldier.

One of his people. He was safe.

BOLAN RELEASED the Galil's trigger when he recognized the pilot of the helicopter as Matt Smiley.

Smiley set the chopper down in the middle of the street.

"We got reinforcements, mate?" Phillips asked at Bolan's side.

Bolan nodded. "Unplanned," he answered truthfully as he surveyed the still-vacant street and wondered where Lee Wingate had gone with the boy. "But that's what it looks like."

"What the hell. They may be unplanned but they're bloody well not unwelcome."

"Hey, Sarge," Smiley yelled from the cockpit. "You got a hell of a lot of soldiers headed this way."

"How many is a lot?"

Smiley grinned. "I was too busy to take my shoes off and count when I flew over. At the time they thought I was a friendly. It ain't going to take them long to figure out different."

Bolan led the way to the helicopter. "Where did you get this?" he yelled over the throb of the rotors.

"Borrowed it," Smiley replied. "Just like I borrowed the cargo plane we'll be leaving in. Saw your smoke and figured maybe things had gotten a little heavier than you'd planned on."

"Not any heavier," Bolan said. "Definitely a little more spread out, though."

"Hey, is that an M-60 you got back there?" Kelley asked as he climbed into the chopper.

"Beats the hell out of me, kid," Smiley answered. "I wasn't kicking tires or looking for engine leaks when I picked up this number. It just happened to be available. You see something you like, knock yourself out."

Bolan watched Kelley move into the back and start checking over the machine gun, attaching it with practiced ease to the door mount as he took his place in the seat. The big gun clicked into place, pointing down at a forty-five-degree angle.

Smiley jerked a thumb over his shoulder toward Kelley. "One satisfied customer already and it's my first day of business. Hell, I may keep this if I can figure out a way to carry it on my boat." He revved up the RPM on the rotor. "Coming on board?"

Bolan shook his head. "Got a few things to tie up first."

The look on Smiley's face was serious. "You don't have a hell of a lot of time, guy. The numbers we were talking about earlier seem kind of low. Looks like Thinh pulled out all the stops for this one."

"Yeah," Bolan said. "Well, I don't plan on leaving any unpulled on our side, either."

"Somehow I knew you were going to say that. I heard a lot of stories about you when you were over here during the war. I guess I made a mistake when I thought a lot of it was made-up." He reached down to shake Bolan's hand, then looked back at Kelley. "You any good with that thing, kid?"

Kelley grinned. "You got time for a reference check?"

"Terrific. Well, you better pucker your ass up next to that seat because the things I'm going to put this bird through shouldn't be done to any self-respecting machine."

"I'll let you know if I get scared."

"You do that." Smiley turned back to Bolan. "I'll try to keep a few of these soldiers off your back, but I can't promise anything. I'm talking about a hell of a lot of troops."

Bolan nodded. "Couldn't ask for anything more. I've got a smoke grenade in my pouch. If I find my missing people I'll set it off."

"I'll be there." Smiley looked at Phillips. "I'll need somebody to ride shotgun if we're going to hang around here for a few of the fireworks. And the kid's going to need somebody to feed him ammo if he's as good as he thinks he is."

Phillips looked as if he wanted to object, but Bolan interceded. "Somebody's got to go with them. I'll find Wingate and your other man, but I've got other things going on here, too. I can't leave until I know they're taken care of."

"Be careful then, mate." Phillips took the copilot's seat and freed his weapons for instant access.

"I'll be seeing you," Smiley yelled to Bolan, "in just a little while."

Bolan nodded.

Smiley increased the throb of the rotors until the skid Bolan was standing on felt light beneath his foot. The warrior moved away as the helicopter prepared to take to the air.

"Here we go, Deadeye," Smiley bellowed back to Kelley.

The helicopter sprang into the air, drowning out all sounds of the soldiers Bolan saw pouring from the end of the street. He started moving, chunks of mud spitting up at his feet noiselessly.

Abruptly sound returned as the helicopter drifted away. He could hear the chatter of the big M-60 as Kelley cut a swath through the first line.

Bolan's adrenaline flow was easing, and he felt his legs grow leaden as he ran through the alley. He was beginning to feel like a rat trapped in a Skinner box, moving endlessly. Only his intended goal was in the box and moving, too. He just couldn't learn the right moves to get the reward.

The only right moves involved here were the ones that kept a man alive and striking.

Scanning the alley leading out onto the next street, Bolan saw a reddish smear along one white-painted wall. He stopped beside it, touched it and found it was still fresh. Lee Wingate? It was possible. But Ho Chi Minh City was filled with possibilities right now.

Peering around the corner, Bolan checked the street for hostile activity. Nothing. As he stepped onto the sidewalk in front of an apartment building, a window overhead shattered and the sound of an automatic weapon knifed into the Executioner's hearing.

A body, dressed in the uniform of Lee Wingate's men, came flying out seconds later, driven by a hail of bullets.

RAPPING ON THE BACK of the truck cab, Lee Wingate got Briscoe's attention. "Stop the truck, Jack," he yelled through the black pain that threatened to engulf him.

The ten-wheeler rocked to a halt as Lee watched Sang disappear down a side street through tear-blurred vision. He could tell by the warm trickle running down his leg that the boy's blow had reopened the wound. Hobbling as fast as he could, he used the M-16 as a crutch and leaned against the support struts.

Briscoe met him at the rear of the truck with a concerned look on his face. "You look like you're in pretty bad shape."

Lee slid to a sitting position on the edge of the truck, then dropped to the ground, gritting his teeth against the impact. Sang was out of sight.

"The boy's gone," Lee grated as he lurched toward the side street the young Amerasian had disappeared into.

"What happened?"

"I don't know. He came at me with my own knife. Damn near nailed me with it, too." The words seemed alien to Lee as he said them, as if they were spoken by someone else. None of it made sense. The boy should have gone with them willingly, and he shouldn't have to worry about what his father had really given Solly Taggert. But Sang had definitely been unwilling—almost to the point of homicide.

Briscoe didn't say anything as he fell in behind Lee. He walked with his weapon up and ready, as quiet as a shadow. Lee felt more secure with the man at his back.

"You got any idea where Phillips and Kelley are?" Lee asked as he limped along.

"Last I seen of them, they were pinned down. I was planning on doubling back for them once I had you stashed and saw how bad you were hurt. I figure they can shake loose on their own."

Lee bit back a yelp of pain as his foot slipped in the mud and he had to throw unexpected weight on the injured leg. "Did you see the boy?"

"No."

"His face was black and blue, Jack. Somebody had beaten the hell out of him. And when Taggert turned him over to me, he was tied up."

"Sounds like he had a lot of say in wanting to come to the States."

Lee paused at the corner of the side street, halting long enough to sweep the area for enemy troops. "He also called us killers—right before he went for me with the knife and after I told him I was responsible for Taggert bringing him here. I didn't want to try to explain about my father."

"You can bet his people weren't too happy about his being kidnapped," Briscoe said. "It wouldn't surprise me if Taggert did kill somebody to deliver him. In fact, several somebodies probably wouldn't be too far off base."

"Yeah. I don't know what I would do if I had the choice. Maybe I'd go after him anyway to fulfill my obligations to my father or maybe I'd let him go. But right now, in the middle of this hellzone, I can't let him go it alone."

"I know," Briscoe said softly.

Lee's leg trembled as he walked, but he forced himself to
go on, thinking of the boy abandoned in the cold heart of
the city. Sang was a pawn to everyone concerned. Even me,
Lee told himself, knowing he had banked on his ability to
recover the boy to earn his father's love. Now none of that
mattered, not even the fact that Sang was Stu's son and his
own nephew. He only wanted to save the boy because Sang
would be used by whoever found him.

Pausing at the corner of the next street, Lee leaned against
the wall to scope out anyone who might be lying in ambush. Sang was gone and the street was empty.

The short hairs on Lee's neck bristled. Office buildings
towered on both sides of the street, rising six and seven
stories above him. The building he leaned against was a hotel with a bar occupying the bottom floor. Lee could see an
old Budweiser sign sitting in one small window halfway
down the length of the building.

Estimating the accessibility of the other buildings, Lee
decided Sang had gone inside the bar.

Lee signed for Briscoe to cover him and stepped around
the corner, his M-16 pointed at waist level. The door opened
to Lee's touch.

Carefully he nudged it aside and slid through the opening. It took a moment for his eyes to adjust to the darkness
of the room. Directly in front of him was a small registra-
tion desk where guests checked in. To the left, down three
sunken steps, were empty tables and chairs that had seen
better days. A wet bar extended the entire length of one wall,
mirrors gleaming darkly behind it as rows of liquor bottles
cast double shadows. A stairway was located through a
small foyer and was nearly hidden by a jungle of drooping
plastic plants.

Briscoe was on his heels.

The stairs led up into darkness, and the silence in the place
seemed to crouch like a live thing poised to strike.

"Come up, Americans," a voice called in English from somewhere above. "We have much to talk about. Like whether or not this whelp will live past this morning."

Lee remained silent, his eyes tracking the shadows for enemy troops. The bar was empty.

The voice was harsher when the man called again. "I do not have all day. Shall I send you a finger or an ear to prove to you I'm serious?"

"Okay," Lee called back. "I'm coming up." He turned to Briscoe. "Clear out, Jack. See if you can find the others and get the hell out of here. This is going nowhere."

Briscoe's face was impassive when he answered. "I can't, Lee. I wish I could, but I can't leave. There was a kid once, the last time I was over here. I could have helped him but I didn't. I'm going to play this one through."

Lee nodded, realizing Briscoe had his own dark ghosts to deal with. He lifted his injured leg and took the first step up the stairs, using the M-16 and the banister to carry most of his weight. He wondered if his father had ever thought it would come to this. Or had he thought the price he'd paid would be enough to guarantee safe passage for them all?

PHAM PUT HIS FOOT on the temple of Taggert's corpse and pulled his knife free. Blood had spewed down the taped handle and he knew he would replace it as soon as he could. But until then he refused to rid himself of any of his weapons. Over the years they'd become extensions of his body. Being without one was unthinkable.

Kneeling beside the body, Pham unbuttoned the shirt and freed the package inside, opening it for a brief inspection. He sensed that he had his hands on the genuine article. He tucked it inside his shirt and walked over to where he'd left the machete taken from the black American.

Pham stood beside the body and spit into the man's face, remembering how he'd awakened in the funeral parlor. He'd been almost dead then, but now he was a rich man. Wealthy beyond his dreams.

A soldier separated himself from the others who were watching from the mouth of the street, calling out his name and interrupting his first swing with the machete.

Pham looked up, letting his annoyance show. He left the machete buried in the corpse's neck. "What is it?"

"Captain Thinh wants you. He has the boy and feels certain the Americans will trail him quickly." The soldier gave the location.

Pham nodded, pleased that the hotel was within easy walking distance. Then he turned back to his grisly task.

"Captain Thinh is sure the Executioner will be there, as well."

Pham nodded again as he picked up Taggert's head by the hair, then Greenberg's. He walked to the end of the street and held the heads out to the soldier. "Hold these for me until I return. And take care of the trophies. I will have the Executioner's head with me when I come back for them."

The soldiers parted before him as he swung the Uzi from under his shoulder and headed for the address Thinh had given his messenger.

Pham could feel the death lust singing inside him as it never had before. He touched the marksman's medal in his pocket. The gods were on his side in this confrontation. He could sense it.

Overhead he heard the thrum of a helicopter's rotors as it neared, heard it lower until he was sure it had landed somewhere close by. Obviously Thinh was bringing more troops into the area. Every nerve was alive as he moved in on the hotel.

SANG STOOD RIGIDLY at attention as the soldier's knife pressed into his throat. Already he could feel a small trickle of blood slipping down his neck.

There were four other soldiers in the captain's group. All of them stood behind the man holding him. The hallway on the second floor of the hotel wasn't large, but it was easy for three men to stand abreast with their weapons up and ready.

From somewhere behind Sang the captain had bellowed orders to the Americans below, and his words had made the young Vietnamese cringe. To lose a finger or an ear, which would be worse? For surely the Americans would not foolishly walk into the captain's waiting guns. And Sang felt sure the captain was not bluffing.

They wouldn't come. Sang was positive. He waited, knowing the knife would draw new blood.

But footsteps sounded on the wooden steps. Sang could hear the limping efforts made by the wounded American.

"We're coming."

Sang recognized the American's voice. Why was he doing this?

Light streamed through a large window in the wall behind the landing, reflecting dully off the metal room numbers and doorknobs. Not the true brightness of day, but it served to mask the faces of the Americans as they came to a stop on the landing in front of Thinh's men.

The American with the beard had his rifle leveled. The wounded one leaned on his, and Sang could feel the man's eyes bore through him.

"Throw down your weapons," Thinh ordered.

The bearded man looked at his companion as if uncertain of what to do. For a moment Sang wondered if he would die by the knife or the bullets that would surely be flying through the hallway.

"Do it now," the captain commanded, "Or the boy dies."

Sang tensed, wanting to make the most of whatever opportunity presented itself.

Then the bearded American tossed his weapon to the floor. In Vietnamese, he said, "You got it. Just let the boy go."

The wounded American's rifle joined his friend's, and Sang watched as two of the captain's men rushed forward to gather them up. As the soldiers moved back, Sang heard the captain give the command to open fire.

19

As the body fell through the window above, Mack Bolan pressed himself back into the wall with the Galil thrusting upward. The man lay only an arm's length away, facedown in the mud. Blood soaked the back of the shirt.

It was hard for Bolan to resist the impulse to reach out to the fallen man, but he knew it would be pointless for both of them to die in the street. When no one appeared in the shattered window, he moved to the body, checking for a pulse. There was none.

Dark anger stirred in the Executioner. The deaths of comrades in arms was a fact of his life. But these warriors hadn't even been given a chance to succeed. Stuart Wingate's finger might just as well have been on the trigger as the Vietnamese soldiers.

Bolan turned the body over gently, recognizing the man as the one who'd driven the fruit truck from the cathedral. He also saw the man had been unarmed. Bolan closed the dead eyes. He looked back up at the shattered window. Lee Wingate and the boy had to be inside the hotel.

Slinging the Galil over his shoulder, Bolan took a collapsible grapnel from a pocket in the blacksuit and whirled it overhead.

The grappling hook caught on the first try, three stories up. Bolan tested the nylon cord and started scaling the wall. There weren't a lot of options once he was on the wall, but he was betting a lot of local forces were inside the building to secure the captive. More would probably be en route to cover their retreat.

Once he drew level with the broken window Bolan peered inside. Lee Wingate stood in the hallway, pressed against one of the dark walls, a Vietnamese captain holding a pistol under his nose. From the way Wingate's wounded leg was shaking, Bolan knew the merc commander had pushed himself as far as he could go.

A soldier farther down the hall held a teenage boy by the hair, a combat knife held laxly against the boy's throat. Four other soldiers were crowded behind him.

Six targets, Bolan thought as he measured the nylon cord in his hands, two of them of immediate concern. He snagged Big Thunder, taking the weight of his body on one hand and his legs. Six targets and seven shots in the AutoMag. Sure, the Beretta held more, but the Executioner was banking on the psychological terror of the booming .44, as well as the man-stopping power of the 240-grain flesh shredders. In the small hallway the Magnum was going to sound like a cannon.

After prepping the .44 for action, Bolan holstered it long enough to reach for the smoke grenade in the pouch at his belt. Holding the nylon cord tautly, Bolan lobbed the grenade to the top of the building, listening for the small pop it made as it released its contents. Thick yellow smoke filled the air above the hotel, threading between the other tall buildings of the business district.

"Where are the plans?" the captain shouted.

"I don't know what the hell you're talking about," Bolan heard the merc colonel reply.

"You lie. It was agreed that you were to trade them for the boy. Where are they?"

"I gave the package to Taggert. Ask him. Sang, look, I'm sorry. I didn't know about any of this."

Bolan heard the sound of flesh striking flesh.

"You're a brave son of a bitch," Wingate taunted. "Threatening kids, shooting unarmed men. What do you do for an encore?"

Bolan didn't wait for a reply.

Kicking away from the building as hard as he could, Mack Bolan swung out at an angle that carried him away from the hotel and straight back at the window. Big Thunder filled his right hand, held across his chest for instant target acquisition.

Out of the corner of his eye, just before he went plunging through the ruined window, Bolan saw approaching troops pointing to the smoke rising from the top of the building.

Then he was inside.

The warrior's first round caught Thinh as the man wheeled to face the unexpected assault, punching him backward. The Executioner slid across the hallway carpet on his knees, levering his right arm out before him as he switched the heavy AutoMag to his second target. The 240-grain hollowpoint impacted in the middle of the guard's face, blowing him away from the boy.

Lee Wingate launched himself from the wall as the remaining troops started to return fire. The merc pushed the boy to the floor, covering his body protectively with his own.

Pushing himself to his feet, Bolan kept the .44 hammering, pumping death into the four men at the end of the hallway, ignoring the crackling automatic fire as it chipped the walls and shredded the carpet in front of him.

Ears ringing in the deafness imposed by the AutoMag, Bolan ejected the spent clip and slammed another home. He walked through his declared hellground and made sure his enemies were dead.

Turning to check on Lee Wingate and the boy, he saw the merc's lips moving, but couldn't hear a word. When the man repeated his question, visibly shouting this time, it sounded like a whisper.

"What about Jack?"

Bolan shook his head.

Wingate closed his eyes and leaned back against the wall, holding the boy tightly in his arms. "Goddammit."

The leg wound had been bleeding profusely, and Bolan wondered how Wingate had managed to stay conscious.

"We've got to go," Bolan said as he holstered his weapon. "Just before I broke in here I noticed troop activity outside."

"Where the hell are we going to go?" Wingate asked as he accepted the Executioner's hand.

"Up," Bolan replied. "Transport should be on its way." He pulled the Galil into position and went back to the first-floor landing. "Take the stairs. I'll follow in a moment."

Wingate nodded as he stood dizzily against the wall. He hooked one of the soldier's fallen rifles by the sling and checked the magazine. "The kid may not want to go with us," Wingate said. "He's already run from me once. It seems my father wasn't as truthful with me as he should have been." There was a grim set to the man's face.

Turning to look at the boy, Bolan asked his name in Vietnamese.

"Sang," the boy replied. His voice was steady and his blue eyes burned.

"Why did you run?"

"Because these men had my grandparents killed when they took me from my village."

"Not these men, Sang. They were told they were coming here to rescue you."

"I didn't need to be rescued."

"They didn't know it," Bolan said. "One of them has died trying to save you. These are good men. The man beside you is your uncle."

"He told me that."

"He's risked his life for yours many times."

The boy nodded. "I've seen that."

"There'll be no safe place for you in Ho Chi Minh City right now," Bolan told him. Down below he could hear the front door banging open. Smiley wouldn't be able to hold the helicopter on top of the building forever. "I don't think he'll be able to make it up the stairs without help. He's already pushed himself further than any man should be asked to. I'm needed here."

"I'll help him." Sang took Wingate's left arm and draped it across his shoulders.

Lee looked at Bolan with surprise. "I don't know how you managed it, McKay, but thanks."

Bolan nodded. "Move out."

Wingate hobbled down to the next landing with the boy's help.

The Executioner waited until four or five soldiers gathered in front of the entrance before wheeling around the corner with the Galil and emptying the clip. Return fire chipped plaster, raked the plastic plants.

Bolan recharged the Galil as he raced after Wingate, hearing the powerful rotor throb of the waiting helicopter.

Phillips and Kelley had left the chopper to help Sang lift Wingate on board. Smiley grinned when he saw Bolan, giving him a thumbs-up.

"Hustle up, Sarge, things in the airfare service are starting to get tight," Smiley bellowed from the pilot's seat.

"We're going to take our dead with us," Bolan said as he came to a stop on one of the chopper's landing skids. He tossed the Galil to Phillips.

"Jack?" the sergeant asked as he tore the old bandage off of his commander's leg. Lee had passed out before they'd gotten him on the helicopter.

"Yeah," Bolan said. He looked back at Smiley. "You game?"

Smiley nodded.

The chopper lifted suddenly, canting toward the side of the hotel Bolan indicated. He motioned Kelley into position on the door gun.

The whirling blades called out Thinh's troops. Between the M-60 and Bolan's AutoMag, they were kept at bay as the chopper landed at the opposite end of the street.

Racing the short distance, Bolan kept Big Thunder in his fist. The big M-60 was a spitting dragon in Kelley's talented hands, chipping brick splinters from the buildings on both sides of the street.

Bolan sensed rather than saw someone above him. He twisted to face his attacker, releasing his hold on Jack Briscoe. But it was too late to completely avoid the attack.

The Executioner went down, the AutoMag skittering away when he hit the ground. Hot pain darted across his shoulders as he rolled away from the attacker. Before he could gain his feet, the man was on him, landing a kick that exploded on Bolan's temple.

His vision swam as he forced himself to his feet, agony lancing through his head just behind his eyes. Instinct and experience guided him in blocking the knife slashing toward his throat. Mere inches separated Bolan from the unknown, one-eyed Vietnamese dressed in black.

The smaller man had a knife in each hand, stilettos that danced in his fingers as he twirled them and caught the light. "So, Executioner, we meet at last. For the second time."

Bolan didn't say anything, aware that time was running out for all of them. Under Kelley's watchful eye no other soldiers were able to come into the street. But it wouldn't be long, Bolan realized, before some of them circled the hotel and came at the helicopter from a different direction.

"You don't recognize me, do you, Executioner?" the one-eyed killer taunted. "I'm Pham, the man who's going to kill you."

Without warning Pham slashed a knife forward in a low blow that threatened Bolan's groin area. As the Executioner twisted out of harm's way, the other knife darted in and slashed his cheek lightly. Only Bolan's speed prevented the man from driving the blade deep in his throat.

The warrior could feel the blood dripping down his face. He kept his eyes away from the twirling stilettos, focusing on the man's evil smile. Feinting with his hands, Bolan launched a kick that connected with Pham's lower ribs. The man grunted with the impact, but Bolan knew he'd been able to avoid most of the blow's force. The knives licked out in search of his body as Pham was transformed into a flail of glittering blades.

"You took my eye years ago, Executioner," Pham shouted. "Today I will take your life. Just as I take the lives of all my enemies. Your head will join Taggert's, a tribute to my abilities. People everywhere will fear me."

New life flowed into Bolan as he faced his opponent. "You have the Star Wars plans," the Executioner said as he stared into Pham's eye.

The killer smiled at him mockingly. "Yes, American, and you will die trying to possess them as Solly Taggert died trying to keep them."

Bolan shook his head. "You missed your chance to kill me when you dived from that window. Now you won't be able to escape me." The Executioner's icy voice was taunting as he spoke.

With a cry of rage Pham rushed forward in a flurry of knife strikes and kicks.

Bolan backed away from the sheer ferocity of the attack, waiting for an opening in the glittering fabric of double-edged steel Pham wove before him. The Vietnamese was good and he was fresh. Bolan's own energy was nearly spent. Time after time he narrowly evaded the slashing blades as they shredded the blacksuit and scored numerous small cuts over his arms and chest. The stilettos seemed to be everywhere at once.

When Pham left the ground in a flashing snap-kick, the Executioner grabbed the striking foot in both hands, yanked and twisted hard. The man had no choice but to release one of the knives in order to keep from smashing face first into the ground.

Dodging back from the remaining stiletto that licked hungrily at his legs, Bolan slipped in the loose mud. Pham was on top of him immediately, blade searching for throat as the man's knees tried to smash into his groin.

They rolled in the mud, locked tightly in a death embrace Bolan knew only one of them would walk away from. The smaller man's strength was fired by maniacal intensity, almost more than the Executioner could control.

Levering an arm under Pham's chin, the warrior tried to force the man's head back, rolling his arm so he could force the killer's face into the mud. But Pham slid beneath him, twisting so he was once more on top and in control.

Bolan landed a solid right jab to the man's face but it didn't seem to have any effect. The mud on Pham's arm caused the warrior to lose his hold, and he watched the killer draw his hand back for a death blow.

"Now, Executioner," Pham said, "now you die."

His arm swept down, the point of the stiletto seeming diamond-bright to Bolan as it zeroed home.

Mustering a surge of strength, Bolan blocked the blow with his forearm, smashing into Pham's inner elbow. The blade missed the Executioner's face by less than an inch. With his right hand clasping the bottom of Pham's, he added to the force of the killer's strike, accelerating the stiletto upward.

Bolan watched with grim satisfaction as the blade drove deeply into the eye patch.

Pham's mouth gaped soundlessly as blood covered the left side of his face. He released his hold on Bolan and tumbled forward.

Pushing the body aside, Bolan forced himself to his feet, conscious for the first time of the numerous cuts Pham had inflicted. He drew in a deep breath and picked the AutoMag out of the mud.

Unsteadily he searched Pham's corpse until he found the package he'd seen Lee Wingate give to Taggert. It was stained with blood, and Bolan wondered sadly how many lives had contributed to the ante as he noticed his own bloody fingerprints mingling with the blood of others.

Then Phillips was in front of him, helping him as he lifted Lee Wingate's dead companion from the mud.

"Here you go, mate, I've got him now."

Bolan nodded and looked over his shoulder. He breathed heavily through his mouth, trying to recharge his oxygen-starved lungs. The AutoMag seemed like an anvil at the end of his arm.

Kelley sent another stream of rounds thudding into the hotel as troops considered rushing the retreating American forces.

Senses swimming from the effort, the Executioner followed Phillips to the waiting helicopter.

EPILOGUE

Mack Bolan let himself into the hospital room and found Lee Wingate in bed, looking out the window. The man looked white even against the stark bed sheets. He'd barely survived the flight from Vietnam to the military base in the Philippines, and it had taken the doctors hours to bring him to a stable condition. An IV bag hung upside down to the right of the bed, dripping slowly into Wingate's right arm.

"Are you leaving?" the merc colonel asked in a weak voice.

"Yeah, I got a flight going back to the States in a few hours." Bolan stopped at the foot of the bed.

"Is everybody else okay? I don't remember much after the helicopter."

"Phillips and Kelley are outside. They've been waiting for you to wake up. They're asleep now and I didn't bother waking them. There'll be plenty of time for talking later."

Wingate nodded and reached for a water cup on a dresser beside the bed. It was just out of his reach and Bolan stepped up to get it for him.

"Where's Sang?"

"Outside," Bolan answered. "Asleep. Waiting like the others."

"Taggert killed his grandparents, didn't he?"

"Yes."

Wingate closed his eyes. "Christ. What's he going to do now?"

Bolan moved over to the window to adjust the blinds, letting more sunlight in. He moved carefully, mindful of the small bandages under his clothes. Only a few wounds had required sutures, but they were all painful. The doctor had wanted to give him medication for the pain but Bolan had refused, knowing that Brognola would arrive soon; he wanted to be clearheaded for the meet. There were still a few things to be done from the big Fed's end.

"What Sang does depends a lot on you," Bolan said. "I've talked to him. There isn't much for him to return home to. His American heritage wasn't popular in many places, and you can't mistake it with those blue eyes."

"I know. He got them from my brother."

"He's going to need someone to look after him. Someone who will care about him and help him over the rough spots. And, from time to time, it will be a bitch."

Wingate rolled his head from side to side. "If you got me in mind for the job, you can forget it. That kid won't come within ten feet of me. He tried to kill me. I'm the last person he wants in his life."

"I've explained what really happened. He doesn't understand everything, but he knows you're innocent of his family's deaths. Who else does he have to turn to?"

Wingate grimaced as he moved his injured leg under the sheets. "My father will stop any attempt I make to stay with Sang. He wants the boy for himself."

"I've got things in motion already, Lee. Your father won't be allowed to come near him."

"My father turned over the plans to the Star Wars defense system, didn't he?"

"Yeah."

"I try, goddammit, I really do, McKay, but I don't understand the obsession my father had with Stu. He would've done anything to bring him back." He looked at Bolan with a pain that didn't come from his wounds. "Will my father go to prison?"

The warrior shrugged. "Hard to say."

"He'll die in there." Wingate closed his eyes.

"Look, Lee. I don't often get the chance to see the good come of things I do," Bolan said. "Usually I take on a mission long enough to nullify a threat. But here I can see good things coming for both you and the boy. I know you've carried a lot of guilt around because of your father. His obsession with your brother nearly killed you and Sang. You can't lay there and tell me you're not going to try."

"I don't know anything about taking care of a kid, McKay."

Bolan walked closer and looked down at the man. "Just because you didn't have a good father doesn't mean you can't be one, Lee.... We've both dealt in death, but I've been in the hellzones a long time. I've probably seen a lot more of purgatory than you have, and I'm real good at being a soldier. But I'm a man, too, underneath all the trappings.... Death is more than just the flip side of life. Of love. Death is easier to control, a sure thing. Life and love, those are different because you can't move confidently through them. Death is an absolute. You have to nurture life, have to want it to grow.... Don't let this boy's needs fall on barren ground, Lee, or you'll never be able to let go of the past that haunts you."

A hesitant knock interrupted the tense silence that followed Bolan's spontaneous speech. He opened the door and saw Sang.

"Is everything okay?" the boy asked.

Bolan gave him a warm grin. "If not okay, young tiger," he said in Vietnamese, "then it's at least a little better."

"Sang." Lee's voice was barely a whisper as it carried across the small hospital room.

The boy looked at him and approached the bed.

Bolan watched as Wingate tried to speak and found he couldn't. Wordlessly Lee held out his arms.

THE PARKING AREA beside the hospital was filled with military vehicles. Bolan walked through it quietly, his emotions swirling. Only a handful of hours had passed since their arrival in the Philippines. He'd burned the Star Wars plans in the plane on the way over, before finally succumbing to the waiting darkness as they flew.

Matt Smiley had been locked up tight in a poker game the last time Bolan had seen him. Phillips and Kelley had both waited outside Lee Wingate's room until they could no longer keep sleep at bay.

Gingerly he adjusted the Beretta's rigging under his suit coat, the AutoMag's holster on his hip.

Movement flickered to Bolan's left. A blond man abruptly confronted him, holding a .45 automatic in both hands.

Bolan stopped, knowing he'd finally met Cary Rolfe face-to-face.

A grin creased the CIA guy's face as he trained the pistol on the warrior. "You know me, Belasko? Or should I call you Mack Bolan?"

"I know you," Bolan replied quietly, thinking about Scotty Williams and his girlfriend, wondering how much agony they had suffered at Rolfe's hands.

"It took me a while to put it together," Rolfe continued. "Your being Mack Bolan and Mike Belasko, I mean. But I know my way around computers."

Bolan noticed the thin sheen of perspiration on the agent's forehead, the mad gleam in his eyes.

"You have a lot of enemies, Bolan. Besides me. You can destroy my career, you know. Of course you know. Your friend in the Justice Department was already taking care of that when I left the States. I knew you'd head for a military base once you left Vietnam. It was the only logical choice for people needing hospital facilities. The Philippines was the closest, so I used a dummy identity, much like yours, and here I am." Rolfe pointed the automatic meaningfully.

Bolan stood ten feet away from the CIA man. Only barren ground was between them. No place to run or to hide.

"I can kill you here and now. You've made thousands of enemies around this world. Without your testimony I have a chance of salvaging something with the Agency. I've already taken care of the listening devices at Wingate's estate. Then it will be my word against your friend's. I'm not going to let you destroy my career. I can survive this—as long as you die. And any one of those thousands of enemies can take the credit."

Rolfe's first and only shot whispered past Bolan's left cheek as the Executioner unleathered the AutoMag. The big .44 boomed in the warrior's fist as he punched three hollowpoints into the agent's chest.

Cary Rolfe was blown backward from the impact, sailing to a rest on top of the hood of a jeep behind him.

Bolan limped tiredly to a military limo and leaned against a fender, holding the AutoMag between his knees. Yeah, maybe Rolfe had been right. Maybe there were thousands of enemies out there waiting for him. But that was tomorrow. For today, the Executioner was one up on them.

Phoenix Force—bonded in secrecy to avenge the acts of terrorists everywhere.

Super Phoenix Force #2

American ''killer'' mercenaries are involved in a KGB plot to overthrow the government of a South Pacific island. The American President, anxious to preserve his country's image and not disturb the precarious position of the island nation's government, sends in the experts—Phoenix Force—to prevent a coup.

From Europe to Africa, the Executioner stalks his elusive enemy—a cartel of ruthless men who might prove too powerful to defeat.

DON PENDLETON's

MACK BOLAN

Moving Target

One of America's most powerful corporations is reaping huge profits by dealing in arms with anyone who can pay the price. Dogged by assassins, Mack Bolan follows his only lead fast and hard—and becomes caught up in a power struggle that might be his last.